THE WITCHES OF CAMBRIDGE

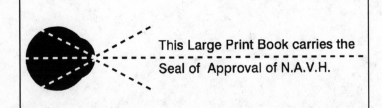

This Large Print Book carries the
Seal of Approval of N.A.V.H.

THE WITCHES OF CAMBRIDGE

MENNA VAN PRAAG

THORNDIKE PRESS
A part of Gale, Cengage Learning

Farmington Hills, Mich • San Francisco • New York • Waterville, Maine
Meriden, Conn • Mason, Ohio • Chicago

LIBRARY OF CONGRESS CATALOGING-IN-PUBLICATION DATA

Names: Praag, Menna van, author.
Title: The witches of Cambridge / by Menna van Praag.
Description: Large print edition. | Waterville, Maine : Thorndike Press, 2016. | © 2016 | Series: Thorndike Press large print women's fiction
Identifiers: LCCN 2016003245| ISBN 9781410490001 (hardcover) | ISBN 1410490009 (hardcover)
Subjects: LCSH: Witches—England—Cambridge—Fiction. | Paranormal romance stories. | Large type books. | GSAFD: Love stories.
Classification: LCC PR6116.R34 W58 2016b | DDC 823/.92—dc23
LC record available at http://lccn.loc.gov/2016003245

Published in 2016 by arrangement with Ballantine Books, an imprint of Random House, a division of Penguin Random House LLC

Printed in Mexico
1 2 3 4 5 6 7 20 19 18 17 16

For my fellow witch, Amanda.
With love & thanks for first
inspiring the story . . .

ACKNOWLEDGMENTS

Epic thanks, as always, to my magnificent agents, Christina Hogrebe and Andrea Cirillo, for keeping the faith and supplying the inspiration. Enormous thanks to Linda Marrow, the loveliest editor a writer could hope to have. Gigantic thanks to all at Random House, especially Elana Seplow-Jolley, Alex Coumbis, and Maggie Oberrender — what an amazing team you are! Massive thanks, as ever, to Alice Jago, for her brilliant brain and eagle eye. Huge thanks to Laurence Gouldbourne for his infinitely inspired feedback. Mammoth thanks to all my readers — your generosity and enthusiasm touch my heart. Great thanks to my friends/students, especially: Leah, Katrin, Vica, Ashley, Sandy, Anita, Stefanie, and Natasha for your enthusiasm and absolute brilliance — you all inspire me so! Thanks to dearest Virginie and to little Héloïse for inspiring big Héloïse. And infinite thanks, as always to Artur, for loving me and making everything possible.

CHAPTER ONE

Amandine closes her eyes as the clock ticks past midnight. She tries to ignore the tug of the full moon and the flutter in her chest as its gravity squeezes her heart. Instead Amandine focuses on her husband's soft snores and wonders, as she has every night for the last few months, why she feels so numb.

When they met thirteen years ago, she thought him the most beautiful man she'd ever seen and he's still a handsome man, strong and lean and dark. Amandine Bisset was so passionate for Eliot Walker that tiny silver sparks flew from her fingertips when she touched him. When they made love her whole body filled with white light so bright Amandine believed she might explode. Now she wonders, when was the last time sex was like that. Before the babies were born?

Now they have two rambunctious, full-blooded, glorious boys and hardly enough energy left at the end of the day for a goodnight kiss, let alone anything else. And any intimacy had quickly evaporated, like wet kisses scattered across warm skin. Thirteen years ago, when they were both undergraduates at Cambridge, Amandine's skin had shimmered at the sight of him. The first time Eliot Walker entered her world she was standing in the foyer of the Fitzwilliam Museum gazing at *The Kiss* by Gustav Klimt and wondering if, among all the glistening gold, she'd ever be blessed enough to feel the passionate desire depicted in that painting.

A moment later, the thought still lingering in her head, Amandine had heard laughter as bright and brilliant as moonshine. She turned to see Eliot standing alone in front of a van Gogh, his laughter flooding the painting and filling the room. Seized by a sudden urge she couldn't explain, Amandine found herself walking toward him. When she reached him she didn't extend her hand and introduce herself.

"Why are you laughing?"

Eliot turned his smile on her. "What?"

She asked again and he shrugged.

"I don't know. There's a quirky joy about it, the sky rolling like waves, the moon and stars like little suns. I think the artist wanted us to smile."

"I don't think so," Amandine said, feeling the need to contradict him. "Van Gogh was a depressive. This painting was the view from his sanatorium window. I doubt he was smiling at the time."

Eliot's own smile deepened, tinged with cheeky triumph. "But he didn't paint it there, did he? It was done from memory, years later. He might have been laughing then."

Amandine frowned, not because he was wrong — indeed she knew for a fact that he wasn't — but because he was so sure of himself, slightly arrogant and argumentative. Just like herself.

"Before or after he cut off his ear?"

Eliot laughed again. "You don't like to be wrong, do you?"

Amandine's frown deepened. "Does anyone?"

"Not me," he agreed. "But that doesn't matter, because I never am."

Now Amandine laughed, despite herself. "Everyone's wrong sometimes."

"Something you know more than most, I imagine." Eliot's eyes glittered.

Amandine was just about to fight back when she realized he was flirting. So she reined herself in, suppressing a smile and giving a nonchalant shrug.

"I'm as wrong about life as anyone, but I'm rarely wrong about art," she said. "And you're not even studying art, are you? I haven't seen you around Scroope."

"Law. Finalist. Trinity." He gave a little bow with a flourish of his hand. "Eliot Ellis Walker-Jones, at your service."

"Ah, so you're one of them." Amandine raised a teasing eyebrow, her glance resting for a moment on his thick dark hair. "I should have known."

"One of whom?"

"A lawyer. A double-barrelled name. A snob."

"The first charge I already confessed to. The second, I can't deny," Eliot said. "But how can you claim the third?"

"Your accent, your name, your knowledge of art even though it's not your subject." Amandine smiled, feeling a sparkle on her skin as it began to tingle. "You probably play the piano disgustingly well and row for Trinity. And I bet a hundred quid you went to Eton —"

"Winchester."

"Same difference."

"Well, not unless twenty thousand pounds a year means nothing to you."

Amandine rolled her eyes, finding it harder

and harder not to look into his: vivid green with flecks of yellow, bright against his pale skin and dark hair.

"So, you're an art historian then?" Eliot asked, shifting the tone.

Amandine gave a little curtsy, fixing her eyes on the floor, hiding her desire to know this man more deeply, though she knew him hardly at all.

"Amandine Françoise Héloïse Bisset."

"Pretty name."

"Merci."

Eliot met her eyes. "You don't have an accent."

A rush of warmth rose in her throat. "My parents are French, but I grew up here."

"Well, I'm glad about that," Eliot said. "Your growing up here, I mean. Well, that you live here right now, anyway . . ."

Amandine stifled a smile. "Yes, me too."

They stood for a while, both glancing at the floor, then back at the painting.

"It's very . . ." Eliot trailed off.

Amandine waited.

"And you — you're, you're very . . ."

And, although he didn't finish his sentence, this time Amandine knew what he'd wanted to say, because she felt the wave of his feelings fill the air like smoke. Joy. Passion. Desire.

She could feel what Eliot felt just as she could feel what van Gogh had when he painted *The Starry Night* in 1889. Every artist — painter, writer, musician — put their spirit and soul into their work, along with their emotions, and Amandine had always been able to feel exactly what the artist had when she looked at a painting or read a book. Music was trickier because the emotions of the musician always mixed with those of the composer, and she was confused and cloudy when confronted with conflicting or unclear emotions.

And, amazingly, though he clearly wasn't a witch, Eliot had been right about van Gogh's *Starry Night,* though Amandine was loath to admit it. Besides, she couldn't say so without also telling him her deepest secret. And she had absolutely no intention of doing that. Even her father hadn't known about her mother. Héloïse Bisset had kept her true nature from her husband and so Amandine had always assumed that it wasn't safe to share such things with people who were purely human. It was likely, if nothing else, to shock them so much that they'd never see you in the same way again.

"I don't suppose . . . ?" Eliot began, tentative for the first time.

"What?" Amandine asked, though she

already knew the answer.

"I don't suppose you fancy taking a cup of tea with a snobby lawyer? My treat."

"Well," Amandine pretended to consider, "since you're not a lawyer yet, I suppose I could make an exception. And if you like van Gogh, you can't be so terrible."

"Ah, high praise indeed. I should ask you to write my references," Eliot said. "And when I am a lawyer, what will you do about fraternizing with me then?"

They began to walk past the paintings and toward the door.

"We'll still know each other then, will we?" Amandine swallowed a smile.

Eliot paused for a moment in front of *The Kiss.*

"Oh yes," he said. "In ten years or so I'll be a London lawyer and we'll be married with two kids. Both boys."

Amandine raised both eyebrows. "Oh, really?"

They began walking again.

"But I don't want children," Amandine said, "so I'm afraid that might put a little crimp in your plans."

"You might not now," Eliot said, "but you will."

Amandine laughed. "Now you're taking arrogance to a whole new level. But I'm

15

afraid you're wrong this time. I admit I might change my mind in many ways in the next ten or twenty years, but not about that."

"Ah, but I told you," Eliot said, still smiling. "I'm never wrong."

And then, with one bold move following another, he reached out and took her hand in his. Amandine almost flinched, thinking perhaps she ought to be shocked, affronted at his arrogance again. But she wasn't. So she let her hand soften in his and, as they walked together, Amandine wished that her mother had given her psychic powers along with extraordinary empathy, so she could know whether it was possible that this man might be right.

Now Amandine lies in bed next to her husband, who has changed so much, from being the light at the center of her life to someone currently trying to hide at the edges. Lately there's something else Amandine has begun feeling from Eliot, emotions coming off him in swells so strong she could swear she can almost smell them. Wafts of guilt and fear float around the house in great ribbons, trailing through corridors and lingering in the air so Amandine could track his every movement if she so chose. Her first assumption, of course, was that he was having an affair. It wouldn't be difficult. He commutes to London every day and often works late and on weekends, no doubt spending time with a wide variety of ambitious young paralegals who might set their sights on a successful and handsome barrister.

However, if Eliot's having an affair then he's as careful and cunning as an MI5 agent. No emails, no texts, no phantom phone calls. Amandine's routine investigations have failed to unearth anything remotely suspicious and she's sure he's neither discreet nor deceptive enough to hide such an obvious secret right under her nose. Eliot Walker is clever, certainly, and as a lawyer he has probably pulled off a few tricks in his time, but as a husband and father he's always been transparent and true. It's just a shame that her gift for feeling what other people do isn't accompanied by the ability to know their thoughts. Empathy balanced with telepathy would make sense. It would provide the whole picture. Without it, sadly, Amandine is left knowing how people feel but not knowing why.

Noa Sparrow has never been much liked by people and she doesn't much care. That isn't strictly true, of course. She tries not to care, she pretends not to care, but she doesn't do a very good job. The problem is that most people don't like to be told the truth. They prefer to hide things from themselves, to act as if everything is okay, to pretend that stuff doesn't bother them when it does. They think, rather foolishly, that what they ignore will simply disappear.

Noa can't help it that she's always been able to see the truth. What's worse, though, is that she's unable to keep silent about what she sees. The words escape her lips, no matter how hard she tries to clamp them tight shut. How often she longs for the ability to feign and fake, to be two-faced, to be a bold and brilliant little liar. Most people seem to manage it easily enough, but sadly it's never been one of Noa's gifts.

She was twelve years old when her need to tell the truth ruined her life. It was two weeks before Christmas and Noa was sitting at the dinner table with her parents, wondering what she'd get in her stocking that year, while they talked about fixing the dripping tap in the sink, when she saw something — a dark truth snaking beneath benign sentences about faucets and the price of plumbers — that she couldn't keep secret. Every day since, Noa has cursed her awful truth-telling Tourette syndrome, wishing she'd been able to keep quiet on that dreadful December night. But, since she can't undo the past, she's spent every day instead hating herself.

Diana Sparrow didn't speak to her daughter for three months after Noa, reaching for more potatoes, suddenly burst out with the fact of her mother's affair with her tango teacher. The shocking secret had just slipped out. Noa clamped her hand over her mouth as the words tumbled into the air, but it was too late. Both her parents had turned to look at her in shock and the stunned guilt on her mother's face was unmistakable.

In the months of earsplitting, heart-shattering pain that followed, Noa prayed every night that she'd be struck down and her "gift" for seeing and telling the truth would be stripped from her. She cut off her long blond hair in penance and denied herself any treats. She took a vow of silence, not opening her mouth to say anything at all, so no hideous, undesirable truths could sneak out. Noa watched, helpless, while her mother relocated to the sofa, then moved out altogether. She listened to her father sob behind his bedroom door in the early hours of the morning. And all the while she said nothing. Not a single word.

Noa had hoped she would somehow be able to go through the rest of her life like that, silent and unseen, never upsetting anyone again. But Noa found that her teachers weren't willing to let her tiptoe through her education undetected, especially when they noticed the quality of her written work. Seeing they had someone rather special in their school, they encouraged her to participate in class, to join in with everyone else. So, in spite of her desperate efforts to remain anonymous, Noa was frequently forced into class discussions, team projects, and group assignments. And, although she tried desperately to monitor her words very carefully in her mind — planning them once and checking them twice — before she let them out of her mouth, every now and then someone's secret would break free. Perhaps unsurprisingly, then, Noa's childhood passed without the comfort of friends.

By the time she reached university to study the History of Art at Magdalene College, Cambridge, Noa had almost convinced herself that she didn't need anybody else, she was perfectly fine going through life alone. She could quite happily spend entire days in the Fitzwilliam Museum on Trumpington Street, passing the morning with Re-

noir, Matisse, and Monet, sharing her
lunchtime sandwiches with van Gogh and
Vermeer, having a quick supper snack in
the presence of Picasso and Kandinsky. But
at night, as she lies alone in her bed, all the
unspoken thoughts of the day pinballing
around in her head, Noa's loneliness is bitter and sharp.

Noa sleeps with the curtains open, allowing as much moonlight as possible to flood
her bedroom, allowing her to see each and
every picture on the walls, if only as a pale
glimmer. It took Noa weeks to perfect the
art display. Reproductions of Monet's
gardens at Giverny blanket one wall: thousands of violets — smudges of purples and
mauves — and azaleas, poppies and peonies,
tulips and roses, water lilies in pastel pinks
floating on serene lakes reflecting weeping
willows and shimmers of sunshine. Turner's
sunsets adorn another: bright eyes of gold
at the center of skies and seas of searing
magenta or soft blue. The third wall is
splashed with Jackson Pollocks: a hundred
different colors streaked and splattered
above Noa's bed. The fourth wall is deco-
rated by Rothko: blocks of blue and red and
yellow blending and bleeding together. The
ceiling is papered with the abstract shapes
of Kandinsky: triangles, circles, and lines

tumbling over one another in energetic acrobatics.

Noa adores abstract art. It quiets her mind; it creates, for her, fewer questions than figurative art. She doesn't wonder — though perhaps she ought — what intention lay behind the placing of a square or the choice of yellow or blue. Noa can simply gaze at the colors and shapes and enjoy the emptiness inside her, the rare absence of thought, together with a feeling of connection — the shadow of something she misses and longs for.

Other than her beloved aunt, Heather, and with the exception of a few cursory words exchanged with librarians and museum curators, virtually the only people Noa speaks with are her professors. So far, to her great good fortune, she's had only two teachers, who have been so boring and lifeless that they harbor no hidden truths for her to blurt out and offend them with. Today though, she's meeting a new professor, Amandine Bisset, and Noa can already sense that she won't be so lucky this time. This new teacher's name alone suggests sensuality and secrets, veiled lives and lovers, concealed longings and desires. Noa imagines her: tall and willowy with long black curls, enormous brown eyes, and lips that have kissed a hundred men and brought them to their knees with whispered French words coated in black coffee and chocolate. Noa is absolutely certain that this woman will be her undoing. After years of carefully clipped silence, she will be unable to contain herself.

It's a surprise, then, when Noa opens the door to Professor Bisset's office and steps inside. The room is large and the walls are bare — a strange quirk for a professor of art history — except for a big, bright poster of Gustav Klimt's *The Kiss* hanging opposite a large oak desk, behind which sits Amandine Bisset, head down, scribbling into a notebook.

"Give me a sec," she says, without a French accent and without looking up.

Noa stands at the edge of the room, not sitting down in her allotted chair, antique and upholstered in dark red leather, wanting to give her new teacher at least the semblance of privacy. While Amandine writes, Noa watches her. She was right about the beauty and the black hair but it's very short, Amandine's eyes aren't brown but green, and she isn't tall and willowy but average height and verging on voluptuous. More important, however, Noa instantly sees that she's absolutely accurate about one thing, the worst thing of all: Amandine Bisset is full of secrets.

"It's strange that your walls are empty," Noa says, before she can help it. "Why do you have only one painting? Don't you get bored?"

Professor Bisset looks up from her writing. "I have a good imagination," she says, her voice a little sharp and a little shocked. "And you have a rather impolite way of introducing yourself."

"I'm sorry," Noa says as she sits. "I can't help it. I . . ."

"Oh?" Amandine's frown deepens, though she sounds more curious than annoyed. She studies Noa, then, about to say something, but seems to change her mind. "I'd get bored looking at the same paintings every day, no matter how much I loved them."

"Except for the Klimt."

"Yes."

Amandine glances back at her notebook.

Noa bites her lip, but she can't stop herself. She sees what her teacher isn't saying as if it were written on a teleprompter that someone is insisting she read aloud.

"Your husband. That's why you keep that painting. It reminds you of when you were happy."

Amandine's eyes snap up again.

"How did you know that?" she says. Her mouth remains open, as if she wishes she could swallow the words back down. She can't, of course. And the truth once spoken is undeniable.

Noa gives a little shrug and starts fishing around in her canvas book bag for her essay. "I've been looking forward to the French Impressionists," she mumbles, hoping her teacher will appreciate the swift change of subject and let her off the hook. If Noa's really lucky she'll be able to get through the next hour without saying something really off-limits, something that will have Amandine refuse to keep her on as a student. It's happened before.

"Fuck the French Impressionists."

Having just pulled her essay out of her bag, Noa drops it. Five pages flutter to the floor but Noa just stares at her teacher, wide-eyed, her fingertips already sticky with fear. Mercifully, the shock empties her mind and silences her mouth.

"Sorry," Amandine says softly. "I didn't . . . of course, that was rude. But you can't say something like that and then expect to start talking about Monet. You have to explain yourself first."

Noa nods. Her mouth is dry. She swallows. "I didn't mean to upset you. It's just . . ." Noa has no idea how to explain herself so that she doesn't sound crazy or scary or both.

Amandine takes a deep breath and sits up. She pulls her long fingers through her short hair. "You don't have to give me a rational explanation," she says. "I'm not a rational person myself. I'm . . ."

It's then that Noa sees what Amandine is. And she smiles, just a flicker at the edge of her lips, but a sense of relief floods her whole body from fingertips to toes. Now she knows it's safe, for the first time in her life, to reveal herself. Noa has only just met this woman, but she knows that Amandine won't judge, reject, or punish her. She knows that it's finally okay to tell her own secret, to be honest about who she is.

"I see things I shouldn't," Noa begins, her voice soft. "I see all the things most people don't want other people to see . . . I don't want to say anything, I want to keep their secrets, but I can't seem to help saying what I see. I don't have any control over it, I don't know why not."

Amandine sits forward. "How do you see what you see?"

Noa shrugs, twisting a piece of her hair around her finger, then smoothing it against her cheek. "I don't know. I've always just known things. That's okay, I guess, but not being able to shut up about it, that's a shame."

Amandine nods. "It doesn't make you many friends, I suppose."

"No," Noa says, "not many."

Amandine sits back in her chair. "You mentioned my husband." Her eyes flicker to the one painting on the wall. "And how we used to be happy . . ."

Noa nods. "Something changed, quite recently. It's like . . . a wall between you." While Noa speaks she looks at her teacher, who's still gazing at the painting. "You don't know what's happened. You wonder if he's having an affair. You wonder if he loves you anymore."

Still staring at the painting, Amandine nods, slowly, as tears pool in her eyes and drop down her cheeks.

"Do you want me to leave?" Noa asks, her voice so soft she almost can't hear her own words.

"No." Amandine pauses, taking a long moment before she brushes her cheeks with the back of her hand and looks up at her student again. "No, I don't want you to leave. I want you to meet my husband. I want you to tell me the truth about him."

Chapter Two

It's been a while since Amandine has practiced any real magic. She can't help what she feels, of course, but since marrying Eliot she's been careful not to cast any spells and to control her body so it doesn't betray her. It hasn't always been easy. When she gave birth to Bertie and Frankie four years ago, her skin got so hot that her sweat burned holes in the sheets of the hospital bed. Fortunately, Eliot was too caught up in rubbing ice cubes on his wife's back and whispering urgent words of encouragement to notice. The midwives did give Amandine strange glances while changing her scorched sheets, after the four-hour-old sleeping babies had been tucked up into bassinets, but didn't say anything. On her wedding day Amandine was so happy that her skin sparkled and her hair shone, but luckily the heavy July heat wave shimmered over all the guests and hid the shining bride. On the wedding night silver sparks dropped from her fingertips onto her new husband's back but he, swept up in love and desire, didn't feel a thing.

On her wedding night, and many times over the past thirteen years, Amandine has almost blurted out her secret to Eliot but, whenever the white-hot words are sitting on her tongue, ready to tumble out and change everything, she swallows them back, choosing to keep everything safely the same for a little while longer. Amandine has no idea how Eliot might react if he knew the truth about her but guesses, based on his practical, rational nature, that he'd be horrified, thinking she was either crazy or a con artist, or both. She should have told him on their first date, or soon afterward; she should have told him the day she knew she was in love. But she didn't want to lose him, and the longer she loved him the harder it was.

Amandine watches her boys closely for signs that they've inherited her particular powers but she hasn't seen anything yet. She wonders what she'll do if she does. How would she explain that to Eliot? Sometimes Amandine feels sad that her husband doesn't know the deepest parts of her. Sometimes she blames herself for the breakdown of their relationship, for the distance between them. After all, starting out with such a big secret to hide doesn't really foster intimacy. Lately, while she watches him move through their lives barely noticing her anymore, Amandine wonders if that's why he finally found a mistress (as she suspects he has): because he never really felt connected to her. But why didn't he say anything? Why didn't he ask if he felt something was wrong? Amandine can't blame him for that, she knows, since she hasn't done the same thing herself.

How can it be that two people who've been together for over a decade, who've shared a bed and two births, who've kissed every inch of each other's bodies and gazed into each other's eyes through tears of joy, unable to believe that this much love was possible, can one day — seemingly all of a sudden — turn into virtual strangers? If it hadn't happened to Amandine herself, she wouldn't have believed it possible.

Now she watches her husband eating breakfast, forking scrambled eggs into his mouth with one hand, flicking through *The Times* with the other. Bertie and Frankie sit opposite their father across the wide oak table on their respective booster seats. The twins chatter away in their own secret language, ignoring their parents and their breakfast.

"Eat your eggs, boys," Amandine says, ruffling her fingers through their soft brown curls, swallowing an urge to kiss their cheeks. When the boys were babies they loved kisses, insisting on at least a dozen a day, but as soon as toddlerhood hit the kisses stopped. Now Amandine is lucky if she can sneak a solitary peck at bedtime.

"Oui, Maman."

"Oui, Maman."

The boys speak in unison, their words simultaneously reassuring and dismissive. Sometime over the last year they perfected the art of superficial listening, absorbing instruction without stopping to really hear the words. As her sons gobble up their eggs, still chattering, Amandine closes her eyes, remembering the days when they used to fix her with attentive gazes of such absolute adoration that she almost couldn't breathe, unable to absorb so much love all at once.

A wooden chair scrapes against the stone floor. Amandine opens her eyes to see Eliot pushing his chair back, tucking *The Times* under his arm, and taking his empty plate off the table. He strides over to the kitchen sink, where Amandine stands, and slips his plate gently onto the white plastic drip tray. He quickly kisses the tops of his sons' heads as he passes.

"Bye, Dad," Frankie says.

"Bye, Daddy," Bertie says.

"Bye, boys," Eliot replies as he reaches the kitchen door, giving a little wave with his newspaper. Then he looks at his wife, while somehow managing not to meet her eye.

"I won't be back till late tonight, maybe midnight," he says quickly. "We're working on the Tredlow case, it's a pain in the arse."

Amandine's eyebrows shoot up and she nods toward the boys. She can see Eliot swallow a sigh and speak through thin lips.

"Sorry." He turns and pushes open the wooden door. As it bumps shut behind him Amandine turns to the sink and starts to wash the pan she'd scrambled the eggs in.

"I'll get a babysitter then," she says softly, "since I'm visiting my mother tonight, though I expect you've forgotten that."

Noa ambles along Bene't Street, past the enormous shining gold clock (an incredible work of art in itself, with an elaborate pendulum marking off the seconds while a fierce metal locust gobbles up time with each tick) and the tiny stone church until she reaches Gustare, the lovely little Italian café at the top of the street. This is her morning ritual. First she stops at the café for an espresso and pistachio cream croissant before dividing her allotted breakfast hour between the two art galleries across the road. Before her first lecture of the day, Noa sips her coffee and nibbles her croissant while the beauty of the art and the peace of the empty, unpeopled place soaks slowly into her skin.

Noa's dream, her deepest desire, is to work as an art curator for the National Gallery. She first found this wish — waiting for her, wrapped in shining gold paper and tied with ribbons of longing and hope — in the gallery of modern art, tucked between Monet's *Le Bassin aux Nymphéas* and van Gogh's *The Church at Auvers*. Her father, a curator at the Fitzwilliam Museum, took Noa down to London to visit the art galleries as a special treat for her seventh birthday. She already knew more about every artist, from Aachen to Zaganelli, than any child, and probably most adults, from the amount of time she spent among the corridors of the Fitzwilliam, gazing up at all the wondrous art contained within its walls. At three o'clock every afternoon after school finished, Noa hurried along Trumpington Street, her bag bouncing on her back, toward her father and the magical world to which he held the key. She spent a blissful few hours away from people, wandering up and down the galleries, absorbing the brilliance of the colors and the beauty of the pictures, with a full heart and a silent mouth.

The Fitzwilliam Museum was the greatest place in the world until Noa saw the magnificence of the National Gallery. She'd never seen anything on that scale before and was — incredibly — rendered speechless at the sight of it all. She walked along each wooden corridor in a daze, grasping her father's hand, until she found the wish.

Noa has treasured this wish ever since that day, and every step in her academic career has been aimed toward this one goal. The only problem is that, in addition to a degree in art history, Noa needs work experience and, given her particular power for seeing and speaking the truth, that might be significantly harder to come by.

She's never spoken to the owner of either art gallery on King's Parade, too worried that she'll blurt out their secrets mid-conversation and be instantly banned from her two favorite places in the world. Noa would love to work part-time as a sales assistant in one of the galleries but she doesn't dare ask. A fellow art history student works in one; she sees him on Tuesday and Thursday mornings, so Noa knows she'd have a good chance of getting in. If only she weren't a social liability. Even if she got through the interview (no chance of that, though, since she's already seen that the owner of Primavera is concealing a gambling addiction and the owner of Atkis is hiding an affair with his sister-in-law), Noa wouldn't be working an hour before she'd insult a customer with an undesired and unsolicited tidbit of truth, something she'd snatch sight of while extolling the talents of the artists they represented or the beauty of the paintings they sold.

Noa pushes open the door to Primavera and smiles at the girl behind the counter, a pretty redhead in a gorgeous green dress, who nods slightly and smiles back.

"Good morning," she says, "I'm here if you need anything."

"Thanks," Noa says, hurrying past her as quickly and politely as she can. The beautiful girl is bulimic, spending her evenings gorging on gargantuan tubs of chocolate ice cream and plates of cookies, then regurgitating it all before bedtime, something she certainly wouldn't want a stranger mentioning in the midst of polite chitchat about the weather and the price of art.

Noa settles herself in the farthest reaches of the gallery, admiring the work of an artist she hasn't seen before. The canvases are large and dark, great splashes of royal blue on black, what appear to be deep purple seas beneath deep red skies. They remind her of Turner's tranquil sunsets, with a slightly sinister edge, as if sharks swim in the purple seas and black crows caw through the red skies. Noa gazes at the painting, leaning closer, careful with her coffee and croissant, to see each brushstroke, the curves and dips of the sea and sky. And then she does something she's never done before in her life, not to the thousands of paintings she's ever seen — Noa reaches out and touches her finger to the paint.

For a split second she imagines she's about to be pulled into the painting, sucked into the purple and red and spat out in another world. Because, so close now, Noa can't believe the picture could simply be a flat surface, it must contain depths hidden to the naked eye. Noa peers at the artist's name on a small plaque beneath the painting: *Santiago Costa — Storm over Bahia — 114" × 98" — £950.*

"What do you think?"

Startled, Noa turns to see a man standing behind her, just a few feet away. She's not sure how he managed to sneak up so close without her feeling his presence. He's tall and thin with floppy black hair, caramel-colored skin, a large nose, and large brown eyes. Noa stares at him. It's not that he's handsome, though he is; it's more than that. He's captivating. When this man fixes you with his brown eyes you want to stare into them for a long, long time. It's as if his heart doesn't reside in his chest but sits, waiting and open wide, just beneath his eyes. And you believe that if you look long enough you'll fall right in.

Noa knows, before he says another word, that he is the artist.

He reaches out his hand, but drops his beautiful eyes to the floor.

"Santiago Costa," he whispers. "It's a pleasure."

Noa slips her coffee and remaining croissant into her left hand and shakes his hand. "Noa Sparrow."

They stand together in silence for several moments.

"Your work," Noa begins, searching for adequate words, "your work is, it's . . ."

"Thank you." Santiago gives a slight bow, a lock of black hair falls over one brown eye. He brushes it back with long fingers.

"I can't really explain why I love it so much, it's just so, so . . ."

"Good, that's the best way," Santiago says. "Too much analysis kills a thing. Art is created from passion and inspires passion. And passion is beyond reason. Don't you think?"

Noa laughs. "If that's the case then I've just wasted the last two years of my life."

Santiago frowns. "Why?"

"I'm studying for a degree in art history. It involves rather a lot of analysis."

"Oh dear," Santiago says, sounding genuinely concerned. "That is a shame."

"I'm going to put it to use," Noa protests. "So it won't be a total shame. It'll be in service to the greater good."

"What will you do with it?"

Noa doesn't answer immediately. She hasn't shared this dream with anyone else, not her parents or her teachers, no one. She glances at his paintings, then back at him. Santiago holds her gaze and Noa sees in his soft eyes the promise of something spectacular. What it is exactly, she can't be sure, but Noa sees enough to want to know more.

"Well, I want to work as a curator for the National Gallery," she says softly, hoping the girl at the counter won't hear. "It's what I want . . . more than anything else in the world."

Santiago smiles. "And I admire you for it. When you could be putting your excellent education to lucrative ends for private clients, you've chosen to work in virtual penury for the public, so everyone can enjoy great works of art. It's a beautiful, noble ambition." His smile deepens. "And one I have every belief you'll achieve."

"Really?"

Santiago nods. "But of course. Don't you?"

Noa shrugs. "I certainly hope so, but I don't know . . ."

Santiago fixes her with his deep brown eyes. "I do. And you can trust me. I can see things in people that they can't see in themselves."

"Oh?" Noa says and, before she can stop herself from asking such a thing from a virtual stranger, she blurts it out. "And what do you see in me?"

Santiago smiles and Noa feels her skin flush. He brushes his fingers through his thick black hair again and Noa feels suddenly overcome with the desire to touch his long, thin fingers, to entwine them with her own.

"Great strength," he says. "The power to do anything you put your mind to."

"Really?"

"Oh, yes." He nods. "And so, when you're a curator at the National Gallery, I hope you'll invite me to exhibit there. I should be most honored."

"Of course," Noa exclaims. "As soon as I'm in place, you'll be the first artist I'll ask."

Santiago places one long-fingered hand on his chest and reaches out the other to her. "It's a deal." He gives a little bow. "And now I have two reasons to hope your dream comes true. First, for you. Second, for me, so that I will see you again."

Then, in a gesture so quick Noa doesn't see where it came from, Santiago plucks a card from his pocket and holds it out to her, between two fingers. Noa takes the little dark purple card and reads, in delicate silver letters, his name and phone number inscribed across the front.

"So you can call me when you get that job," he says. "I hope it will be soon. I have a feeling it will be sooner than you think."

And, with that, Santiago turns and walks away. When Noa blinks again, he's gone and she's left standing next to his paintings in the empty shop.

It's only when she's walking back along Bene't Street that Noa realizes she hadn't seen any of Santiago's secrets. She'd looked deep into his soft eyes and seen nothing. It certainly wasn't because he didn't have any secrets. Everyone has secrets, even little fears and facts they won't tell another living soul. Noa has never met a person for whom this wasn't true. It's what has made her life so difficult up to now. And Santiago is no exception. If anything, she'd guess he has more secrets than most. So why couldn't she see them?

Amandine is scared of heights. Which wouldn't matter ordinarily, except that she's president of the Cambridge University Society of Literature and Witchcraft, which meets on the first Friday of every month, at midnight, on the top of various university turrets, each one at least fifty feet from the ground. This means that, for twelve days of the year, Amandine has to take a dash of valerian and a sprinkling of passionflower in her tea before she leaves the house, which serves to stop her legs shaking and her heart beating quite so fast.

Three women and one man are members of the Cambridge University Society of Literature and Witchcraft, all professors and all witches, but only one is afraid of heights. In the early days Amandine had suggested the group meet in a more conventional location, a library or café, but she'd always been voted down by the others, who prefer places that afford better views. Each professor takes it in turn to choose the book and host the event at the highest point of their respective colleges. A month ago George Benett had chosen E. M. Forster's *Maurice* and discussions took place on the roof of Pembroke Chapel, just next to the ornate silver weather vane. It was the first of April, a chilly evening with a cool breeze, but the weather didn't affect the witches, who are not subject to petty physical limitations.

In three days' time, on Friday, it's Amandine's turn. By rights it should be her mother's, but Héloïse Bisset hasn't attended a book group meeting or taught a tutorial for nearly two years now. She's hardly left the house since her husband died. For many months, Amandine had let her mother sink into her sorrow. She brought her food and forced her to eat it. She wiped her mother's nose while she sobbed, she held her while she shook, she made sure she washed and dressed every few days. For fourteen months she allowed her mother to fall apart, along with the scattering pieces of her shattered universe. But, six months ago, Amandine decided that enough was enough. Héloïse is still young, not yet sixty, and it was time for her to start living again.

Perhaps Amandine's decision was partly selfish; she could no longer cope with feeling her mother's pain so acutely every day, trying to shed the heavy cloak of sadness when she came home at night so she could be with her husband and boys and feel joy as she hugged them close. Perhaps she'd reached her limit of self-sacrifice. So, for the last six months, Amandine has stopped pandering to her mother's pain and agoraphobic tendencies and instead tried to force her out of the house and back into life among the living. She took her on walks, packed picnics, dragged her into cafés and cinemas. Amandine has chosen her book — *She Came to Stay* by Simone de Beauvoir — in a bid to tempt Héloïse back into the fold by picking her favorite author. So far, sadly, it hasn't worked. But Amandine hasn't given up, nor will she.

Amandine has picked, as their meeting place to discuss the book, a nice discreet turret at the back of Magdalene College far from the street, just in case any curious passersby happen to glance up, although she knows from experience that normal people rarely look very far above their own noses. After eight hundred years in existence, the Cambridge University Society of Literature and Witchcraft has only been spotted by the public a handful of times. People don't look up. They scurry about, lost in their thoughts, and rarely consider slowing down and gazing at the sky. It's a shame, Amandine sometimes thinks, since they miss so much. She's always particularly shocked at how many of her own students, who should be drawn to architecture, haven't noticed the incredibly intricate turrets and towers crammed into the city.

Amandine has been gazing up at the colleges of Cambridge since the first day she arrived as an undergraduate. Now, in her thirty-seventh year, she knows every single carving, every stone spire and sculpture. She knows all 149 gargoyles by name, having named them one weekend when she wasn't in the mood to stay at her desk and mark essays.

Amandine joined the group as soon as she was admitted to the university. She attended her first meeting on the evening of her matriculation, finally achieving a dream she'd been dreaming since she was a teenager. On the eve of her thirteenth birthday Amandine had followed her mother, Professor Héloïse Bisset, out of the house and under the cover of a cloudy sky.

Every month Héloïse went out and Amandine always wondered where she was going.

She knew it was somewhere special because she felt the anticipation and delight that bubbled inside her mother on the morning of the day she was set to go out. Little Amandine begged Héloïse to tell her, but her mother always refused, telling her she was too young, that she'd tell her one day but not yet. By the time she was nearly thirteen, Amandine finally got fed up with the waiting and determined to find the truth for herself.

She followed Héloïse to Emmanuel College, crept up the stairs of the north wing on tiptoe, and alighted on the rooftop. There sat three other women and a man sitting in a circle, each hovering five inches in the air, holding a book and a cup of hot chocolate. Amandine watched as Héloïse went to join them, finding her place in the circle, mysteriously producing a book and, even more mysteriously, a hot chocolate of her own as she sat down. That night Amandine watched and listened. The book they talked about was one she'd never heard of but, after hearing all its salacious details discussed in depth, she borrowed it off her mother's bedside the next morning and spent her birthday reading it cover to cover.

Amandine hadn't really been surprised by the strange things she saw that night: the sudden appearance of marshmallows and chocolate on sticks, along with a tiny elevated fire, flickering and spitting a few inches off the roof, upon which to roast them. She didn't gasp in shock when the strangers themselves hovered a few feet in the air whenever they laughed or argued. She didn't wonder why, when it started to rain, none of her mother's friends got wet.

Amandine had always suspected there was something different about her mother. Unlike her father, her mother seemed to know what would happen *before* it happened — she picked up the phone the second it started to ring, she started to pack before they had to move house, she made tea with lemon and honey just before her father started sneezing and complaining of a cold. Amandine also knew there was something different about herself quite early on, quickly realizing that other people didn't feel their fellow human beings' feelings in the same way she did. But it wasn't until the night that she turned thirteen that Amandine finally confronted her mother.

When she saw that the book group was coming to an end, when the marshmallows had all been eaten and the little fire went out, Amandine scampered back down the staircase — treading as lightly and quickly as she could — then waited for Héloïse around the corner so she could catch her on her own.

"So," Héloïse said, before she saw her, "*ma petite fille* is ready to grow up now, is she?"

"Can I join your book group, *Maman,* can I, please?" Amandine asked, running along to catch up to her mother.

"Not yet, *ma petite,*" Héloïse said. "But yes, in time, you can."

"When?"

Héloïse gave a small sigh then, as if deciding whether to tell her. A few hundred feet away the golden stone clock on King's College chimed one o'clock. Each note pierced the air around them.

"Please, *Maman,*" Amandine begged. "I'm thirteen now, I'm very much old enough."

"Are you now?" Héloïse laughed. "All right then, you'll join us after you turn eighteen, when you're accepted at Magdalene College."

Amandine stopped walking, eyes wide. "Really? I will, are you sure?"

Héloïse nodded. "Yes, *ma petite,* I'm sure."

"Brilliant! Brilliant!" Amandine exclaimed, her voice echoing through the emptiness, excited words bouncing off ancient buildings. She started to skip down the street. "I can't wait!"

CHAPTER THREE

Héloïse wakes just before dawn, as she always does, the sun pulling her out of bed. Sometimes, now that she no longer has a husband to take care of, Héloïse wishes she could sleep in. But it's a habit she doesn't mind very much, since the stillness and silence of the early morning suit her.

She sits up, slowly stretching her arms above her head with a yawn, then picks a brush off her bedside table and brushes her short bob flat, tucking stray wisps behind her ears. It's entirely gray now. She stopped dyeing it back to black when François died. Now, nearly two years later, she can hardly remember what she used to look like. A vague image of beauty and glamour lingers at the edge of her memories but the taint of guilt and death have darkened it.

Tu es plus belle ce matin, ma chérie.

"I am not, darling," Héloïse says, curling her fingers at the ends of her hair. "But it's sweet of you to say so."

Héloïse slides her bare feet into slippers and shuffles across the wooden floor to the window, to sit and watch the sunrise. The weather is warm enough to sleep without a nightgown and Héloïse doesn't bother pulling one on now. No one can see her from across the street, and she doesn't mind how she looks, no matter that her breasts, buttocks, and stomach sag now, no matter that her skin is wrinkled and spotted with age. Perhaps it was François's doing, the way he'd stroked his fingers along the lines that multiplied over the years, how he'd kissed her breasts so tenderly, held her middle-aged hands so softly, cupped her cheeks and kissed her lips . . . Probably. But Héloïse can also credit her own mother's example. Virginie Ghanimé was forty-five when her first and only child was born. Héloïse remembers sitting at her mother's coiffeuse, pretending to put on rouge. Until she died in her eighties, Virginie looked and felt herself to be beautiful.

C'est un beau matin.

"Yes," Héloïse agrees, glancing outside at the sunshine. "I suppose it is."

She sinks into the armchair by the window. It's soft, deep, and striped in her favorite colors: dusty pink and green. Nearly a year and a half after François died, Amandine insisted on redesigning the bedroom and, although Héloïse protested at the time, she's grateful for it now. The room is a fairy tale, an escape from reality, a reminder of the romance of the past instead of the grief of the present. The bed is wrought-iron with white sheets and a canopy of cream gauze. The desks, bookshelves, and matching wardrobe are all original Victorian antiques painted white. With the touch of a sparkling crystal chandelier, Amandine created a room that gives Héloïse a tiny smile of pleasure every time she wakes. Until a few seconds later when she remembers that François isn't waking up with her and never will again. Héloïse used to relish the transition from unconsciousness to consciousness. She loved those few moments floating into reality on the edges of her dreams, but now the reawakening is too cruel, too much of a shock. At night she dreams that François is alive and vibrant and young. At daybreak, when she opens her eyes, he dies all over again.

Sometimes Héloïse wonders if the heartbreak of her husband's death — along with the fact that it was her fault — would have killed her, if she hadn't had her daughter's deep love and sprinkling of magic as support. She needs both from Amandine now, since François's death, along with silencing Héloïse's heart, seems to have switched off her own magic. For the first year or so she neither noticed nor cared, but lately she's started to miss it. It's a sign, perhaps, that Amandine's efforts to bring her alive again are beginning to take effect, at least a little.

Amandine gently pushes open her front door, wincing as the hinges squeak into the silent night air. Frankie can sleep through a parade but Bertie is a light sleeper and she's forever in danger of waking him. Slipping in through the smallest crack she can squeeze through and softly clicking the door closed behind her, Amandine tiptoes down the hallway. She's still pulling off her coat when she steps into the living room. At first she doesn't see Eliot huddled on the sofa, his head tucked into his knees, but she hears him. His voice is muffled into his hand. At first Amandine thinks he's talking to himself and then she realizes he must be speaking into a mobile phone.

"I want to see you more too, of course I do, but I — I can't tell her yet, I —"

A cough rises in Amandine's throat, tickling and scratching her windpipe until she can't swallow anymore and the cough splutters into the room. Eliot turns his head as if he's just been caught robbing a bank. An iridescent glow of guilt rolls off him and hits Amandine in the chest with such force that she almost falls over. Eliot snaps the phone shut.

"Who were you talking to?"

"Spencer. He wanted a file I had. I'll see him tomorrow."

Amandine feels a flush of fury that he's lying to her. She almost wants to slap him in the face and insist on the truth. At the same time the idea of learning something that would mean the inevitable breakup of her family is almost too terrifying. Still, she can't just let it go.

"Why did you hang up without saying goodbye?"

Eliot shrugs and Amandine is surprised by how easily he lies; even his body doesn't betray him at all. Were it not for the echo of secondhand guilt still shuddering through her, she might believe what he's telling her, that what she just witnessed means nothing.

"Spence and I don't bother with formalities."

I heard you. The words are on her lips. *You don't speak like that to Spence. Tell me who it was.* But, unlike the cough, Amandine manages to swallow the words. The truth is still too scary to contemplate and, for once, she's grateful that she can only feel people's emotions and not know the why behind them.

Eliot stands and crosses the room. When he reaches her, for a split second Amandine thinks he's going to give her a kiss, perhaps pull her into his chest and hold her tight, but Eliot just passes by, twisting his body slightly so he won't have to touch her as he leaves the room.

During the past few weeks waking up in her bedroom, Héloïse has begun noticing that the room is becoming more animated than she is — which, no doubt, was Amandine's intention all along. Perhaps it's been active for the past year, but she simply hasn't noticed before.

It shifts around on a whim while she sleeps. When she wakes the armchairs turn up at the other side of the room; the two desks rotate in shifts to sit under the windows, taking it in turns to soak up the light; the bed tests out different corners of the room, the bookshelves different walls. Some mornings, new pieces of furniture materialize and old ones disappear: a reminder of the cycle of life and death, possession and loss. It's not something Héloïse particularly wants to be reminded of and yet sometimes the new things delight her.

Two days ago Héloïse woke to see a brass hat stand next to the door, complete with three wooden, ivory-handled, silk-edged umbrellas at its base and three straw hats hanging from its arms. The next day five paintings appeared on the wall opposite her bed: four of Monet's gardens at Giverny and one by an artist she doesn't know (Amandine tries to educate her mother about such things but Héloïse has never cared who the painters are, so long as the paintings are beautiful) of a thatched cottage with sunflowers under the windows and chickens in the yard. It reminds her of home, growing up in the Dordogne, and brings her comfort for a moment or two.

The room, Héloïse knows, is Amandine's way of telling her to stop staring out of the window and start stepping out of the house. And yet she can't, and won't be able to until she finds a way to switch off her thoughts, her memories, her longing. So far, she hasn't had much luck. She still thinks of François every few minutes. The first time, about a week ago, when a whole half hour passed without him in it, Héloïse found herself gasping for breath when she thought of him again, like a drowning swimmer.

Most of the time she thinks of the mundane things — the way he ate toast: nibbling around the edges until he reached the middle; the way he sneezed: squeezing his eyes shut and swallowing the sneeze before it exploded; the way he looked at her every evening before switching out the light: as if she were twenty years old on their wedding night. In thirty-five years of marriage they'd had their fair share of fights, of course, but, judging by her friends' critiques and complaints about their husbands, Héloïse had been far happier than most of them. And yet they'd all been allowed to keep their husbands, while she had lost hers. Her François. Her short, sweet, portly, balding, devoted François.

She sinks into the memory of him again and smiles as she feels his breath on her cheek.

Certainly devoted, mais oui, he says. *But not entirely bald. At least, not until the last few years.*

Tears fill Héloïse's eyes. She grips the armchair and blinks them back. She must find the strength to stop listening, she must find the strength to let go. Or else what's the point of being alive at all? She might as well close her eyes, open her veins, and let the warm, bloodred grief slowly pull her under. And perhaps she would, if it weren't for Amandine and the boys. So Héloïse shakes her head, like a dog shaking off water, in a halfhearted attempt to free herself from the grip of grief, to slowly pry its tight fingers from around her throat.

Non, not yet. I'm not ready. S'il vous plaît, non —

François has been whispering these particular words into Héloïse's ear every day since the day he died. Of course, one day, it must stop. Or one day she must stop listening. Because, despite her sorrow, Héloïse has always believed that life has meaning. She believes that since she's still alive it must be for a reason. Or, if not, then she at least owes it to François, to life itself, to make the most of the breath in her lungs and the blood in her veins. There are still things (on her best days) that she wants to do, or had wanted to do. She'd like to visit her birthplace again. She'd like to travel. She'd like to see more of the world. As an undergraduate, she'd been offered a scholarship to study in San Francisco, at Berkeley. She'd been wild with delight and had, with François's blessing, immediately begun making plans. They hadn't worried about being apart for a year. They believed in their relationship, in the strength of their feelings; it wasn't a concern. And then, three weeks before she was set to leave, Héloïse discovered she was three months pregnant.

Now she reaches up to press her palm against the window. The cool dewy glass against Héloïse's skin suddenly snaps her out of the past, so she's sitting in her enchanted room once more. Slowly, she turns in her pink and green armchair to face the painting of the farmyard and, still feeling the brush of François's breath on her cheek, Héloïse whispers these words to herself, over and over again: *Let go, let go, let go . . .*

When term ends, or Noa runs out of money, or is feeling particularly lonely, she doesn't go home to either of her parents but visits her aunt instead. Ostensibly this is because Heather Sparrow lives less than a mile from Magdalene College, on Park Street in a tall Victorian house overlooking the river, while her mother lives three hundred miles away in the Lake District and her father (Heather's brother) in a rather grimy street in London. In truth, it's because Noa's mother — now separated from her lover — still blames Noa for ending her marriage, even though she won't admit it to either her daughter or herself. And Noa's father doesn't know how to deal with a daughter who can see more about him than he can. Both Noa's parents prefer to pretend that things aren't the way they are and they don't take well to people — especially their own flesh and blood — pointing out emotions and secrets they take great pains to hide.

Noa's aunt, on the other hand, is nearly as blunt as Noa. She appreciates her niece's ability to see the truth and say it without censorship. Indeed, she's often voiced the desire to have Noa's strange sense for herself.

"I wish you could have it," Noa says, for what feels like the seven hundred thousand sixty-second time in her life, as they sit in Heather's kitchen drinking tea and eating blueberry scones. "I'd give it to you in a second, if I could."

"I don't understand why you hate it so much," Heather says, taking another gulp of tea, then slathering another scone (her fourth) with butter and clotted cream. "I've spent my life wishing I had some sort of extraordinary gift so I wouldn't be so bloody boringly normal."

"It's hardly a gift," Noa says, sipping her tea. "I've got no friends and I'm starting to doubt I'll ever, ever have an actual relationship with a man. Anyway" — Noa smiles — "you're hardly normal."

"True." Heather nods, gobbling up her scone and licking her lips. "God, these are delicious. Well, if men can't handle the truth, why don't you give women a try?"

Noa smiles again at her beautiful, portly aunt's five thousandth attempt to convert her. "If women were any better at hearing their secrets spoken aloud, then I might very well give it a go," she says, "but I'm afraid to tell you that they aren't."

"I suppose you're right." Heather sighs. "Still, maybe you'll see sense yet."

"Or maybe you will," Noa teases.

Heather nearly snorts up her fifth scone. "Hardly. I've tried men and they've tried me and we simply don't suit each other."

Noa sighs. "Well, lucky you, getting to try everything and everyone. At this rate, I'll die a virgin."

"Pish!" Heather exclaims. "Don't be ridiculous. Give it time, you just —"

"Yeah, yeah," Noa says. "It'd be okay if I was a teenager, but I'm twenty-three. In Austen's time I'd be an old-maid governess by now, fit for nothing but other people's children."

"Well, then, it's lucky for us both that we don't live in Austen's time, isn't it? Anyway,

I couldn't live in a place without ready access to chocolate. Can you imagine?"

"You'd die," Noa admits, "or become a highwaywoman stealing illicit sugary substances from the rich."

"Your chocolate or your life? Sounds about right to me." Heather laughs, licking her fingers. "These scones are too delicious. Who'd have thought that the simple addition of frozen blueberries could turn something bland into something irresistible? But, really, when you find your perfect match, you won't have to worry about your gift, or your curse, or whatever you think it is, because they will love you for all that."

Noa humphs into her teacup. "I doubt it."

Heather shrugs. "That's only because you've never been in love, so you've no idea what it means. Lily loved the joy I took in eating, she loved that I didn't squash myself for social events and could always be counted on to blurt out something silly that most people would be too shy to say."

"Do you miss her too much?"

Heather nods, her eyes filling. "Every day." Then she smiles. "But it used to be every minute of every day, and now a good ten minutes can pass without memories of Lily, so progress is being made."

Noa gives her aunt a little smile and takes

another scone.

"That's when you'll know love though," Heather insists, "because you'll feel more yourself and happier in your own skin than you ever did before."

Noa laughs. "That wouldn't be love, that'd be a bloody miracle."

"Yes." Heather smiles, dipping her finger into the cream. "Exactly."

Amandine fell in love with Eliot by degrees. And the day they married Amandine knew she loved him more than she'd ever loved another human being and believed then she'd reached the heights and depths of her capacity for love but, as the years passed, she realized that day had only been the beginning. Sometimes another degree of love snuck up on her. She'd catch sight of Eliot cooking dinner — the way he lost himself so completely in the act — and suddenly her heart would swell anew and she'd find tears falling down her cheeks, her body unable to contain her feelings.

Sometimes she was (fairly) ready for it, though the impact still surprised her every time. The night the twins were born and she watched Eliot holding them both in his arms — still squalling and bloody — Amandine was overcome again. Witnessing the man she loved falling in love deepened her love for him more than she could have possibly imagined. And, although people told her she'd soon love her children in an all-consuming way that she would never love Eliot, Amandine hadn't yet found that to be true. While her heart had immediately expanded to include her sons, her husband hadn't been ousted in the process. If anything, she only loved him more: as a father as well as a man.

Whenever Amandine heard other women complaining about their own husbands, who regularly seemed to forget about birthdays and foreplay and housework in varying and woefully negligent ways, she felt a fresh swell of secret love and gratitude for Eliot, who forgot none of these things and always remembered considerably more on top of it — cups of tea in bed, foot rubs, her love of yellow roses, and secret kisses before bedtime.

All of which, unfortunately, only serves to make the present condition of her marriage all the more painful. Perhaps, Amandine thinks, if she'd had a slightly negligent husband to start off with, she might have been better prepared for the drastic decline that was to come.

Héloïse sits on a park bench, halfheartedly throwing peanuts for a squirrel, trying to tempt him out of a tree. She dips into the bag and pulls out another fistful. It's the same bench in the Botanic Garden, next to the rock garden, overlooking the little lake, the one she visited every day with François for five years. They'd planned on doing this for another twenty years, before he died so suddenly. After Amandine graduated and left, and he retired and she semi-retired in order to join him, just doing the odd tutorial now and then, they spent breakfast-time sharing their cold buttered toast with the birds.

We had such a time here, didn't we, mon amour? Do you remember when we adopted the robin and he visited us every morning?

Héloïse doesn't answer. She wants to. Her reply is on the tip of her tongue, the smile on the edge of her lips. But, with great effort, she swallows her words. The squirrel scuttles down the tree, leaps across the grass, and picks up a peanut at Héloïse's feet. Slowly, she uncurls her fist so a palmful of peanuts is open on her lap. She doesn't have the energy to throw them anymore. The promise she made to herself yesterday is already broken. She stepped outside, on Amandine's insistence earlier that morning, but she doesn't have the energy to let go. Not now, not yet.

Let me stay, he says. *Please, let me stay a little longer, s'il vous plaît . . .*

Héloïse looks out at the park, at the trees against the Tupperware sky, at the light drizzle beginning to fall. And suddenly she feels more alone than she's ever felt in her life, filled with a deep black emptiness heavier even than the day François died. As if every moment of despair over the past two years has been spun together, woven into a blanket that falls over Héloïse, suffocating her, breath by shallow breath.

Je t'aime. Je vous aimerai toujours.

The squirrel stops nibbling at her feet and glances up, darting its head from side to side, then jumps up and scurries along the bench, snatching a peanut out of Héloïse's hand. For a second the squirrel looks at her, black unblinking eyes fixed on hers, before darting off the bench and springing back up the tree. As Héloïse watches the squirrel, Amandine ambles across the grass toward the bench. When she rests her hand gently on Héloïse's shoulder, Héloïse yelps.

"Sorry, *Maman,*" Amandine says. "It's

only me."

"Oh," Héloïse gasps. "I didn't see you."

"Sorry, I shouldn't have scared you." Amandine nods at the bench. "May I?"

"Of course," Héloïse says, "you're the one who dragged me out here in the first place."

Amandine sits, resisting the impulse to roll her eyes. Instead she takes her mother's hand and holds it gently in her own.

"It'll get better, *Maman,* day by day, you just have to keep trying, keep bringing yourself back into this world and, one day, you won't have to try anymore, you'll just be here, it'll happen all by —"

"How do you know? You've never lost anyone you loved."

"He was my father —"

"He was *my* lover, my best friend, the man of my life."

"Yes, I know, but —"

"Non!" Héloïse exclaims. "You have no idea. *Se taire. C'est conneries!"*

Amandine wants to stand, she wants to bite back, to tell her mother to snap out of it, to tell her it's been long enough now, it's time to move on, to forget him (or, at least, not remember him every second of every day) and to forgive herself. Instead, Amandine tells herself, yet again, to be patient.

"Désolé," Héloïse says. "I didn't mean to

65

say, to be . . ."

"It's okay, *Maman,* I underst— I mean, I don't, of course, but that doesn't mean I can't help you, it doesn't mean —"

Héloïse nods. "I know . . . I know you want me — you think I'm holding on too tight. And I try. But . . . when you've loved and lived with a man for thirty-five years, it isn't so easy to let him go just like that."

Amandine takes a deep breath. "I just —"

"I know," Héloïse says, squeezing her daughter's hand. "And I will. I am."

"Okay," Amandine says softly. "I just want you to be happy. You're still young, you can still love again, or —"

A smile creeps to the edge of Héloïse's lips. "Don't finish that thought, *s'il vous plaît, non.*"

"Oh, *Maman,* you're such a prude." Amandine squeezes her mother's hand, flooded with hope at the sight of her mother's first smile since her father died. "And you're still at the center of your life, even though you act as if you're circling the edges of it, you can still have pleasu—"

"Oui, oui," Héloïse says, "enough of that."

Amandine nudges Héloïse gently with her shoulder, grinning. *"Je t'aime."*

Héloïse is about to answer but instead starts to laugh. At first it's a little giggle at the back of her throat, then a full chuckle so her shoulders shake with delight. And, while she laughs for the first time in a very long time, Héloïse feels free. And the blanket of grief and guilt begins to lift a little and let her breathe.

Amandine seizes the moment. "*Maman,* will you come to the book group tomorrow night? We all miss you and I'd —"

Héloïse looks at her daughter, her laughter dried up, but its echoes still in her voice. "I haven't read the book."

"You have. It's *She Came to Stay.* You've read it at least five hundred times."

Héloïse snorts. "Hardly."

"Don't tell me you couldn't recite it by heart."

"Perhaps."

"Please, *Maman.*" Amandine draws out the syllables *maman,* as she did when she was a little girl. "Please come."

Héloïse waits, torn. She can feel François's breath on her cheek.

Je t'aime. Je vous aimerai toujours.

She wants to listen. She wants to pretend he's still sitting next to her on that bench. She wants to hold his hand. And then she looks back into her daughter's eyes.

"*D'accord,*" Héloïse says at last. "I will come."

CHAPTER FOUR

When Cosima Rubens was eight years old
her teacher asked the class what they all
wanted to be when they grew up. And, when
they'd decided, they had to pick a role
model who had that job and interview them.
Cosima didn't have to think twice, she
didn't have to weigh her options or investi-
gate the possibilities; she'd known since she
was four years old what she wanted to be: a
mother. Unfortunately, she didn't have a
mother of her own to interview on the
subject, only her big sister, Kat, who refused
to answer her questions, claiming — perhaps
rightly — that she didn't have the necessary
qualifications. And so, instead of finding
someone else's mother, Cosima pretended
her own mother was still alive and answered
the interview herself on her mother's behalf.
Cosima told her teacher that this experience had only further convinced her that

she had indeed chosen the right path for herself.

As a little girl, Cosima spent much of her time practicing the art of mothering. She dressed her dolls in different outfits every morning, brushed and plaited their hair, and served them a nutritious and balanced diet of imaginary food for every meal. Sometimes she asked Kat's advice about certain things she wasn't sure of, like how to make a neat bed with hospital corners, or how to bake an imaginary loaf of bread, or how to explain to her doll daughters that some people died before you'd even met them and never came back.

At twelve years older, Kat was fully able to furnish her sister with all the required information and knowledge. And, even when she didn't feel so inclined, when she'd rather be chatting with her friends or doing her homework, she still did it to the best of her ability. Kat took care of Cosima because it was her duty and she believed in such things as duty, honor, and family. She also loved her sister. When Cosima hit puberty and began looking at boys, Kat, by then studying for her PhD in Applied Mathematics at Cambridge University, advised her to keep looking for the best and not marry her heart to the first one she met. Fortunately, as a teenager, Cosima heeded this particular piece of advice well, recovering easily from rejection and heartbreak and quickly renewing her search — once she'd shed her tears — for a better specimen of boyhood. Her standards were high and her mission a pressing one, so she couldn't afford to stay fixated for long on anyone who failed to be a perfect fit. By the time Cosima turned thirteen, she'd dated and discarded every boy in her class and a good many boys in other classes too.

Kat, on the other hand, as is so often the case with people who give great advice, didn't follow it herself. At twenty-five, she suffered from an inability to fall out of love with her best friend who, she was pretty certain, didn't return her affections. Not wanting to damage her credibility as a good role model, Kat kept this information a secret from her sister. She added it to the other, far more dreadful, family secret she'd recently discovered on a routine visit to her doctor. Kat kept this secret for another year, every day unable to break her sister's heart. It wasn't until Cosima turned fourteen and got her period that Kat finally told her: she wasn't allowed to have children.

Cosima's heart remained impervious until

she turned eighteen and met Tommy Rutherford. She'd just finished her A-Levels and was wondering what to do next when she saw him playing cricket on Midsummer Common one Saturday afternoon. Tommy was tall, broad, and blond and Cosima couldn't take her eyes off him. She completely forgot that she'd been on her way to meet her sister for lunch and so, while Kat was left waiting at Fitzbillies, Cosima settled on the grass to watch the man who, she was quite sure, would become the love of her life.

By a lovely stroke of luck the cricket ball rolled straight into Cosima's lap after Tommy bowled out an irate member of the opposing team and, when he ran over to collect it, she struck up a conversation and let him convince her to wait and take her for a drink after the sun had set and the game was over. She went home with him that night and by the time the sun had risen again she knew that this was it: he was The One. She prayed to Hera, the Greek goddess of love and marriage, that he felt the same way because Cosima knew that, this time, for the first time and quite against her will, she'd given her whole heart and wouldn't be getting it back, at least not in one piece.

They moved in together six months after they met. He proposed on her twenty-first birthday and they married in Venice while traveling around Europe. They fell in love with the city and stayed, living in a beautifully dilapidated room overlooking a canal and ten minutes' walk from St. Mark's Square where Tommy spent his days as a waiter and his evenings drinking espresso in the red velvet booths of Florian's Café, imbibing the spirits of Henry James and Mark Twain and hoping to pen his own masterpiece there. Cosima found a job as a kitchen porter in Café Del Gusto and, finding to her surprise that she enjoyed cooking, rose slowly up the ranks to sous chef in charge of puddings and pastries. On Cosima's twenty-fifth birthday Tommy's manuscript was accepted by an agent and sold to a publisher for a good sum, enough to enable them to return to Cambridge, rent a nice flat, and allow Cosima to open her own café. A year after that, the novel *Lost for Words* was published to great acclaim and Tommy soon spent much of his time in London and touring. Cosima sometimes complained that she no longer saw enough of him, but really she was happy and proud of her husband. Sunday, whenever Tommy was in the country, was their day together.

"What are you thinking about?"

Cosima sighs and gives him a wistful smile. "Babies."

Tommy strokes a strand of hair back from her face. "I thought so."

"Am I that predictable?"

Tommy grins. "I'm afraid so."

Cosima blushes. She still can't really believe she got so lucky, that she still finds Tommy Rutherford to be the most beautiful boy in the world — more than ten years after they first met. But, since he's tall, broad, blond with big lips and big blue eyes, she suspects a few other women might agree with her.

"Don't worry, it'll happen soon," Tommy says, pulling her into a hug. "And, until it does, we'll just have a jolly good time trying."

"Yes," she says, "of course we will."

Cosima and Tommy sit on Midsummer Common, under a tree on the patch of grass where they first met. As is their tradition, Cosima has baked a plethora of goodies: sour cherry and chocolate cupcakes, goat's cheese and pesto pizzas, orange oil cannoli, and — Tommy's personal favorite — lemon and lavender cake. Cosima doesn't simply bring leftovers from Gustare, she bakes everything specially, since each contains a secret ingredient selected to facilitate fertility. Despite the fact that Cosima and Tommy have been eating these special goodies nearly every Sunday since returning to England, the magical properties have yet to take effect.

Cosima fingers the hem of her dress, tipping her head down so her long black hair falls over her face. "I just wish, I wish it wasn't taking so long. I mean, I don't mind waiting — well, not too much — but every month that passes I get more scared that it might never happen."

Tommy reaches for Cosima's hands, holds them to his chest, and kisses her fingers over and over again. "I know you do, my love. But I promise you, it will be okay. You will get your dream. I just know it, I do."

Cosima looks up from under her bangs. "Really?"

Tommy nods. "I know it."

And, as Cosima looks into his big blue eyes and smiles, she feels a twinge of guilt over the secret she's been keeping from him all these years, the one she knows she'll never tell him. Because, if Tommy knew the great risks involved in Cosima getting pregnant, he'd never let her do it. Never. And she couldn't bear that.

■ ■ ■ ■

The first time Kat met George was at a summer party in Trinity College gardens. She was studying applied mathematics and set to get a first. She was young and beautiful, with long legs and long dark hair and every boy in the math department wanted to date her. Kat, being of a democratic state of mind, had given them all a chance but none really took her fancy. Henry Hamblion, being the least boring of the set, was granted license to take her out every Friday night and sometimes Saturdays too. They went to the cinema and to dinner, they kissed in her college bedroom with the lights off and sometimes went further, though Kat's heart was never really in it.

She barely noticed George the first time. He was standing at the drinks table, choosing between the small selection of soft drinks on offer. Her eyes swept over him — short, round, and bespectacled, with a mess of mousy brown hair, wearing a gray cardigan with patches on the elbows — to settle on the dashing professor who'd taught her advanced trigonometry that term. Leaving Henry to discuss the golden circle with his classmates, Kat strode across the grass to snatch up Dr. Brown before someone else did. But, when she reached the rows of glasses filled with red wine, George stepped in front of her and, not looking up, spilled his orange juice down her T-shirt.

"Oh, gosh, oh gosh, I'm so, so," he mumbled, "so sorry, I didn't see you."

"You weren't looking." Kat scowled at George, who was fumbling for a tissue in his pocket. He held it out, brushing it in the general direction of her breasts. She snatched it from him. "Stop! It's fine, I'll sort it out."

"Yes, yes, of course, sorry."

"Stop apologizing."

"Sorry." George blushed. "I mean, sorry. Gosh, I'll shut up now."

Kat ignored him, patting the tissue to her chest.

George dropped his hand as he stared fixedly at the ground. In the next moment, he glanced up to see that the T-shirt was already dry and the stain had evaporated.

Kat inwardly cursed herself, not having meant to do something so obvious. But sometimes such things happened when she wasn't paying attention. George had stared at her chest and, just as Kat was about to swat his chin, he opened his mouth.

"Oh," he said. It wasn't an exclamation of

surprise or shock, but of understanding. "You — you're like me."

Of all the things Kat might have imagined he was about to say, that certainly hadn't been one of them.

"What do you mean?"

George smiled a smile of deep recognition, of joy, of delight.

"You know," he said. "You know exactly what I mean."

Kat sits in her study in Trinity College. She's had it adapted to her personal taste, so three walls are made of blackboard and covered from ceiling to floor with mathematical equations. Her favorite, the fundamental theorem of calculus, is framed in silver and glass above her desk:

$$f(x) = a_0 + \sum_{n=1}^{\infty} \left(a_n \cos\frac{n\pi x}{L} + b_n \sin\frac{n\pi x}{L} \right)$$

Every inch of the other wall, above her desk, is lined with textbooks. On the fourth shelf, in the corner, sits a picture of Albert Einstein with wild white hair and sticking out his tongue that Kat remembers to study whenever she feels herself getting too serious — at least once an hour.

Kat is top of her field. She's had more than fifty research papers published in the last ten years. At forty-one, she's the youngest departmental head of applied mathematics at Cambridge University. And yet . . . it's not as if Kat isn't a beautiful woman. It's not as if she isn't still propositioned by men, even, sometimes, by her own students. Unfortunately, since Kat, aged twenty-one, gave her unrequited heart away to someone else, she hasn't had much luck on the dating front. Even before that, her love life was slightly pitiful, as she's always had the tendency to fall for unobtainable men. Kat's first crush was on her math teacher, a tall, floppy-haired, bespectacled man who spoke so passionately about compound fractions that she wanted to listen to him for the rest of her life. It was an unrequited and unfulfilled desire. For Kat, it's all been downhill from there.

Kat puts down the piece of white chalk she was pressing between her fingers and thinks about love. Why is it that her sister got so lucky and she got so unlucky? Why couldn't she fall in love with someone who'd be a perfect fit? Or, at least, an approximate one? If only life were like a perfectly balanced mathematical equation.

Sadly though, at least for one Rubens sister, it isn't so. Which is exactly why Kat spends more of her time with equations than she does with people.

If Kat spent the rest of her days alone in the Department of Applied Mathematics, she'd be okay. Not exactly joyful, perhaps, but a lifetime of heartbreak and disappointment has taught Kat to keep her standards — and thus the probability for further heartbreak and disappointment — very, very low. Having learned her lessons in life early, Kat is spending the rest of her days (from her early forties to forever) being careful not to expect anything more than she already has, which, all things considered, is really quite a lot.

As a result of this careful lifestyle, Kat worries a great deal about those she loves. When Cosima wanted to open a café in the center of Cambridge, Kat urged her to reconsider, warning her sister that the town was already soaked with coffee shops, that 60 percent of small businesses failed within the first year, that she might not be able to cope with the work needed to make the café a success. And yet, to Kat's great relief and surprise, in less than a year, Cosima had created a gorgeous little Italian café on the corner of Bene't Street and Peas Hill and already made a great success of it.

Kat has to admit that she's always under-
estimated her little sister, probably since
she was the one (with the sporadic assistance of assorted nannies employed by
their heartbroken father) changing Cosima's diapers, wiping her bum, cleaning her
spit-up, teaching her how to walk and wash
and eat. And when you've done all that for
a person perhaps you'll always see them as
someone who needs help, who can't func-
tion alone in the big, bad world.

Occasionally, Kat detects the aftertaste of
a spell in Cosima's cooking — one to add
extra flavor or mask the bitterness of being
burned on a slice of cake or a pistachio
croissant — but nothing too serious. As
children, Kat had taught Cosima a few
tricks now and then, including the odd baking spell, but her little sister had always been
more interested in playing with her dolls
than learning the magical properties of flowers and herbs. Cosima's games always
involved weddings starring Snow White,
Sleeping Beauty, or Rapunzel marrying
Prince Charming. Kat had watched, warning her against giving her whole heart to
one man. Of course, her lucky little sister
had found her Prince Charming; Kat just
hadn't found hers.

■ ■ ■ ■

"What's the occasion?" Cosima asks, grinning. After a busy shift at the café, she's stepped through her front door — sweaty and exhausted — to find the kitchen table set with candles and a bottle of Bollinger chilling on ice next to a bouquet of yellow roses.

Cosima drops her coat on the sofa. "What have I done to deserve this?"

In all the years that they've been together, Tommy has never cooked more than tomato pasta or cheese on toast. Not that Cosima ever minded — he's more than made up for his deficiencies in the kitchen by his dedication in the bedroom — but she's deeply touched he's made the effort tonight.

Tommy pokes his head out of the kitchen. "Just sit down, my love, your steak en croute is on its way."

Cosima raises an eyebrow. *"Steak en croute?"*

Tommy grins. "I bought a book. So far, so good. It'll be edible, at least."

Cosima sits at the table, smoothing a red linen napkin across her lap. "So, are you going to keep me in suspense?"

"What?" Tommy calls from the kitchen.

"Can't a man cook his wife dinner once in a while, just as an act of love and devotion?"

Cosima laughs. "Some men, yes, but you've never done it before in your life. You tend to have . . . other ways of expressing your devotion. And this champagne must have cost a couple of hundred quid, so —"

"Three hundred and forty five, actually."

"What?" Cosima squeals. "Oh, my God. What's going on?"

Suddenly the shriek of the smoke alarm blares through the little flat. Cosima jumps up from her chair and Tommy runs out of the kitchen, smoke billowing out behind him. Frantically waving a dishcloth to clear the air, Tommy runs around the kitchen table while Cosima laughs, yanking the alarm off the wall and pulling out the batteries.

"Thank goodness for that." Tommy sighs into the silence. He leans over his knees to catch his breath. "I'm so bloody unfit, it's ridiculous."

Cosima peeks into the kitchen to examine the charred steak. She returns to Tommy and pats his back. "Honey, I think we'd best skip dinner and take the champagne straight to the bedroom. Then you can tell me your news."

Tommy stands, still holding his tea-towel,

and grins at her. "BBC Films just optioned my book. For rather a lot of money."

Cosima gapes at him. "Really? Oh, my God, that's amazing! Congratulations! I'm so happy, I'm so happy for you."

"For us, Cosi, this means we can buy the flat outright and you can own your café and —"

"Seriously?" Cosima gasps. "That is a *lot* of money."

Tommy grins. "That's what I said."

"We could use it to pay for IVF, so we don't have to wait forever."

Tommy pulls Cosima into a tight hug and kisses her. "Whatever you want, my darling, whatever you want."

Cosima is sighing a sigh of deep contentment, and thinking that this is the happiest moment of her life so far, when a phone begins to ring. Tommy roots around in his jeans. When he sees the number, he frowns.

"Sorry, sweetheart," he says, stepping away, "I've got to take this. It's . . . my editor."

Cosima nods as he walks out of the living room and into the hallway, and starts unwrapping the champagne. The cork pops across the room when she hears Tommy exclaim then begin saying "Oh, God" over and over again. Still holding the bottle, Cosima hurries into the hallway to find Tommy leaning against the staircase, tears falling down his cheeks.

"What's happened, my love, what's going on?" Cosima rushes up to her husband and hugs him. "What's wrong?"

Tommy pulls away, shaking his head.

"What is it?" Cosima persists. "What's wrong?"

Tommy crumples onto the stairs. After several very long minutes, he wipes his eyes, takes a deep breath, and looks up at her.

"I'm so sorry," he whispers. "I've done something unforgivable."

Silence stretches out between them.

"What is it? What have you done?" But, even as she says the words, Cosima knows. She can't believe it, not for a second, but she knows.

Tommy drops his head to his knees. "It was over. A long time . . . months ago. It was just a silly flirtation. Nothing was going to happen . . ."

"But, but, but it did," Cosima says, unable to understand how she can still speak while her world is falling apart. "Didn't it?"

Slowly, Tommy nods.

"How . . . how many times?"

Tommy looks up. "Only once. I promise. It was only once."

"Only?" Suddenly Cosima shrieks, her voice almost as piercing as the smoke alarm. "So, so, that makes it all right? Because it was only once?!"

"No, of course not," Tommy says, stricken. "That wasn't what I meant, I just, I just . . ."

"What?" Cosima's voice breaks. "You what? You broke our vows. And you're breaking, breaking my heart . . . and you what? What are you going to say?!"

Tommy shakes his head and lets out another sob. "I'm so sorry, I'm so, so sorry."

Cosima looks at him, still unable to believe it. "I don't, I can't . . ."

Her head is spinning, she can't catch her breath, her palms are suddenly sweaty, and she's shaking. Cosima starts to hyperventilate. She bends over to drop her head between her knees.

Tommy leaps up and puts his arms around her shoulders. "Oh, Cosi, I can't, I can't bear to —"

Cosima pulls away from him as if she'd just received an electric shock. "Don't. Touch. Me."

"Sorry, I . . ."

Cosima shakes her head. "No. You don't ever get to touch me again. Ever."

Tommy shakes his head, tears running down his cheeks. "No, no . . . Please, I couldn't stand it, I couldn't . . ."

Cosima sobs. When she looks at him, all she can see is her Tommy, her boy, her love, and the thing he says he's done seems suddenly impossible. It was once. One horrible thing. And if she takes it away, if she rubs out the stain and forgets it was ever there, then he's still as pure and beautiful as the day they met. Once. Only once.

"Cosi . . ."

Tommy reaches up to her and, all of a sudden, Cosima is overcome with the need to touch him, to hold him, to make him hers again. She drops to her knees and rests her head in his lap. As Tommy strokes her hair, so softly, so tenderly, she feels the fall of his tears on her cheeks and she believes, for the briefest of moments, that everything will be okay, that their love will be strong enough to heal everything, to swallow this hurt, to absorb it, to eventually forget it altogether. They are strong enough to do this, she is strong enough, Cosima knows this. And then, she realizes something.

"But . . ." She pulls her head from his lap and looks up. "Why are you telling me all this now? If it was — the phone call? What was it? What happened?"

Tommy drops his head again. His voice is muffled, almost inaudible but Cosima already feels sick, already knows.

"She . . ." Tommy whispers, "she — she's . . ."

And, even though he can't bring himself to say the word, Cosima still hears it, a piercing cry in the silence, signaling the death of her hope and the complete shattering of her heart.

CHAPTER FIVE

Noa hurries along Magdalene Street toward Heather's house. It's late, nearly midnight, but it's also Friday night, which means her aunt will be baking bread. She's been doing it since Noa was a little girl, filling the house with the gorgeous scent of doughy yeast until every room smelled like a bakery. Noa loves baking night, not the actual weighing and measuring and kneading, but sitting in the breakfast nook with a milky coffee to keep her awake while watching Heather bake.

In the distance she hears the King's College clock chime the twelve strokes of midnight, and starts to run. Just before the bridge, Noa stops to catch her breath. Her hands on her sides, she tilts her head back to look up at the sky when she's splashed with liquid. Noa wipes her face with the back of her hand and frowns. It isn't raining. Then she realizes it isn't water, but wine. Noa squints up in the darkness, thinking she sees a shadow of someone up in the turrets of Magdalene College, and then another someone, and then another.

"Hey!" Noa calls out. "What are you doing up there?"

The shadows freeze.

"I can still see you," she yells. "I've already seen you."

Silence.

And then the moon slips out from behind a patch of cloud and Noa can see one of the shadows more clearly, though she can hardly believe it.

"Professor Bisset? Is that you?"

A faint curse echoes from the turret, then a hushed voice.

"Wait there."

Noa, wondering what on earth is going on, waits.

When Amandine pushes open the heavy wooden door of the college and steps out onto the pavement, she hurries straight over to Noa, who's frowning.

"Professor Bisset? Are you drunk?"

"No, of course not!"

"Then why are you sitting on the rooftop? Or, rather, hovering above it."

Instead of answering, Amandine whispers a simple forgetting spell she learned from

Kat a few years before.

"Reminiscere quod vidi. Oblitus quod vides. Reminiscere quod vidi. Oblitus quod vides."

"What are you doing?" Noa raises an eyebrow as she sees another of Amandine's secrets. "You're trying to cast a spell on me."

While Noa gasps, Amandine sighs. Of all the people who could have seen them, it had to be her strange student, the one who can see people's secrets. When confronted with awkward questions from overinquisitive passersby before, she'd always been able to cover her tracks and protect the book group with forgetting, mystifying, or confusion spells. But she can see none of them will work on Noa.

"What are you doing up there?"

Seeing she has no other alternative, Amandine answers.

"That's pretty cool," Noa says. "Can I join?"

Amandine starts to shake her head and form her lips into the word no, but somehow finds herself nodding and saying yes instead.

"Great, thanks." Noa smiles. "How do I get up there? You don't fly, do you?"

Amandine casts her student a curious glance, wondering if she may be a witch after all, or a very rare and subtle sort of enchantress.

"We go up by the stairs," she says, turning. "Follow me."

"I hated it. I read it two years ago, and I hated it," Noa says. "Sorry," she adds, seeing the looks the other members of the Cambridge University Society of Literature and Witchcraft are now fixing her with. "I mean to say, well, it wasn't quite to my taste."

Héloïse looks at the newest member of their little book group, wondering why Amandine had agreed to admit her, and regretting her impulsive decision to rejoin the group. It's too soon. It's far too soon.

"I'm not sure you picked up the subtleties of the story," Amandine suggests, seeing how suddenly distressed her mother looks. "Or perhaps you don't remember the story very well. In a sense it's —"

"Pretentious rubbish," Noa says. "That is to say, I mean . . ." She glances to the other two, still-silent, members: Kat and George. Kat raises an eyebrow in her direction while George examines his feet, flexing his toes in his shoes. Kat glances at George's feet too.

"You're talking about Simone de Beauvoir," Héloïse snaps, in heightened hushed tones, each word as sharp as a spike of ice, as if Noa had just blasphemed during

91

confession. Suddenly, her fury momentarily eclipsing her sorrow, she feels sparks of angry passion at her fingertips. "She was the pioneer of modern feminism. Without her, you would be chained to a kitchen sink with fifteen *petits enfants* tugging at your apron strings."

"Yes, true," Noa says, "and I'm very grateful for that." *Don't say it,* she tells herself, *don't say it. Keep your mouth shut. Please.*

"So," Noa begins, cursing herself as she speaks but unable to stop, "you're the sort of friends who just nod and smile and don't really tell one another the truth, right?"

A little sigh escapes Amandine's lips.

"I'm sorry, what?" Kat asks.

"You are all so suppressed," Noa says. "You're practically dead to the world."

"Mademoiselle," Héloïse slowly pulls herself up, "I am not sure you realize this privilege, being invited to join our group. We can easily uninvite you, so be aware, *s'il vous plaît.*"

"Sorry," Noa says, "that came out wrong. I didn't mean . . ."

"What did you mean?" Amandine asks.

Noa gives her a grateful look, wondering how on earth she's going to explain her outburst without giving herself away. "Well," Noa says, scrambling, "I just meant to . . .

to inject a little life into the group, a little passion and vigor, a little *joie de vivre* . . ."

Kat adjusts her glasses. "I assure you, we've all got quite a lot of that, and we certainly don't need lessons in living from a teenager who's lived half as long as the rest of us."

"I'm not a teenager," Noa objects softly.

"Almost," Héloïse snaps. "I am probably three times older than you."

"Exactly right." Kat nods. "Well, actually 58.2 into 23.5 is 2.47, so not quite, but close enough."

Noa frowns. "How do you know how old I am?"

"I've got two PhDs in applied mathematics," Kat explains. "I see everything in numbers."

George gives a quiet cough. "I'm afraid I've got to be up early for a lecture tomorrow." He stands and edges toward the parapet. "So, if we're not going to discuss Ms. Beauvoir's novel, I'll leave you ladies to discuss . . . whatever it is you're going to discuss." And, with that, he disappears down the ladder.

"He's so timid I'm surprised he can get out of bed in the morning," Noa says. She turns to Kat. "How long have you been in love with him?"

Kat stares at Noa, her eyes suddenly as wide as her glasses. Héloïse splutters and Amandine is silent, averting her gaze to the rooftop.

"I'm sorry," Noa says, "but you are, aren't you?"

Kat spins around to Amandine. "What did you tell her? I never said — have you been reading my feelings again? You promised you wouldn't do that anymore."

"I didn't say anything," Amandine says. "And I wish I could stop doing that." Her voice drops so low they can barely hear her above the breeze. "I can't."

"You told me," Kat protests, "you told me you could."

Amandine gives an apologetic shrug. "I'm sorry, I can't really help it."

Kat turns to Héloïse. "Did you know?"

"Bien sûr." Héloïse gives a slight shrug. "You forget my psyc— at least, before . . ."

"Bloody hell." Kat sighs and sinks her head to her knees. She looks up. "At least Cosi doesn't know. And, God forbid, George."

"Cosi?" Noa asks.

"My sister. Luckily she's neither an empath nor psychic," Kat says, casting dark looks at Amandine and Héloïse in turn. "And George, well . . ."

Noa regards Kat more closely. Then she stands. "Well, I guess I'd better go. I didn't mean to ruin your book group. I don't mean to be a bitch. I just, I can't seem to . . . whatever I see, I just say it." She turns and walks toward the ladder. When her left foot is on the first rung she turns back to the three witches. "Please forget what I said."

"You're not a bitch," Amandine says. "You just see what you —"

"Shouldn't," Noa finishes. "I know. I don't want to . . . I see things about people, it rises up like a sneeze, and I just can't swallow it back down, no matter how hard I try."

"You don't need to go," Amandine says.

Noa sighs. "I already told you that you think your husband is having an affair with some sexy lawyer at his firm. Also, you haven't had sex with him in nearly two months." She looks at Héloïse. "You still talk to your dead husband at the breakfast table every morning and every evening you wonder if you should swallow that bottle of paracetamol in your bathroom cabinet." Noa looks at Kat. "And the real reason —"

"Enough," Kat snaps.

"I'm sorry," Noa says. "You see, I'm no fun to be around. No one wants to be friends with a human lie detector test." She climbs down onto the second rung of the ladder. "Thank you, Professor Bisset, it was kind of you to invite me to your book group. I'm sorry I spoiled the meeting." She steps down to the third rung. "Apologies to you all."

And, with that, her blond bob disappears behind the red brick.

"I feel awful for the poor girl," Amandine says. "Can you imagine living like that?"

"That's your problem," Kat says with a sniff. "You're too nice."

"I am not," Amandine protests. She can't stop thinking about what Noa said about the paracetamol, but she's nervous to ask her mother if it's true. "I absolutely am not."

Héloïse pats her daughter's knee. "I'm afraid you are, *ma petite,* you always have been. When you were a little girl I had to teach you not to apologize all the time. At school, if a child trod on your toes, you'd say sorry. If someone stole your lunch-box, you'd say sorry . . ."

"Okay, okay," Amandine says. "I get it."

The three witches sit in a booth at Gustare, drinking coffee and eating pistachio cream croissants for breakfast. After the book group fiasco the night before, Amandine had persuaded them to meet again the next morning to settle themselves and partake of a little caffeine and empty but delectable calories. Kat didn't need much persuading and together they dragged Héloïse along.

"She's an interesting case," Kat admits. "That's quite a brilliant gift to have, being able to see people's secrets, if slightly less brilliant for the people being seen."

"I feel for her," Amandine says. "It can't be easy going through life like that; I'll bet she doesn't have many friends."

Héloïse sips her coffee and sighs. "*Exactement.* You worry about a stranger. You should worry instead about your own marriage."

Amandine tears off a large piece of croissant and chews it slowly. "I've asked her to meet Eliot," she says. "I'm hoping she'll tell me what's going on."

Kat sits forward, leaning across the table. "Are you sure that's wise? She's your student, you don't want her knowing the intimate details of your marriage."

"I can trust her," Amandine says, reaching for the remainder of the croissant. "She won't tell anyone what she finds out."

"How do you know?" Kat asks. "Since she says everything she sees, maybe she won't be able to help it."

Amandine shakes her head. "That's only

to the person whose secret she sees, not the whole wide world. At least, I hope so."

"*Moi aussi,*" Héloïse says.

Amandine catches her mother's eye. "Can't you tell me what's going on with Eliot?"

"*Désolé,*" Héloïse says softly. "I would, if I could, of course. But since your father . . . I still can't . . ."

"*Maman?*" Amandine asks, tentative. "Is it true?"

"*Quoi?*"

"What she said about the — pills."

Héloïse gazes into her coffee cup. Amandine waits until her mother at last looks up.

"I won't do anything," Héloïse says. "I can promise you that."

"But you want to?"

Héloïse gives another little shrug. The blue silk scarf on her shoulders ripples and slides down across her breast. She picks it up and turns to Kat.

"So this girl is right in everything, is she?" Héloïse says. "You will not tell George again how you feel?"

"Shush!" Kat hisses, glancing around the café.

Amandine giggles. "I don't think he has spies hiding around corners, he's not the subterfuge type."

"It's his favorite café," Kat snaps. "And if my sister overheard, she'd tell him in a second. She's forever trying to fix me up."

"Is Cosi working tonight?" Amandine asks. "I haven't seen her. I'll say hello."

Héloïse smiles. "You're just hoping she'll give you free cakes."

"Well, there is that too, of course."

Héloïse looks at Kat. "So, will you tell George?"

"Of course," Kat says, picking at the flaky pastry of a croissant. "One day. When I solve Hilbert's eighth problem or Kepler's $M = E - \epsilon \sin E$."

Héloïse raises an eyebrow. "And am I right in supposing that this will not happen especially soon?"

"It's a delicate situation," Kat says. "And there are other factors to consider, it's not just a simple matter of declaring oneself. It's complicated."

"Ah, *oui*." Héloïse smiles. "Of course it is."

"Shut up," Kat snaps. "I'm waiting for the right time."

Amandine fixes Kat with a coy smile. "And a perfect opportunity hasn't happened to crop up in the two decades you've known each other, is that it?"

Kat glares at her.

"*Alors,* so you're not really scared," Héloïse says. "You are simply being strategic, *oui?*"

Kat starts shredding the croissant. "You two don't know what you're talking about. There's a lot more to it. For starters, he wants children, and I can't have them. And, anyway —"

"That's not a deal-breaker," Amandine says. "You can adopt."

"I'm sure he wants his own," Kat protests. "And I can't ask him to compromise that, it wouldn't be fair —"

"You could ask him," Héloïse suggests. "That might be a first step."

"Hey," Kat snaps, "when was the last time you put your heart out there to be stamped on? You were married forever, to a man who adored you — you never had to risk anything."

A silence falls over the table and the three women all avoid one another's eyes. Amandine sneaks a sideways glance at her mother, wondering if she should say something to deflect the subject and fill the silence. But then Héloïse looks up.

"*C'est vrai,*" she says. "But I'm no longer married, am I? So what's left of my heart has now been quite thoroughly stamped on, wouldn't you say?"

Kat nods, ceasing her shredding of the unfortunate croissant.

"But I am learning," Héloïse continues, "that hiding my heart away from the world — for risk of further stamping — is to give up on life. I'm afraid I cannot recommend it."

Kat nods, taking the older woman's hand and squeezing it. "I'm sorry. And I'm glad you're back. We missed you."

"Yes," Héloïse says softly, "me too."

Amandine takes her mother's free hand and Kat's. The three women sit together, holding one another tight and falling into silence again.

Ten sleepless nights later, Cosima still slips into unconsciousness only at dawn, then wakes an hour later. And, for one blissful moment, she forgets. She still thinks Tommy is sleeping beside her, still believes in true love, still has an unbroken heart. And then, in the next terrible moment, she remembers.

Every morning Kat visits, bringing treats and things she hopes will help to heal her sister. She force-feeds Cosima chocolate brownies for breakfast, baked to her own special recipe: a pinch of powdered Michaelmas daisy for farewell, two pinches of dried magnolia for dignity, three drops of jasmine for separation, and celandine for joys to come. This, along with four drops of witch hazel in her glass of warm milk, ensures Cosima's relatively easy recovery. Of course, Kat isn't a miracle worker and broken hearts will only fully heal when their owners finally want to forgive and forget, but incredibly, on the eleventh morning Kat is able to persuade Cosima to return to the café.

And, when Cosima is again holding a bag of sugar and a jar of dried daisy petals over a fresh, warm batch of sour cherry and chocolate cupcakes, she makes two vows: she will never give her heart to a man again and she will take her destiny into her own hands.

In six months she'll turn thirty and Cosima knows that a woman's fertility drops drastically after that fateful birthday. The clock is ticking. Now that she's lost Tommy and sworn off true love, she needs to find a man who shares her dream of parenthood. She's given up on the idea of being loved; she's no longer looking for Prince Charming, she's just looking for a man who's happy to impregnate her, a man who wants to be a father. Given what Kat told her all those years ago, Cosima understands the enormous risks of such a venture, which is why she's being extra stringent in her standards. She needs to find the best possible father for her baby, to compensate for the worst-case scenario that she won't survive to be its mother, just as her own mother didn't for her. And since she's failed to find and keep romantic love by natural means, Cosima decides that morning to settle for platonic love by magical means instead.

Cosima stands at her oak-topped counter, absorbing the scent of a batch of walnut and stilton bread she's just pulled out of her oven. As she sniffs the air, Cosima contemplates her plan. She's decided to add a deeper dimension to her baking spells, putting a pinch of dried honeysuckle and purple rose petals into everything — savory and sweet — in order to help find a suitable father for her child. The spell won't change a man's desire, only highlight it for Cosima to see. It'll make spotting a potential candidate much easier; then she can better pick the one she wants before asking him to sit down and discuss the details. The spell will also highlight those with the necessary credentials, so she doesn't waste precious months on someone who wants a child but sadly can't help create one. In her wildest dreams, she might still be hoping for the whole package — love and a baby — but she's quite happy to settle for a confirmed bachelor who wants a child but not a wife.

As the milky early morning sun slips in through her kitchen windows, Cosima plucks the blossoms off her yellow squash and begins to make her way through today's menu: courgette blossom and artichoke pizza, wild mushroom and tomato bruschetta, lemon and pistachio cake, vanilla and orange oil cannoli, espresso and hazelnut tart . . . And into each bowl she sprinkles a generous pinch of paternal love, protection, and devotion. If she's right, this will bring her a brilliant batch of potential fathers before the week is out.

CHAPTER SIX

George nods absently, sneaking a glance at his watch. He's still got forty minutes of listening to first-year students muddle their way through the meaning of the archaeological sites of Christianity in ninth-century England. Forty minutes until lunchtime, until he can consume one of Cosima's delicious pizzas and a divine cannoli.

"Go on," he directs the third student, whose name escapes him.

While she continues in a dull monotone, George looks down at his stomach, significantly rounder than it was three years ago. He's never been slim but certainly wouldn't be quite so fat now if not for Cosima's cooking. Every afternoon he dines on pizza slathered with rich sauces and rarely a vegetable in sight. At this rate he'll be dead before he hits fifty.

George has never been a particularly powerful witch, with only a slight dose of magic passed down on his father's side, just a sprinkling of the supernatural in his otherwise human blood. He can move things with his mind, insignificant objects like pens and spoons; he can hear the occasional thought and invoke the odd simple incantation. But he's not an empath like Amandine, a psychic like Héloïse, or a master spell caster like Kat. George has one supernatural skill and that's the ability to keep secrets — one particular, personal secret — free from the prying eyes of psychic witches. That's been pretty useful, he supposes. But he's always longed for a little more power (Kat has always theorized that his magical powers, like his self-confidence, are locked up deep inside and he just has to unlock and unleash them) and he's never been able to find it. Which is lucky, perhaps, or he'd be tempted to work a bit of magic in his own favor to cancel the calories of the delicious food he consumes in excess every day, for example, or to find true love. And he knows the dangers of self-serving spells, the probability that they might backfire or cause general havoc and mayhem.

Less than an hour later George is standing in line to buy another deliciously decadent lunch. He's pretty sure Cosima puts something in her food to seduce her customers into coming back again and again, though he can't be certain. He'd ask her outright, if he had the guts, but he's always found Kat's sister a little bit intimidating. As he edges closer to the counter, standing in the heat of the pizza ovens, a light sweat gathers on his brow. George opens his wallet and starts counting out his cash.

"What can I get you today, Georgie?" Cosima asks. "The usual?"

"Thanks." George nods. He leans forward. "Are you okay? Kat told me . . . I'm really sorry . . ."

Cosima shakes her head. "I don't want to think about it. But I'm okay, I mean, I'll be okay."

"That's good," George says. "You deserve it. To be happy, I mean."

Cosima smiles. "Thank you. You're sweet."

Picking up a slice of squash blossom pizza with a pair of tongs, Cosima tucks a stray black curl behind her ear and adds a dusting of flour from her fingers to her cheek. George watches as she bags it up, then adds two vanilla and orange oil cannoli for luck.

"Espresso?"

George nods. "Double, thanks."

Sometimes George wishes that Cosima were his type. How glorious it would be to combine love and food, two physical and emotional delights wrapped up in one human being. Perfection. Perhaps it's a good thing, saving him from a premature heart attack.

"Try this," Cosima says, handing him a sliver of lemon-pistachio cake. "While you wait."

George's eyes widen as he takes it. "Looks delicious." He gobbles it down in one gulp. "Incredible."

Cosima laughs. "You barely tasted it."

"I have highly sophisticated taste buds," George explains. "They only need a passing lick of something in order to fully appreciate the delicate subtleties of its flavors."

"Oh, really?" Cosima smiles. "Okay then, try this and tell me what's in it." She hands him a slice of wild mushroom and grape tomato bruschetta. "Every single ingredient."

"All right then," George says, as he begins to chew. "You're on." He swallows. "Okay, in addition to the obvious: basil, garlic, olive oil, black pepper, salt . . . a splash of lemon juice and a dash of rosemary."

Cosima studies him with a raised eyebrow and a curious smile. "That's very impressive. Anything else?"

"Nope." George shakes his head. "That's

what my extremely sophisticated taste buds are telling me."

"Well then, they're pretty damn good, but not absolutely flawless."

"Really?" George asks. "What have I missed?"

"That'd be telling." Cosima grins.

"Oh, come on," George says, "that's cheating, you've got to tell me."

Cosima shakes her head. "No I don't. Trade secrets."

George smiles. "Tease."

Cosima regards George curiously. Is she sensing a frisson of flirting? She's known George since she was a kid, and she's never noticed any such thing before. How curious.

"That'll be nine pounds and eighty pence then," Cosima says. "Including the freebies and the being-Kat's-best-friend discount."

"Thanks." George grins and reaches for his wallet. "Oh, bugger," he says. "I've left my cash behind, just give me a sec."

And, before Cosima can protest, or wonder what's going on anymore, he runs out the door.

Parles. Me parler.
Héloïse shakes her head. She's sitting in her favorite armchair, it having migrated

across the living room overnight. An extra umbrella, cream with gold edges, has sprouted in the hat stand. "I shouldn't, *mon amour*," she says. "I will never let you go if I keep acting as though you are still alive."

Ne me laisse pas partir. So, don't let me go.

Héloïse is silent.

You let me go once, he protests. *Twice is too cruel.*

Héloïse feels her heart contract and momentarily stop her breath. She's having a hard enough time forgiving herself without having him remind her.

"I'm sorry," she whispers. "You know how sorry I am."

She feels his hand on her cheek, his lips on her lips. She sighs. For a moment she sits, breathing him in, then she stands.

"I must go."

Où?

"Just out," Héloïse says softly. "I just need to go out."

When she steps outside, holding the gold-edged umbrella, her high-heeled feet hitting the pavement, Héloïse doesn't know where she's going. She turns randomly down streets and walks across them, without any purpose or direction. Almost an hour later, having taken an extravagant detour through town, Hloïse finds herself outside the gates of the Botanic Garden.

Despite herself, she smiles. "Even my feet can't forget you."

It's a cool day, the sun sneaking off behind thick layers of cloud. But as she stands on the pavement, wondering in which direction to turn next, the clouds slip away and Héloïse feels the warmth on her skin. It is, perhaps, a perfect day to walk in the park.

Once inside the gardens, Héloïse quickly crosses the lawn and skirts the lake. She won't sit on their bench today. A few minutes later she's hurrying over a small stone bridge stretching over a stream. On the other side, she finds herself in a hidden cave of willow trees. Around the edge is a dirt path of dry woodchips. Héloïse follows the path, slowly at first, gazing up at the trees, at the leaves blown by the breeze. Then she begins to walk a little faster, and faster, frustration pushing her on, and soon she's too hot.

Héloïse stops and pulls her black cashmere sweater over her head, leaving only a silk camisole. She feels rather exposed, having not flashed this much skin in public in more than a decade. But the path is empty, Héloïse is alone, so what does it matter? She bends down, pulls off her high heels, and settles her bare feet on the path. The woodchips are dry but the soil is wet beneath her skin and soon Héloïse finds that she rather likes the sensation. As a girl she never went barefoot. Indeed, she never went anywhere without silk socks and satin shoes. Elegance was always something Héloïse cherished and never thought to question, yet now she feels that perhaps being swathed in silk and cashmere all her life cut her off from experiences that were even more sensual.

Two swans waddle toward Héloïse on the path and she slows to pass them. She remembers reading that swans, along with penguins and wolves, mate for life. She can almost hear François's whisper on the breeze, his laughter rustling the leaves high above her head. She takes a deep breath and starts striding along the path again, using the gold-edged umbrella as an elegant walking stick.

Two hours later Héloïse is red-faced, sweating, and feeling more alive than she has in a very, very long time. Her heart hits her chest hard, her limbs throb, her muscles ache, and she's never been so aware of her body and quite how incredible it is. And, for the first time in nearly two years, she's spent hours without thinking of, or hearing, her beloved François. Her mind has been completely empty. All thoughts of him, indeed all her thoughts, have dissipated. For almost two hours he hasn't been sitting inside her head. And, instead of feeling bone-achingly lonely, as she'd been terrified she would, Héloïse only feels free.

Cosima is standing behind the counter serving another customer when she glances out the window and sees George on the other side of the road, about to cross. He's standing on the pavement, waiting for a gap between the cars, next to two women chatting, one of them holding the hand of a small boy. The boy looks up and says something to George, who grins. And then, before Cosima can blink, the boy lets go of his mother's hand and runs into the road. Just as she's about to scream, George reaches out and snatches the boy back to safety, folding him tightly in his arms for a few seconds, then passing him to his startled, grateful mother.

"Oh my goodness," Cosima says, as George enters and strolls over to the counter. "That was amazing."

For a second he seems confused. "Oh, right, well . . ." He shrugs and hands Cosima a ten-pound note.

"You were so fast, it was incredible."

George frowns slightly. "Hardly. Anyone

could have done the same."

"I doubt it," Cosima says. She feels a sudden and unexpected flash of hope rise up in her chest. For a moment she thinks of Tommy, then suppresses the thought. "George? Do you want children?"

George's frown and confusion deepen. "Yes, I . . . I always have, actually, but the opportunity hasn't arisen."

"It still might," Cosima says. "You've got time. Men can wait as long as it takes."

George laughs. "Maybe so, but I'd rather not be one of those ancient fathers, and anyway . . ."

"What?"

But George doesn't reply, he just looks at Cosima, her long black curls tied loosely, falling down her back and framing her face, puffs of flour dusting her apron, fingers, and flushed cheeks, dark eyelashes framing her brown eyes.

"Are you okay?" she asks.

Slowly, George nods.

"Are you sure?"

George opens and closes his mouth like a trout.

"Do you want a glass of water?"

Slowly, George shakes his head. "You know, a recent excavation at an archaeological site in Ireland suggests that moat water held spiritual and cosmological significance for the inhabitants of medieval castles during Anglo-Saxon times."

"Excuse me?"

"You mentioned water and I thought perhaps . . ."

Cosima smiles, relieved he's speaking again and making some sort of sense. "I wasn't offering you moat water."

A few people in the queue behind George snicker softly.

"Of course not," George says. "How silly of me."

Cosima hands George his coffee, pizza, and cannoli. He reaches out so their fingers entwine for a moment.

"Did I ever tell you, you look like Sophia Loren?" he asks.

"Sorry?"

"I can't believe I never noticed the resemblance before."

Cosima gives George a quizzical look. "Well, thank you."

George shrugs. "It's the truth."

Cosima hands George his change but, before she can drop the coins into his hand, he shakes his head.

"Keep it," he says, stumbling half-dazed out of the door, still shaking his head and mumbling something to himself.

Cosima watches him go, wondering what on earth is going on. And then, quick as a flash, she realizes.

"Oh, no!"

The customers in the queue regard her curiously. Cosima glances down at the little stack of enchanted vanilla and orange oil cannoli on the counter. One more is missing. She glances around the café and sees, on a table by the window, a man drinking an espresso and about to take a big bite.

"No!" Cosima screams. She dashes across the café and snatches the cannoli away before it touches his lips. The man scowls up at her.

"What the hell?"

"I'm sorry," Cosima gasps. "Bad batch. I'll get you five pistachio croissants, on the house. Okay?"

She scurries off, grabbing the plate of enchanted cannoli off the counter before another unfortunate soul inadvertently eats one, and tips them all into the kitchen bin. Disaster averted, Cosima thinks back to George. What had she done wrong? What mistake had she made? Had she mixed up the flowers? Had she added a little too much honeysuckle and not enough purple rose petals? What was it? What the hell had she done to make George Benett fall in love with her? And how the hell was she going to undo it?

Every morning for the past week Noa has hoped to see Santiago again in her favorite art gallery. She spends a full hour in there, neglecting the other one, just in case he might show up again. Such was her disappointment by Friday that she almost asked the girl behind the counter how she might accidentally bump into him again, but embarrassment stopped her at the last moment. Now, on Saturday morning, Noa stands in front of Santiago's paintings wishing she had the money to buy one, thus giving her a perfect excuse to contact him, with the added bonus that she'd get to gaze at his work — the second-best thing to gazing at him — every single day.

Noa stops looking at the *Storm over Bahia* and focuses on another painting, *Amazonas:* swirls of turquoise, teal, and olive and a river of midnight blue snaking through the forest of green. Unable now to take her eyes off it, Noa reaches out a finger, very slowly, toward the blue.

"You didn't call."

Instantly, Noa drops her finger and, before turning, quickly suppresses the smile of absolute delight that spread across her face

117

the second she heard his voice.

"Hey." Noa steps slightly to the side of the painting, hoping to give the impression that she's here to enjoy all the art in the little gallery and hasn't spent the last five days staring solely at his.

"You came back to see my pictures, I'm flattered."

Noa gives a slight shrug. "Well, yeah, of course. I mean, your paintings are beautiful, but I'm always visiting galleries and museums to see everything I can, for my studies, you know . . ."

"You're a terrible liar." Santiago smiles. His mouth is wide, his teeth perfect and white against his golden skin. "Did you know that?"

Noa sighs. "Yes, it's the bane of my life."

Santiago's smile deepens. "I think it's sweet."

"Oh, no, not 'sweet,' " Noa says. "Next you'll say I remind you of your little sister."

"Not at all. And my sister is far from sweet. If you reminded me of her, I'd be scared." He takes a tiny step closer and drops his voice. "And that isn't the way I think of you at all."

"Oh." Noa holds her breath then begins to feel a little faint. She sucks in a gulp of air, then begins coughing and can't stop.

Santiago reaches out his hand and lightly cups her elbow.

"Are you all right?"

Noa nods, still coughing. A flush of warmth rises up her arm and she's overcome with a blissful, soft sense of relaxation that sinks into her skin.

"Wow," Noa says, her voice just a puff of air. "What was that?"

"I learned some healing, back in my country." Santiago raises an eyebrow and matches it with a slightly wicked smile. "I've been told I'm quite good with my hands."

"Oh, really?" Noa attempts a slightly wicked smile of her own, but ends up scowling instead. "So, um, which country is that?"

"Brazil. I'm from Bahia."

"Ah," Noa says, wishing she were better at geography.

Santiago takes another step closer, so she can almost feel the heat of his skin and the breath of his words. "It's on the east coast, on the edge of the Atlantic Ocean."

"Right, um, right," Noa says, wishing he would just grab her and kiss her. "I, um, bet it's beautiful."

"Yes," Santiago says, "beautiful and hot. Not raining every day as it is here."

"But," Noa says, trying to focus, "you don't have an accent."

"My mother is Brazilian, my father is English," Santiago says. "He brought us here when I was five. So I'm bilingual and quite used to the rain."

"Are all your . . . paintings of your home?"

Santiago shakes his head and fixes her with that gaze again.

"Not all, no. I also paint nudes, from time to time."

"You do?" Noa says, her tongue thick in her mouth. "Ah, okay."

Santiago smiles, as if he knows exactly the thoughts in her head since he just put them there. "Look, I just popped in here on my way to Gustare for a coffee. Want to join me?"

Noa nods, though two cups of coffee in one morning will probably send her into a frenzy. Especially since she's already in one. "Yes. Yes, I'd love to."

As they walk down King's Parade toward Bene't Street, Noa taking two steps for every one of Santiago's, they talk about Noa's dream of working at the National Gallery. When they sit down at a table looking out toward the market square and old courthouse, he reaches out and touches her hand. He drops his voice to a whisper.

"You know, I can get rid of that pesky tic of yours that you hate so much," he says with a little smile. "If you'd like me to."

Noa's breath catches in her throat. "What do you mean?"

Santiago's smile deepens. "You know what I mean."

"Gosh, well, yes, but," Noa mumbles, "how do you . . . know?"

Santiago sits back in his chair and slowly sips his coffee. "There are things I just know, I can't explain it. But then, isn't life better that way? Faith is so much more magical than knowledge, don't you think?"

Noa considers. "Yes, I suppose so." She takes a gulp of coffee to fortify herself and burns her tongue. "But how can you help me to stop . . . doing what I do?"

Santiago sits forward, his elbows on the table and his face close to hers. "In Brazil my mother was a *macumbera,* a white witch. She taught me many things, many skills, and I believe I can help you. Perhaps you will let me try?"

Noa cradles her coffee cup, squeezing the comforting warmth into her fingers. She wonders what to make of this stunning stranger. How does he know? Can he really help her? Noa never believed in magic (she always thought there must be a rational explanation for her odd quirk, if only she could find it) but that was before she met the Cambridge University witches. And, even if he can't, at least it's a chance to see him again.

"Okay." Noa nods. "Okay, why not?"

CHAPTER SEVEN

"Higher! Higher!"

Amandine laughs as she pushes Frankie, his little four-year-old legs kicking with sheer delight, through the air.

Next to her, Eliot pushes Bertie, very lightly, so the swing barely gets above a forty-five-degree angle.

"Carefully, Daddy," Bertie says softly, when Eliot applies a touch too much pressure and sends him a little higher.

Amandine glances over at her husband, seeing the distracted glaze in his eyes that has been so typical lately. She wonders, yet again, what he's thinking about and wishes that even if it's another woman he could put it aside and be present with his children. The thought of Eliot having an affair causes her heart to heave with hurt, but it's almost as painful seeing how he seems to have forgotten his own children.

After the twins were born, it gave Amandine as much joy to see how much Eliot loved them — to watch him stroke their fluffy little heads so gently and change their diapers so carefully, as if he might hurt them with his big man hands — as to feel how much he loved her. In those days Eliot's whole world revolved around his new family. He dashed home from London as soon as he could leave the office; he took long weekends so often that his boss finally intervened. Eliot called her three times a day and was always happy whenever Amandine called him, his voice lifting with joy as he answered the phone.

"I want to get out. I want to get out."

"Love, he wants to get out," Amandine tells her husband, her voice stronger and more focused on its target than the soft plea of her little boy.

"Oh, right, sure," Eliot says, blinking his way out of his daydream, then scooping Bertie out of the swing and popping him onto the grass.

"The slide now," Bertie says, grabbing his father's hand and pulling him in the right direction. "But you have to come with me, okay?"

Amandine watches Eliot being pulled across the park by their son, who nearly trips over his feet in delighted eagerness to get to his desired destination. She wonders why she still calls him by the endearments they've always shared — "Love, Babe, Ellie" — since there seems to be so little love between them nowadays. It's habit, she supposes, a verbal tic, not dissimilar to swearing, though it sounds so different.

"Higher, Mummy! Higher!" Frankie squeals, making sure he still has her attention.

"Okay, sorry sweetie," Amandine says, pushing him higher. Her boys might not be magical but they've always had an acute ability to tell whenever their parents' attention wavers off them for a moment. Last week, while they were having dinner, Frankie was telling her, in intricate detail, about the lifestyle of a T. rex, and she was nodding along and making noises in all the right places. Then he stopped and said: "Mummy, you're not listening." And she'd had to admit she hadn't been, not really. It's strange, Amandine thinks, how her students and other adults aren't able to tell the same thing. Or perhaps they can, but they're just too shy to say anything.

Amandine hasn't fixed a date to introduce Noa to her husband, she hasn't even worked out how she might make it happen — when was the last time they had a dinner party?

— and she dearly hopes that, after the book group disaster, Noa will still be willing. They're meeting tomorrow for another tutorial, so Amandine can ask her then. Across the park Bertie glides down the slide on Eliot's lap, giggling with glee. A shot of sadness, tinged with hope, pierces Amandine's chest and she prays to the moon goddess Mama Quilla that Noa will say yes.

The next morning Héloïse spends a few hours puttering around the house, reshelving books, doing a little light dusting, eating what's left in her fridge from Amandine's last visit, generally doing not much of anything at all. She thinks of François often, of course, since his spirit — despite Amandine's efforts — is still scattered all over the house. When Héloïse enters the living room, her eye catches on his high-backed brown leather chair, the one he sat in every evening to read Proust (it stubbornly having refused to move at all). For the last decade or so François had been trying to make it through *À La Recherche du Temps Perdu* but would always fall asleep before finishing two pages. In the kitchen she's stopped short by the last of his coffee cups. In the bathroom, his shaving brush. In every room, his words dance in the air.

Je t'aime. Je vous aimerai toujours. I love you. Ne me laisse pas partir. Don't let me go. Please . . .

Having the house full of François has given Héloïse much-needed comfort over the last two years, enabling her to pretend that he's still living, that he's just left a room as she's entered it, that he's always around a corner or down the hall. And yet, for the past few days, ever since her turn in the park, Héloïse hasn't felt just comforted but also claustrophobic.

Today their little house feels too small for one woman and one dead man. She finds that François's presence has suddenly somehow expanded, that he's sucking out all the air and squeezing her into the edges of the rooms. Something is changing.

For the past week, Héloïse has left the house at least once a day. And, with each day that passes and each step she takes outside, Héloïse finds that she's returning to herself. When she's not in the house, she doesn't hear François's voice. It's only at night now that he talks to her. Sometimes he tells stories, re-creating tales from the favorite books they shared, putting his own twists into plots he's forgotten. Although Héloïse is getting better at not talking to him, she can't stop at night. The lights go out and the darkness presses against her chest and her hands, perfectly fine by themselves during the day, want nothing more than to reach out and hold his.

When milky morning light fills the little bedroom, Héloïse is brave once again and ready to venture out into the world alone. This morning she decides to walk to the market for breakfast. When François was alive they'd gone to the market every Sunday, buying fresh buttered baguettes for breakfast, sitting out in the sunshine when the weather was warm, scurrying back to the house if it was cold or wet. On sunny days, after eating, they toured their favorite stalls, hand in hand, lingering over French cheeses, Spanish chorizo, and bags of salted almonds that never seemed to last until lunchtime.

Héloïse's favorite stall in the market has always been the secondhand-book stall, owned by a man called Ben, who inherited it from his father, Theo. Héloïse has been visiting the bookstall since she was a PhD student at Newnham, when Theo was in charge and Ben was a baby, occasionally brought to the bookstall to visit his father. As an eager student, Héloïse had shared many wonderful discussions about literature with Theo, learning a great deal from the man who, though only a few years older, seemed to have read every book ever published, many that hadn't been. A subtle flirtation had always skimmed the surface of their conversations, but it had never gone anywhere since they'd both been married then.

The years passed and Héloïse stayed on to teach and Ben grew up among the market stalls, learning the book trade and getting to know the desires and delights of the regular customers. By the time she was a professor of French literature and he was working full-time on the bookstall, Ben knew Héloïse's literary tastes almost as well as she did, offering her new books on every visit and telling her what she would and wouldn't like before she even picked it up.

Héloïse hasn't been to the market or the secondhand-book stall since François died. After drinking a double espresso, she leaves the house and, twenty minutes later, arrives first at the fresh bread stall to buy a croissant. Cambridge croissants aren't the same thing as Parisian croissants, but they'll do in a pinch. Nibbling the crusty pastry, Héloïse wanders through the four lanes of food, trinkets, arts and crafts before at last arriving at Ben and his books. She finds him kneeling on the cobbles, sorting through a large cardboard box.

"*Bonjour,* Ben."

He looks up, frowning, but instantly upon seeing her he grins and stands.

"Lou, you're back! It's great to see you."

For a second they stand together, then Ben pulls Héloïse into a hug.

"I'm sorry about François," he says softly into her shoulder. "We all miss him."

When they pull apart, Héloïse nods. "Yes, me too."

"How are you doing?" Ben asks, casting an eye up and down her. "You look beautiful as ever, I must say. But then you are the most glamorous person I know." He glances down at his own scruffy T-shirt and jeans. "I've never had the touch for glamour myself. I didn't know when you'd come back. I'm glad you have."

"Thank you, so am I. How is your papa?"

"He's well. I'll send him your regards."

Héloïse nods. "Please do." She steps toward the planks of wood covered with books that form his shop. Gazing at the jumble of colors and words, she runs her finger along some of the spines and feels herself starting to breathe more easily. What is it, Héloïse wonders, about the comfort of books? Just by touching the printed words she already feels sparks of excited curiosity begin to wake up her brain. She picks one up and holds it out to Ben.

"Any good?"

He nods. "I stayed up till four o'clock in the morning finishing it."

Héloïse smiles. "I can't remember the last time I did that."

Ben scuffs his feet in the dirt. "Well, I suppose you've had other things to . . ."

"Yes, I suppose I have." Héloïse holds the book, her hand hovering to slip it back among the others. Then, changing her mind, she presses it to her chest.

"I'll take it," she says. "It's about time I stayed up until four o'clock in the morning for a reason other than just missing my Frankie."

"Hey, Cosi, is it *seicento* grams of ground almonds instead of flour?"

Knocked out of bitter thoughts about Tommy (who'd called the night before to say that he was going to try and make a go of it with the harlot for the sake of the baby — Cosima had hung up on him), she glances up from her mixing bowl to see her sous chef, Marcello, standing in the doorway. She hired him for his Sicilian roots and huge brown eyes. The female customers adore him. They gaze at him when he asks

131

for their orders, lost in those eyes, imagining whether their future children would have his thick black hair and olive skin. He draws a crowd when he flips dough in the kitchen, women gathering on the pavement outside the windows to watch, nudging one another and giggling like schoolgirls. But sadly, for all his beauty, he lacks brains, so his genetic code is wanting. Ten times a day Marcello asks for clarification on her recipes and she's had to throw out dozens of batches of lemon-basil biscuits because he burned them. Still, Cosima can't bring herself to fire him.

"Instead of flour, Marc, otherwise the cake'll be too dry."

"Ah, certamente," Marcello says with a smile, *"perfetto. Grazie."*

When he's gone, Cosima opens her special cupboard and removes a glass jar filled with one of her special spices. Twenty-one glass jars sit in her cupboard, each unlabeled, though Cosima knows what's in every one. Now she sprinkles a dash of fennel flower (strength), scabiosa (unfortunate love), and striped carnation (I cannot be with you) over her orange and poppy seed muffins, mumbling a little incantation. This is the tenth batch of enchanted biscuits she's baked for George — in an attempt to undo this first spell, the one that has him mooning over her every lunchtime — and she hopes against hope that this might at last be the one that works.

"I know, Kat," Cosima says softly. "I know I shouldn't have done it. I know you always warned me about practicing magic for selfish purposes and I'm sorry, okay? I'm trying to make it better, but it's trickier than I thought."

All her life Cosima has felt her big sister watching over her. She's always heard Kat's voice in her head, reproving her use or misuse of magic (enchanted breakup brownies are one thing, fertility cannoli quite another) and critiquing her business decisions. Kat would have a heart attack if she knew what Cosima has been doing with the baking spells lately; she'd kill her if she knew what Cosima had accidentally done to Kat's best friend. So Cosima had better fix that, and quickly.

Marcello pokes his head around the door again.

"*Mi scusi,* Cosi, am I meant to add cream to the cake mixture before it goes in the oven? I'm sorry, it is a bit . . . thick."

Cosima smiles. "Yes, Marc, just as it says on the recipe, okay?"

"*Perfetto,* chef, *grazie.*" He nods, grinning,

and turns to go.

"Wait," Cosima says, and he does, lingering in the doorway, that hapless smile on his face. Why not give him a chance? Perhaps . . .

"*Sì,* chef?"

"Marcello." Cosima rolls her tongue around the three syllables of his name. "Would you like to work late tonight?"

Noa steps inside Santiago's flat. Her aunt Heather wouldn't like to think she's gone home with someone she barely knows, someone who claims to have the ability to rid her of the habit she hates most about herself, someone who talks about magic as if it's something he has at his fingertips. The rational, sensible side of Noa is a little nervous but even though she can't see his secrets, and even though she's not entirely sure she can trust him, when she's looking into those deep brown eyes she doesn't really care.

"Take off your shoes," Santiago says, as they reach the end of the hallway.

"Of course," Noa says, slipping off her trainers.

"Follow me," he says, reaching for her hand.

Noa allows herself to be led down the

hallway and into the living room. As Noa looks around, it takes every ounce of her depleted social graces not to gasp. The room is like a cave, like the catacombs underneath a twelfth-century church carved out of stone and painted with the faded frescos of Catholic saints. The walls are windowless and white — in places. She'd expected Santiago's pictures to be hanging everywhere but instead he's painted them directly onto the walls. Between dark green forests, deep red fields, and purple sunsets are dozens of shelves lined with hundreds of different objects. Noa can't identify even half of them immediately, though she feels she's stepped into an exotic antiques shop filled with mysterious, magical objects from all over the world.

"It's taken me thirty years to build up this collection," Santiago says. "I've been acquiring art for longer than you've been alive."

"Really?" Noa frowns. "But I thought . . . how old are you?"

Santiago smiles. "A little older than I look."

"Oh, okay," Noa says, not wanting to pry. It's still strange to her that she can't see inside him as she can with every other person she meets. Strange, but rather a relief.

Santiago crosses the carpet and, when he reaches the closest set of shelves, picks up a wooden object and brings it back to Noa. She takes it from him, tentatively examining the little statue of a naked boy, features carved into his face and what appears to be a shock of dark human hair sprouting from his head.

"It's a birth baby," Santiago says. "My mother made it after I was born, to protect me."

"From what?"

"There's black magic in Brazil, many people believe in it. We are a Catholic country, but the traditions of our ancestors still run deep in our lands."

"Oh," Noa says. "I see."

"My mother was a powerful woman," Santiago explains. "Some people were jealous of her power and wanted to hurt her. They knew, of course, that the best way to do that would be to hurt me."

"Oh," Noa says again, wondering what the right response to such information should be. "I see," she repeats, though of course she doesn't at all.

Santiago smiles, takes the little wooden statue from her hands, and places it gently back on the shelf.

"Would you like a drink?"

Noa nods. "That'd be lovely."

Santiago walks through the living room and into the kitchen, gesturing for Noa to follow. She stares at the shelves, taking in as many mysterious trinkets and magical treasures as she can before they're all out of sight.

After the magnificence of the living room, the kitchen is fairly normal, containing all the usual things one might expect and nothing much extra, except for the fact that the cupboards and walls are painted the colors of Santiago's sunsets: dark reds, deep purples, and royal blues.

"I will make you a tea from Bahia," Santiago says, opening a purple cupboard and plucking out a small tin. "We use dried leaves from various herbs and then sweeten it with local honey."

"Lovely," Noa says again, lacking any better adjectives for a curious concoction she's never tried and only hopes she manages to consume without throwing up. Noa has never had a particularly solid stomach.

Santiago pulls open a dark red cupboard and takes out a glass jar. He unscrews the lid, dips in one long, thin finger and holds it out so his fingertip, coated in thick honey, nearly touches Noa's lip.

"It's the sweetest, most delicious honey

you will ever taste," he says.

Noa looks up into soft eyes. Slowly, she opens her mouth, inviting Santiago to slip his finger between her teeth. Her heart beating so fast she can feel it in every inch of her body, Noa curls her tongue around his finger and sucks at the honey. And it is, indeed, the sweetest and most delicious honey she's ever tasted.

CHAPTER EIGHT

"You are so beautiful, so, so beautiful."

Noa smiles. She has, indeed, never felt so beautiful in her life. She glances down at her body, at the curves of her breasts, the curve of her belly, the puff of hair between her thighs. She can't quite believe that she actually offered to pose for a painting — naked — but, fortified by the splash of rum in her tea, she did.

"Tilt your face up, just a little."

Noa does so.

"That's it, perfect."

Noa looks at Santiago out of the corner of her eye, watching him standing behind an easel with a paintbrush in his right hand. His own eyes shift between gazing intently at the canvas and snatching glances at her. Noa conceals an astonished smile of delight. She had imagined — hoped — when she went home with him that they might end up in bed together, but she never for a moment imagined *this.*

"Beautiful," Santiago murmurs again, as if he can't quite believe it either, "absolutely beautiful."

As she lies there Noa is amazed at how incredibly . . . powerful she feels. Just as strong and magnificently powerful as Santiago promised her she was the first time they met. Perhaps this is his gift: an ability to make women realize the gifts they're hiding from themselves. Noa breathes deeply, realizing that she also feels calmer and more serene than she's ever known in her life. These feelings are so rare and extraordinary, almost as extraordinary as being painted naked by a virtual stranger, that Noa's smile spreads right across her face.

"What was in that honey?"

Santiago laughs. "You think I drugged you?"

"Perhaps," Noa says. "Either way, I wouldn't mind getting a pot of it myself."

"We'll have to see about that," he says. "Now, I'm afraid you have to stop smiling and stay still, or I can't paint you."

Noa swallows her smile. "Sorry."

"Shush."

"Okay, just one last thing."

Santiago smiles. "What?"

"After this, are we going to sleep together?"

Santiago's eyes widen. "Well, it's not a compulsory part of the process. But, if you really want to, then I'm sure your wishes can be accommodated . . ."

Noa laughs at the blush sinking down into his chest. "Well, okay," she says, feeling a fresh and glorious flush of power. "Let's see how the painting turns out first, shall we?"

Santiago averts his eyes to the floor and nods.

"Oh, and what about your promise to me?" Noa asks. "Can you cure me of my curse?"

Santiago leans toward his canvas until his nose is nearly touching it. He adds two more strokes, then steps back and smiles.

"I already have," he says. "It's done."

George has been walking around in a daze. He's not sure what on earth's going on but something has changed. He's been knocked off center. Drastically. All he can think about is Cosima. Which is really very strange. Somewhere, deep in the uncharted depths of his unconsciousness, he wonders if he might be under some sort of spell. But this question is a faint little light, blinking blindly in a pitch-black ocean, so he doesn't pay it any attention. And why should he?

He's got far more exciting things, both gorgeous and delicious, to focus on.

"Hey!"

George looks up. "Oh, hi, Kat, sorry, didn't see you there."

Kat frowns at him. "I'm not surprised, you've practically got your eyes closed. What are you doing, wandering around the streets like you're stoned?"

George smiles. "I was coming to visit you."

Kat brightens. "You were? Great. Have you got time for a coffee?"

"Yes, absolutely." George nods, a little too vigorously.

Kat regards him with suspicion again. "Are you sure you're okay?"

"Of course," George trills, "never better. Shall we go?"

"Oh-kaay, then," Kat says. She grabs George by the arm as he heads off in the opposite direction. "It's this way."

"Right, right, of course."

When they reach Bene't Street they can see the line of customers stretching onto the pavement out of Gustare.

Kat mumbles a curse under her breath.

"It's popular today," George says, hurrying down the street. "I hope they'll have some cannoli left for us."

They reach the end of the line and wait.

"Gosh," George says. "I've always loved your sister's food, but this is crazy." He grins. "I guess she's getting famous. It's a beautiful name, Cosima, isn't it?"

Kat frowns. "I suppose so."

"What's her favorite food?"

She shrugs. "I don't know. She loves bread. Probably walnut and stilton. Why?"

"Oh, no reason," George says, "just wondering. She spends all this time feeding everyone else, it just occurred to me that I didn't know what she liked to eat herself."

They stand in silence for a while.

"This line isn't moving," Kat says. "Let's go across the street."

George shifts from one foot to the other. "No, let's wait."

Kat fixes her best friend with a microscopic stare. "You are acting very strangely. What's going on? Are you stoned?"

George laughs. "Of course not."

"Well, I wish you'd tell me, because you're creeping me out."

George smiles.

"It's like you've been taken over by zombies or something."

George giggles. "Don't be silly."

"Me being silly? I'm not the one being silly. You're being strange."

George shrugs. "Why don't you go, then?

Go and sit in the sunshine and I'll get the drinks and snacks and meet you there."

"Where?"

"Wherever you want. How about outside King's College?"

Kat narrows her eyes. "Are you trying to get rid of me?"

"Of course not. *Now* you're being silly."

"I think we already ascertained that was you," Kat says. "Right, I'm off, I'll see you in — however long it takes you to get through this insane line. Please be normal when you return."

George grins inanely again and Kat stomps off down the street.

Amandine waits impatiently for Noa, tapping her fingers on the desk, chewing the caps of her pens, pacing up and down on her Persian rug. Noa's tutorial was set for nine o'clock in the morning. It's already five past nine. It's unusual for Cambridge University students to be late; if anything they're usually early, overeager and overprepared. It's something, perhaps, to do with being the intellectual cream of the country; such people tend to be highly strung.

Amandine stops pacing to see *The Kiss,* thinking, given the current state of her marriage, that she should probably take it down.

Happy memories are all very well and good when you're happy enough to enjoy them but, being as bereft of cheer as she is right now, Amandine can hardly handle being reminded that she and Eliot loved and found such joy in each other once.

Despite herself, Amandine glances at the painting, letting her gaze fall on the woman's eyes closed in ecstatic surrender to her lover's embrace. Unbidden, a memory rises up. Two years ago, on her thirty-fifth birthday, Eliot bought plane tickets to Paris for a long weekend of eating cheese and chocolate, visiting the Louvre and the Musée d'Orsay and making love in an expensive hotel room overlooking Notre-Dame. Héloïse, though she protested that she and François wanted to take a Parisian trip of their own, had briefly moved into their house to take care of the twins.

But, when Eliot and Amandine reached the airport, she couldn't get on the plane. It would have been the first time she'd been away from the boys for more than a day. And, though she trusted her mother, she couldn't cope with the fact that, should something go wrong, she wouldn't be able to dash straight home to sort it out. The beautiful thing was that Eliot didn't argue, not for a moment, not for a second. He didn't roll his eyes or let a little sigh slip from his throat. Instead, he looked at his wife and smiled and said: "So, where would you like to go?"

They ended up in Waterbeach, a little village thirty minutes from Cambridge. The name was misleading since there was no beach, though it was a very pretty village on the edge of the water. They stayed for three days and nights on a riverboat, rented out to them by two old hippies who camped on the banks of the river. Every afternoon and evening they ate in the village pub, sitting outside under the willow trees, watching the ducks patter past on the lawn.

"Ducks are like us," Eliot said. "They mate for life."

"Do they?"

Eliot smiled. "I'm not sure, perhaps I'm making it up."

Amandine laughed. "But I don't think most humans mate for life."

Eliot bent over and picked up Amandine's blue silk scarf, which had slipped onto the floor. As he hung it over the back of her chair he brushed her arm with his fingertip, from her shoulder to wrist.

"I didn't mean humans, in general," Eliot said. "I meant us, in particular."

"Oh." Amandine's smile deepened. "Do

you think the boys are running rings around Mum?"

"Of course, and she'll be loving every minute of it."

"True . . . You know, sometimes I see the twins together, chattering away in their own private language, and I wonder how it feels to be so close to someone, to —"

"Hey," Eliot protested, "aren't you that close to me?"

Amandine smiled. "Oh, yes, I just meant, it'd be nice to have someone you'd shared your childhood with, someone who'd experienced every little detail you had, all the things that made you the person you became."

"Well, I know I wasn't there, but you could tell me about it now," Eliot said. "I know it's not the same, but it might help."

Amandine glanced down at her plate, piercing a piece of potato with her fork. "In ten years we'll have lived together longer than I lived with my parents. Isn't that weird? I can't believe how old we are."

Eliot laughed. "We're not old, we're just well matured."

Amandine smiled. "Are we?" She ate the potato. "I can't believe the boys are already two. They'll be going to Magdalene before you know it."

"Trinity."

"How's about Bertie goes to your college and Frankie goes to mine?" Amandine suggested. "That'd be fair."

Eliot shrugged. "Or perhaps we shouldn't be such pushy parents and let them decide." Then he groaned. "Maybe they'll rebel against us altogether and go to Oxford."

"Maybe they'll rebel by not going to college at all."

"Oh, no." Eliot held his hand to his chest. "Don't break my heart."

Amandine giggled. "They might not be little swots like us. You have to prepare yourself for that possibility."

Eliot let slip a little sigh. "I know. Anyway, I don't care what they do, as long as they're happy."

"Liar." Amandine laughed. "If they wanted to be rave DJs or dustbin men or . . . anything less than doctors or lawyers, you'd be miserable, let's be honest."

"Hey, that's not true," Eliot said. "Well, okay, maybe if one became a doctor and one became a lawyer, that might be all right."

"I knew it." Amandine reached across the table and touched his chin. "Are you finished? Because I do believe there's a bed on

148

a boat with our names embroidered on its sheets."

"Yes," Eliot said. "We'd better wash those sheets before we leave."

He stood and reached for Amandine's hand. She took it and, as she stood, she saw that look in his eye.

"What?"

"Nothing," he said. "I'm just wondering what I ever did to get so lucky with my life."

"I don't know," Amandine said, as they walked slowly across the lawn together, stepping around the ducks, "by rights all lawyers should be burning somewhere very hot, shouldn't they?"

"Yes," Eliot said, pulling her into him until their lips touched. His voice dropped to a whisper. "Well then, I suppose I'd better enjoy all this while I still can."

Amandine's cheeks are wet with tears when the memory falls away from her. A moment later, she reaches up and rips the poster from the wall.

A knock on the door interrupts Amandine's memories and she turns sharply, as though she'd just been caught doing something naughty.

"Come in."

The door opens quickly and Noa nearly

falls into the room.

"I'm so sorry I'm late," she says, "I was, I was . . . traffic."

Amandine frowns. Noa's college is only ten minutes' walk from Magdalene College. Nobody drives around the center of town, and students cycle everywhere, often on the pavements, much to the chagrin of the locals.

"No problem," Amandine says, walking over to her desk. "Why don't we get started?"

"Yep," Noa says, slipping into her designated red leather chair and opening her book bag. "I focused on Manet this week, with some references to Jean-Léon Gérôme and Alexandre Cabanel."

"Excellent." Amandine sits back in her chair, wondering how long she should wait before she can politely bring up the subject of her husband. "Would you like to read it out?"

Noa would not. She's shy when it comes to public speaking, especially when she always worried about the inappropriate truths that might slip out of her mouth. But, even as she tries to decline, to ask for an alternative, she finds herself unable to grasp hold of the words.

"Sure," Noa says, and begins mumbling

her first few sentences, introducing her critique on Manet's early works, but before she's finished the paragraph, Amandine blurts out an interruption. Noa looks up.

"Sorry to interrupt, but I just have to ask . . ." Amandine pauses, trying to keep the note of desperation from creeping into her voice. ". . . Are you still willing to meet my husband? I was thinking" — she hurries on before Noa can answer — "that you could come to dinner next Saturday night?"

"I can," Noa says, tentative, "but . . ."

"But?" Amandine feels hope starting to seep out of her fingertips. She clenches her fists. "You don't want to? Of course, I —"

Noa shakes her head. "No, it's not that. It's just, I don't know if it'd do any good."

"What do you mean?"

"Well," Noa says, trying not to sound too happy about it, "I don't think I can see people's secrets anymore."

Amandine clenches her fists so tightly that her knuckles blanch. "I don't understand, how could it happen just like that?"

"I met a man who said he could take away my curse and somehow he did."

"What? How? How do you know?"

Noa shrugs. "You're the first person I've seen since last night and, well, I can't see anything about you at all."

"Really?"

Noa nods.

"Nothing at all?"

Noa nods again.

"Oh," Amandine says. "Oh, bugger."

And, with that, her last molecule of hope is gone.

CHAPTER NINE

Amandine has contemplated all her options, those involving courage and honesty and those involving cowardice and dishonesty, and has decided to opt for the latter. So it is that she finds herself in Eliot's private office in the middle of the afternoon, while the twins are at nursery and she should be in her own office at Magdalene marking exam papers on Renoir and Degas.

Amandine has only been in Eliot's office on rare occasions, usually when she's popping in to ask him something or, when they'd just moved into the house, to have sex on his desk. Generally though, she leaves the space as Eliot's own, not letting the boys encroach either, just as none of them go into her attic office at the top of the house. So when she steps inside, Amandine feels a shot of guilt. It's so strong that she almost shuts the door and turns back. But she knows that if she doesn't do it now she'll do it later. She has to. It's either this or actually asking Eliot to tell her the truth.

It's strange, Amandine thinks, that you can have lived with and loved someone for so long, have shared the most intimate moments of your life, have told them (nearly) everything about yourself and yet, one day, find that you're incapable of asking them a simple question. But while the question "Are you having an affair?" is quite simple, the consequences of an answer in the affirmative are rather more complex and devastating.

Amandine can't even contemplate what splitting up their household would do to the boys, let alone her own heart. Would she ever be able to trust and love another man again? Would she even want to? Probably not. Amandine has always considered herself like her mother, a one-man-in-a-lifetime kind of woman. Would she be able to forgive Eliot and forget? Amandine has no idea. The probability of even having to contemplate the question has always seemed so nonexistent before — less than the odds of winning the lottery — that she simply does not know.

Amandine steps farther into the room and shuts the door behind her. Even though no one is in the house, nor will be for several hours, she feels the need to hide herself, as if in some strange way it lessens the impact of what she's about to do.

None of Eliot's desk drawers are locked, so Amandine searches through each one methodically, pacing herself (though she's impatient to be over and done with this sordid task), being sure to check every single slip of paper for clues. For two hours she searches and finds nothing. Most of the papers are legal documents covered with terse and turgid prose that she just glances at to be sure they aren't relevant. Fearful thoughts flash through her mind: the possibility of an extra will bequeathing money to mistresses, hidden bank accounts to subsidize a secret life, telephone records that validate her worst imaginings. And yet, as the sun starts to set, beginning its descent slowly behind the garden trees, Amandine has finally finished searching every piece of her husband's private life and found no evidence of anything untoward.

Turning to the door, the beat of her heart at last starting to lighten, Amandine glances behind her to do one more sweep of the room. Nothing. She places her hand on the dull brass knob and begins to twist it open, but something stops her: a little warning light, a flickering of awareness tucked inside her mind. She turns back once again for another final sight-search of the room, taking her time, inch by inch.

A tiny triangle of paper is tucked under the chest of drawers in the corner, a little white flag of alarm calling out from the tidy room. A gulp of breath catches in Amandine's throat and she holds it there while quickly crossing the carpet and snatching the cause for alarm off the floor. It is a slice of lined paper, torn from a notebook, ripped along one jagged edge. And along each and every line is written one word, over and over again, in a vast variety of styles:

Sylvia. Sylvia. Sylvia. Sylvia. Sylvia. Sylvia. Sylvia. Sylvia. SYLVIA. Sylvia. Sylvia. Sylvia. Sylvia. Sylvia. Sylvia. Sylvia. Sylvia. Sylvia. Sylvia. Sylvia. Sylvia. SYLVIA. Sylvia. Sylvia. Sylvia. Sylvia. . . .

"Hi, Cosi."

"Hi, sis." Cosima wipes flour-and-sugar-dusted fingers across her eyes. On seeing George standing next to Kat, she grins. "Hey, George." Cosima picks up a little ball of sticky dough, studded with almond flakes and blueberries and holds it out to him: her fifteenth attempt to undo the spell. "Try this. Let me know how you like the recipe."

George's eyes light up. "Thanks."

Marcello pokes his head out of the kitchen, his own huge brown eyes bright with triumph. "*Ciao,* Jorge! *Come stai?* I make some pizza sauce for you — with my new special spice. You will love!"

George looks up, cookie halfway to his mouth. "Really? Is it extra garlic? Or a touch more basil? I've been thinking you could try a touch of paprika in the Himalayan sea salt —"

"It's a surprise," Marcello says, grinning. "You'll have to come and taste." And, with a little wave of his hand, he pops back into the kitchen.

"Sis?" Cosima holds a ball of dough out to her sister.

"No, thanks." Kat shakes her head.

"Come on, sis. Why don't you have a couple of pistachio cream croissants? It looks like you need a sugar rush to cheer you up."

Kat frowns, then glances at George — who has his eyes closed in a euphoria of cookie dough. When he swallows, George opens his eyes again. He fixes Cosima with a dazed, delighted gaze.

"You are . . . incredible. How does your baking get more and more delicious every time I taste it?"

Cosima sighs softly. She'll have to try again. "Thanks, George."

"Can I have another?"

Cosima shrugs, supposing there's no harm in it. "Sure."

She holds out another sweet treat. But, instead of taking it from her, George leans forward and opens his mouth. Cosima rolls her eyes slightly, but feeds it to him and then — in a movement so subtle almost anyone else would have missed it — George curls his tongue out over the biscuit so the edges brush against Cosima's skin.

Kat's eyes widen and a stone drops on her chest, knocking all the air out of her lungs. George's eyes are half-closed, the shadow of a smile of pure bliss on his lips.

He is *in love* with her.

Kat stares at them both, breathless. How is this possible? It can't be. And her sister only just split up with her husband. She's not even divorced yet. Kat's world is turning on its axis, flipping her over on her face. What the hell is happening?

George opens his eyes and gazes at Cosima.

"Delicious. Absolutely delicious."

"Well," Cosima says, raising a bemused eyebrow at Kat, as if sharing a sisterly joke, "you obviously *do* have supreme taste buds."

Kat feels tears filling her eyes and darkness seeping into her chest. *Don't. Don't. Hold it together. Be strong. Be strong. Just for now. Just until you're alone again.* And, because Kat has always been good at hiding her feelings — how else can you be secretly in love with your best friend for so long? — she manages it now. Kat knows that once she's back in her rooms at Trinity College, once she's slammed the door shut behind her, she'll fall to the floor and sob. She will sob until her throat hurts nearly as much as her heart. But it doesn't matter. It only matters that she doesn't do it now.

Cosima's still looking at George, so she doesn't notice the despair in her sister's eyes. And then — all of a sudden — she thinks: *Why not?* Instead of trying in vain to fight it, why not just surrender to it?

"Hey, George, why don't you come back after closing tonight?" Cosima says. "I've got something to ask you. And I'll make chocolate and pistachio cream cupcakes, if you're still hungry after all your lunch."

When George grins as if he's five years old and has just been given a puppy for his birthday, and nods and says, yes, he'd love to, Kat just stares at them both. She wishes she could cast a forgetting spell to erase what just happened, to reverse time, to leave it all unsaid. If she could, she'd expunge the whole encounter, so they wouldn't be meeting tonight, but since George has somehow — how did she miss it? — developed feelings for her sister, what would be the point? Unfortunately, Kat's forgetting spells can only erase memories, not emotions.

Noa has never been so happy. Not because she's a little in love with Santiago Costa, though there is that, but because she's finally and suddenly in love with her life. She can be with people and not see too much of them, not scare them away. She can hold ordinary conversations without some unspeakable secret slipping out of her mouth. She can stop permanently censoring herself. She can relax at last.

Now she sits in Gustare, surrounded by people — each, no doubt, with at least one, perhaps several, secrets they don't want anyone else to see — focusing on the calm she feels. Her spine, once as taut as a piano wire, is as soft as her newly relaxed shoulders; her stomach has stopped churning, her heart no longer thumps in her chest like a panicked bumblebee caught in a glass jar. This must be how normal people feel all the time, Noa thinks, absolutely unaware of how utterly lucky they are.

She watches the chefs busy behind the counter, pulling pizzas — bubbling with cheese — out of ovens, sliding them onto flour-dusted surfaces, then drizzling lemon oil or balsamic glaze across toppings of thinly sliced squash or Parma ham. One chef, a tall, beautiful Italian (so Noa supposes), glances every few minutes at another chef — a voluptuous woman with long black bouncing curls, enormous brown eyes, and an air about her that suggests she's somewhere else, not in the café rolling dough but standing in a wheat field in Italy with her face turned up to the sun. For a moment, Noa wonders what her secrets are, along with those of the man who watches her. Then she remembers that she can't know these things anymore, that she's blessedly and gloriously normal.

Noa glances back at the book in front of her, *Monet and the Impressionists,* and flicks through a few pages. The pictures begin to blend together as she stares at them, lost in thought, the pastel colors seeping into one another until Noa has to shut her eyes against the blur.

And then, in the next moment, Santiago is standing in front of her, speaking in a language she doesn't understand, and smiling.

"Hi," Noa says, trying to suppress the sparkle of her sudden delight, and finding, to her surprise, that she can. She has never before been able to conceal anything. Just as she'd suffered from always having to say everything she saw, this transparency had, perhaps inevitably, extended to her own thoughts and feelings as well. Noa has never been able to lie and she's not entirely disconcerted to discover that she can now. As she arranges her face into a carefree smile, Noa experiences a rush of excitement, just as she imagines a baby must feel on finally learning to walk. She's joined the world of adults, of fully functioning social beings; she can do everything they can do.

"*Olá, gata,*" Santiago says, sitting down in the chair opposite, blocking Noa's view of the chefs. "How are you?"

"Happy," Noa says, "and now happier still."

Santiago smiles. "What are you reading?"

Noa flips the book closed so he can read the cover. "It's for my essay on Monet and his position in the French Impressionist movement of the late nineteenth century."

"Ah," Santiago says. "Sounds fascinating."

Noa nods. "It is."

Santiago stands again. "Would you like cake with your coffee?" He takes a few steps toward the counter. Then, suddenly, he turns back and leans toward her across the table, fixing her with those deep brown eyes. Noa holds her breath.

"Unless . . . ?"

Noa exhales. "What?"

"Unless you'd like to come home with me, for something better than cake?"

Noa hides a smile. "Better than cake? How's that possible? I hope you're not selling yourself too high."

"Well, I suppose you'll have to be the judge of that."

"Yes, I suppose I will." Noa grins, unable to hold in her joy any longer. "But, I'd better warn you, I have very high standards."

Noa can hardly believe what she's saying, even given her past propensity for saying absolutely everything she's thinking. She has no standards. She'd have nothing to compare Santiago to.

"That's good," he says, "I like a woman with high standards."

"Ah, and just how many women have evaluated you?"

Santiago smiles. "A few."

"More than that, I imagine."

"Perhaps."

"Well then," Noa says, standing. "Let's see if practice makes perfect."

It takes only ten minutes to reach Santiago's house, and another five to reach his bed, but to Noa, who's been anticipating this moment since the night he painted her, it feels like ten hours. He'd only kissed her that night and, since the intimacy of what they'd done together had felt so deep, it had been more than enough. Now, however, Noa can hardly wait.

When they are both naked, Santiago lays Noa down on his bed and begins drawing his tongue in tiny circles down her neck to her collarbone. By the time he reaches the dip between her breasts, Noa can no longer find the strength to care about her safety, all she cares about is this second, feeling Santiago's chest against her, his legs between her legs, his hands in her hair. All she can think of is how she's never felt a man touch her like this: his tongue warm and wet and slow in one moment, then cold and quick in the next, her skin tingling under his fingertips, her body opening with every touch until all Noa wants in the world is to have him inside her.

Héloïse gathers her long skirt, lifting the linen so she can see the blossom petals scattered in soft blankets along the pavements. May is her favorite month of the year, when thousands of flowers all over the city burst into bloom and the naked winter branches of the trees are suddenly, one morning, clothed in circles of pink and white. Last year she missed spring. Sitting in a dark house with the curtains drawn turned every day into winter. She's so glad she didn't miss spring a second time.

As Héloïse walks along Bridge Street, her step feels so light she fears she might be floating and she glances down at her feet to be sure they're still on firm ground. Before François died, before life folded in on itself, Héloïse had to be careful to contain her effervescence around ordinary people, because whenever she was flooded with emotion her body did things that weren't entirely normal. From the moment she was born, Héloïse took an extra special delight in the world. When she first opened her eyes, the brightness of the light had made her blink. When she'd taken her first breath, the sweetness of the air had made her splutter. When her mother's fingers touched her fresh skin, the warmth had made her shiver. When the chatter of voices tickled her ears, she'd giggled. So it had been on that first day of life, and every day after that. Until

François died. Yet, day by day, she can feel her sense of delight slowly starting to return.

"C'est un beau matin," Héloïse says, expecting his answer to be in agreement. She's a little surprised, even though she hasn't heard François during the day lately, when he doesn't answer at all.

Héloïse takes her time along Silver Street, dipping her toes in and out of the blossoms, smiling as they puff up in tiny clouds around the hem of her skirt. She almost wants to run to the market, eager to see what fresh books Ben has acquired for her. But the pull of the petals slows her down, bringing her back to the warm spring breeze and the smatterings of color on every patch of grass she passes.

Walking slowly means it takes nearly half an hour to get from Magrath Avenue to the Market Square and, when she arrives, Héloïse can feel the tips of her fingers buzzing with excitement and desire to hold their next favorite book. It's only when she's standing at the stall, skimming her impatient hands over the covers of secondhand books, that Héloïse realizes she's holding her breath. Exhaling, she takes a fresh breath, filling her lungs with the deliciously musty smell of love and literature emanating from the old books.

Catching sight of two young lovers kissing on a book cover, Héloïse is surprised to find herself wondering if she will ever experience love again. Is it possible that her heart might one day be patched up again — the cracks healed, albeit with scars still showing? It's extraordinary to Héloïse that she can even entertain the idea of feeling anything for another man, of letting a stranger take up a square inch of space in her heart when for thirty-seven years François has had permanent residence there.

"Morning, Lou." Ben sidles up. "Isn't it a beautiful one?"

Héloïse pulls her gaze away from the books to smile at Ben. "It is."

"I've got something for you." Ben reaches under the tall wooden stool he's sitting on, pulls out a brown paper bag, and passes it over to her. Héloïse opens it.

"A Moveable Feast," she reads. "I've not read Hemingway before."

"You'll love it. I promise you that, or your money back."

"Parfait." Héloïse laughs. "It's a deal."

She stands at the stall, her gaze flitting over the books before her, their spines turned up so she can read all their titles. This is how she knows, in the absence of Ben's specific recommendations, which ones are for her. Some might think Héloïse shallow, selecting all her literature on the basis of titles and covers, but actually her instinct and intuition are so finely tuned these are the only clues she needs. Héloïse has never needed Ben's help at all in selecting the books she'll love, but she lets him because it brings them both pleasure. It's something she's missed, this sense of connection with a similar soul and her own intuition.

After buying *A Moveable Feast,* Héloïse stays awhile, just to be among the books and the chatter of the customers as they greet Ben, taking his recommendations and discussing their favorite authors. She never fails to be astonished at how well read he is, far more than any of her fellow professors and, indeed, anyone else she's ever met.

Ben, and his father before him, has always been the main reason Héloïse buys her literature from the bookstall, rather than visiting one of the shops on the high street or the many university libraries. She had to frequent the latter for work, for obscure texts on French literature, but for everything else she'd always gone to the stall. Héloïse has always been drawn to used books far more than new ones. She loves to hold them and wonder who else has done so; she's excited to find notes in the margins or pages folded over, showing that someone has loved this particular moment of the story especially. Secondhand books have a sense of history, a smell of a life well lived that their newly minted counterparts do not. This is why Héloïse gathers them around her like strangers who tell their most intimate secrets.

It's not until she's in bed — it having now settled nicely next to the bay window — that night that Héloïse finally opens *A Moveable Feast*. She begins just before nine o'clock, and at one o'clock in the morning she's finished. It's not simply the memoir that has her so captivated, it's the annotations in the margins. In tiny dark green script, someone has composed a complete and complex commentary of their opinions, thoughts, and feelings on the book . . .

Where Hemingway had written: *People were always the limiters of happiness except for the very few that were as good as spring itself,* the green pen had added: *Yes! Yet so few realize the power they have to decide their own happiness. And though it's always initially easier, more effortless to be sad than happy, it takes just the same amount of energy to maintain either state.*

Hemingway: *All you have to do is write one*

true sentence. Write the truest sentence that you know.

Green pen: *Isn't it so often the case that we lose the power and purpose of our speech scurrying about with so many sentences, trying to find our point. The fewer words we use, the more closely people will listen when we say them.*

Hemingway: *There you could always go into the Luxembourg Museum and all the paintings were sharpened and clearer and more beautiful if you were belly-empty, hollow-hungry.*

Green pen: *Yes, if one is too full of food, one cannot feel so much. But, of course, if one is too hungry then one is too distracted by the desire for food to feel much of anything else either. Just being on the edge of hungry, then, is best to experience what H. did.*

And so it went on.

Handwriting covers every page and, when Héloïse has at last deciphered the final green line and letter, she's shocked and delighted to discover that she shares every single opinion, thought, and feeling.

George can barely contain his excitement. How did this happen? How does he have a date — is it a date? He certainly hopes so — with the beautiful and supremely talented

Cosima Rubens? He's not entirely certain it is a date; after all, she's still technically married and, given his long history of romantic disappointment, he wonders if he might have got it wrong. He's also not exactly sure how they went so suddenly from being friendly acquaintances to potential partners, but for some reason it feels sort-of-right, so he's prepared to go with it. And there is the plenitude of chocolate and pistachio cream cupcakes to consider.

Reaching the closed café, George adjusts his tie, straightens his jacket, and brushes his sweaty palms on his thighs, then knocks on the glass door. A moment later, Cosima opens it.

"Hey there, George." She steps back. "Come in."

"Thank you." He walks into the empty café, then sees the table she's set up for them: atop a white linen tablecloth is a spread of treats that makes George salivate: tomato breads, zucchini blossom pizza, vanilla cannoli, Sicilian salad, red wine, and, of course, a plate of chocolate and pistachio cream cupcakes.

"Oh," George gasps. "Is this for me? Incredible."

Nervous, Cosima steps over to the table and picks up a cupcake and starts to gobble it up. Cakes, even unenchanted ones, have always had a wonderfully soporific effect on her. George watches as her teeth sink into the dark green pistachio cream, as her lips disappear until she pulls the cake away and chews slowly and nods, closing her eyes. George stares at Cosima's lips, half-covered with cream and cake crumbs, and thinks he has never seen a more beautiful sight. How can a woman be quite so beautiful, so sensual, so unbelievably and utterly irresistible? How can he be quite so lucky?

"I always eat dessert first," Cosima explains. "It's how I like to live, without waiting for the future." This statement, though she believes it brings happiness, reminds her of the risks she's taking, the risks that hover on the horizon, refusing to disappear, much as she'd like to forget them. Cosima takes another bite, swallowing her fears along with the cake and returning to George with a smile. "Your turn."

George steps toward her and picks up a cupcake. "You're like Eve in the garden of Eden, only you've got cupcakes instead of apples. A much better choice." He bends his head to take a bite; swallowing, he stares at her, unable to say anything.

Cosima frowns. "Is something wrong?"

He shakes his head.

"Are you okay?"

George just gazes at her.

"What? Do I have cake on my nose?"

George shakes his head again. "You are the most beautiful, the most lovely, the most magnificent woman I've ever met in my life."

He says it so simply, so matter-of-factly, so without reservation or consideration, that his words — even though she knows they're the result of a spell — drop straight into Cosima's heart, before she's able to think about, analyze, or question them. Cosima is used to compliments, though they are rarely so sincere. She'd received one that very afternoon from a tall, thin, breathtakingly handsome man who'd slipped her a purple business card with his name written in silver. But she knew men like him, she encountered them every day; they flirted their way through life, stealing hearts with every word, snatching up looks of adoration and infatuation and stuffing them into their pockets to pore over later. George is different. He is honest and true, a good man right down to his marrow.

Forgetting everything else, Cosima leans forward and kisses him.

CHAPTER TEN

Shaking a little, her heart thumping, her breath tight in her chest, Cosima reaches a sweaty palm out toward George and takes his hand.

"I want to ask you something. It's really important you tell the truth, okay?"

George nods.

"Do you want to have children?"

George doesn't take much of a moment before answering. "Yes," he says, a slightly wistful smile on his face. "Yes. I do. But . . ."

"But?" Cosima's heart beats faster still. "You can't have them?"

George shakes his head. "No, it's not that, I just never thought I would, given . . ."

"What?"

"I don't . . ." George frowns, focusing. "I can't quite remember."

"Well, that's all right," Cosima says. Perhaps it isn't, but she so desperately wants it to be that she ignores all signs to the contrary. She takes a deep breath. "Would you — would you like to have a child with me?"

"You want a baby?"

"Yes." Cosima sighs. "More than anything in the world."

"But . . . are you doing this because your husband is having a baby with another woman?"

"No, it's not like that. It's not for revenge," Cosima says. "I've wanted babies forever. We were trying for years . . . Now I've lost him, I can deal with that, but I can't lose my chance of having a baby. And I will love her more than anything else in the world. I promise you that."

"Her?"

Cosima shrugs. "Just a feeling I have."

George considers. There's a reason, something that lingers at the edges of his mind, in his memories, why he should say no. Yet he can't think of it, no matter how hard he concentrates. He does, after all, want children. And he's certainly not getting any younger.

"Okay then, let's do it."

When Cosima smiles, George knows he's said the right thing. He's never in his life seen someone so happy at the result of something he's said.

"It'll be wonderful, I promise," she says, dearly hoping she's right. It doesn't matter that she doesn't love him. It doesn't matter that he's under a spell. It'll work out. In time, it'll all work out. "Everything will be wonderful," she says again, with a little more conviction. "It'll be perfect."

"Yes," George says, his other thoughts forgotten. "Yes, it will."

Cosima kisses him again, then takes his hand and leads him into the kitchen.

"What are we doing?"

Cosima smiles. "I'm going to show you how to bake a spell."

George nods. "Oh, okay."

Cosima begins lining up her ingredients.

"Kat taught me," she says, stirring a handful of bright, butter yellow celandine petals into the flour. She picks a glass bottle labeled *Cinquefoil* off the counter, untwists the cap, and adds three spiked leaves. "Kat taught me the meanings of all the flowers and herbs, and how they best complement each other."

"When did you learn?" George asks, feeling a twinge in his chest at the mention of Kat.

"When I was about four, I think. And I loved it, baking, instantly. And Kat was a great teacher." Cosima opens a bottle labeled *Starwort* and sprinkles a few tiny green leaves and white petals into the mix. "I felt as if I was being included in some sort of special big-sister club. She was going to tell me all her secrets and I couldn't wait."

George smiles. "Were you very close?"

"Very. I adored her. Idolized her. She was the first person I ever loved. I suppose . . ." Cosima sighs. "Pass me that jar."

George passes her a jar marked *Sorrel,* filled with puffs of red. He waits to see what she might say.

"Kat probably told you about our mum, that she died after giving birth to me." Cosima sprinkles the sorrel onto the flour, then adds a pinch of dried moss. She carries on, without waiting for an answer. "And Dad was so devastated he virtually abandoned us for years. I mean, he didn't leave, but he was never really at home either. Kat had to look after me for the most part. I clung to her. She was a teenager with a screaming baby sister. It's a wonder she didn't try to smother me in my sleep, but she was amazing. Really and truly. I should probably tell her that more often . . ."

"How did your mother die?" George asks.

"A brain hemorrhage. All the women in my family have a blood-clotting disease. It's pretty serious. We have to take medicine for it every day. And pregnancy is a great risk factor, that's why Mum —"

"Wait," George says, "if that's the case, then surely you shouldn't be putting yourself at risk too? I know you want a baby, but it's not worth . . . You could adopt, or —"

"Don't worry," Cosima says, swallowing down another bubble of doubt. "I'm managing it. I've got it under control. I take herbs every day and" — she smiles — "I have my magic."

"I don't know . . ."

"Trust me, it's fine." Cosima plucks a few fresh flowers out of a vase and hands them to George. "Pluck the petals off these."

"What are they?"

"Daisies and dittany."

George examines the delicate pink and white flowers. "Are you going to teach me the secrets of your baking spells, then?"

"Maybe." Cosima winks. "Though usually husbands aren't told these particular secrets, only daughters."

"Oh?" George smiles. "Is that so you can cast the spells on us?"

"Perhaps."

It's only then that George notices Cosima has just — sort of — referred to him as her husband. His shock reverberates, humming at the edges of the hours while they wait for the bread to rise and bake. It's only when he's eating his first slice that George realizes he doesn't even know the nature of this spell. He chews and swallows. Whatever it is, it must be something joyful, since the bread is delicious.

"So, what was the spell?" George asks. "Will you tell me the secret now?"

A look of dismay passes over Cosima's face. "But — I thought you knew."

"No, sorry, I didn't . . ."

"After we spoke about children, I just as-sumed . . ." Cosima says. "It's for . . . fertil-ity. It's for fertility."

"Oh." George is wide-eyed. "Oh, I see."

Since seeing George looking at her sister like that, Kat's been walking around in a depressed daze, unable to focus on any-thing, even numbers. Things that would normally have excited and delighted her no longer have any effect at all. Even her favorite PhD student, Hamish — a slightly eccentric but undeniably handsome chap who speaks in mathematical equations, never seems to eat or sleep, and has an extremely infectious laugh — can't rouse her from this fog.

She hates to think of what might have happened that night. And she hasn't seen either George or Cosima since that afternoon. She's been ignoring their calls and has had to resist a strong urge to read her sister the riot act and ask what the hell she's thinking, seducing George on the rebound. It's an idiotic move and it'll all end in tears — mostly Kat's own. The worst of it is that she can't talk to her best friend about how she's feeling, since her best friend is the cause of it all.

Kat calls Amandine and Héloïse, hoping for a chance to unburden herself, but neither answer. So, after pacing up and down by her chalkboards, Kat decides to visit Amandine, since her college is only just down the road. She takes the back route to Magdalene College, avoiding the center of town, where she might bump into George or, worse, George and Cosima together, to follow the path of the river running through the fields behind King's and Trinity Colleges.

As students Kat and George spent many lazy afternoons sitting on the banks of the river, on the bench at the edge of Trinity College's lawns (avoiding the glare of the porter guarding his patch from unsuspecting tourists foolish enough to ignore the "keep off the grass" notices) watching the punts glide past. Mostly they sat in silence, waiting to see who'd fall into the river first, listening to the (sometimes invented) facts the tour guides would dispense to the tourists.

Kat had fallen for George on their first afternoon, when they'd talked about witchcraft and feeling lonely and trying to find their places in the world. Admittedly, given the difference in their levels of attractiveness, Kat had rather assumed that George would reciprocate her feelings with happy appreciation. Unfortunately, not only did he not fall for her, but he never even seemed to notice her subtle romantic overtures.

For a little while Kat lied to herself, almost believing that she was perfectly happy just to have George as her best friend. She even dated a stunningly handsome American scientist, who bore an uncanny resemblance to Clark Gable, for a few months, but had to give the ruse up when he started getting too serious, wanting to talk about the future and all that rot. Since then Kat had been biding her time, telling herself that one day, somehow, everything might fall into place, fortuitously, serendipitously, miraculously. Without her having to say anything. Without her having to skirt humiliation. Without her having to risk her heart. More fool her.

"*Bonjour,* Ben," Héloïse says. "Have you any more Hemingway?"

Sitting on his tall wooden stool, Ben glances up from the book he's reading.

"I may have," he says, "I can take a look."

Héloïse smiles. *"Merci."*

Héloïse stands at the bookstall, attempting to appear nonchalant, to keep the note of hope out of her voice, to act like a sensible fifty-eight-year-old instead of a jittery teenager. She wonders what François would say if he's watching her now — would he be pleased or jealous? She hopes the former but fears the latter, so decides not to think about it. There's no guarantee that another book by the same author will yield the same results, but Héloïse considers it her best chance. Hopefully Ben will have bought a batch of books from the person with the green pen, not just one, and it's possible that someone who owned one Hemingway would own a few others too. Héloïse could significantly increase her odds of success and simply ask Ben outright. But, despite how well they know each other, she's a little too shy to tell him her silly tale.

Ben gets down from his stool, placing his book carefully on its smooth seat, and begins searching through the boxes of books stacked underneath the wooden tables that form his stall.

"I don't think I have any more Hemingway," he calls up to her, voice muffled. "But I've got something else I thought you might like." Ben comes out from under the table holding a book. He hands it to Héloïse.

"*The Travelling Hornplayer.* Sounds interesting," she says, though right now, even the most brilliant work of literature wouldn't hold her attention, not unless it was annotated with notes and comments in green pen.

"Wait a sec, I just remembered . . ." Ben ducks under the tables again. Héloïse's heart lifts at the sound of wood scraping against stone. A second chance. "Oh, yes, here we go."

Héloïse holds her breath as Ben emerges. She isn't sure what she's expecting will come of all this — does she really think she'll meet the man who wrote out her own thoughts and feelings with his little green pen? Does she imagine they might meet and fall in love? It's a ridiculous notion. And yet, when Ben offers Héloïse a copy of *The Old Man and the Sea,* her fingers tremble slightly as she takes it.

"So, you loved the last one, did you?" Ben asks.

"*Pardon?*"

"*A Moveable Feast.*"

"Ah, *oui,* of course. *Superbe.* I want to read all his work."

"Good." Ben beams. "I love introducing new authors to my favorite customers."

"*Merci beaucoup.*" Héloïse returns his smile. "I'm glad you do."

The Old Man and the Sea glows in her bag as Héloïse carries it back home to Magrath Avenue. All along Market Street and Sidney Street, over Magdalene Bridge and the river, she feels the book beckoning her to stop, snatch it out of her bag, and read it right there on the street. But, summoning up every molecule of willpower, Héloïse resists. If the book is what she hopes, she wants to postpone the pleasure of reading it. If it isn't, she wants to postpone the disappointment too.

Nearly slipping on a loose stone slab on Granchester Street, Héloïse slows. If she falls and breaks a hip, she'll be reading the book from a hospital bed, which will dilute the pleasure somewhat. When she at last reaches her room, Héloïse postpones the moment even longer by making herself a strong cup of Earl Grey tea, no milk, no sugar. She sinks into her favorite armchair (it being exactly where it had been the day before, the furniture having settled down lately), and Héloïse can hardly open the book, her fingertips are tingling so with excitement.

"Calme. Calme," she whispers to herself. *"Calme, ma petite."*

As the word comes out of her mouth, François pops back into her head; it was one of his favorite terms of endearment. For a moment, her heart constricts, absorbing sorrow like a sponge. Then, taking a deep breath, Héloïse shifts her focus onto her new mystery. She knows it's silly to be so abuzz with something that's solely in her imagination, but she also knows it's really a gift from God, a little adventure to distract her from her sorrow and help her heal. It's a shame, though, that her grief has suppressed her psychic ability, or she'd be able to track down the man with the green pen.

With the book sandwiched between her palms, Héloïse shuts her eyes and whispers a little incantation for luck. Then she opens the book. Flicking through the first few pages she sees nothing and then a flash of faded green catches her eye. Héloïse stops. In the top right-hand corner of the title page someone has printed the letters T.S., along with a date: 24th March 1979.

Her twenty-first birthday.

Héloïse holds her breath. Surely it must be a sign? It can't be a coincidence, it simply can't be. The letters seem to glimmer as she gazes at them and, for a moment, Héloïse is filled with such a rush of hope that she presses her forefinger to the words, closes her eyes, and whispers a little plea to Athena, Hecate, Saraswati, and Thoth. For nearly a minute she sees nothing and then, still begging inspiration from the assorted gods and goddesses of knowledge, an image starts to take shape: a tree and a wooden bench in a graveyard, and on the bench is a book.

Héloïse strains to see the title. The letters are blurred. Then a male hand closes over the cover and picks it up. She waits, hoping to see more of the man than just his fingers. Then everything goes black.

"I want to take you home and do very bad things to you."

"You do?" Noa smiles. "What sorts of things, exactly? I think I should know in advance what I'm getting into, before I say yes."

Santiago frowns. "Not at all. That'll entirely take the fun out of it."

Noa raises an eyebrow. "Maybe for you, but I like to be prepared."

They are sitting side by side at a table in Gustare, two untouched cups of hot chocolate and two uninjured pistachio cream croissants in front of them. Noa slowly leans her head on Santiago's shoulder; wrapping her hair around her fingers, she pulls it back and exposes her neck. She knows what he'll do next and the anticipation sends little shivers of delight down her body.

Santiago leans over until his lips are almost grazing her skin, so she can feel the heat of his breath, and whispers. "You want me to kiss you now?"

Noa smiles and closes her eyes.

"You want me to kiss you now, in front of all these people, you want me to make you sigh and moan and . . ."

"Yes," Noa mumbles, "yes, please."

She can't believe how brazen she has become with him. She would plead with him to kiss her, to tear off her clothes and lay her across the table, to lick every inch of her bare skin until she was begging him to fuck her. She really wouldn't care.

"No," he whispers. "I won't."

"Please."

Santiago's breath is hot on her neck and his tongue so close to touching her skin.

187

"I'll give you a thousand anticipated kisses, to magnify every one I'll give you after, when I finally have you in my bed."

Noa smiles. "Let's go. Now."

Amandine hasn't had a moment of peace since discovering the Sylvia note. She'd had to teach two classes and give a lecture that day and she'd managed to get through them, though she has no idea how, since every neuron of her brain was taken up with the thought of Sylvia. Who is she? What does she look like? Is she stunning and twenty-three? Probably. That's the cliché, and why shouldn't Eliot fall into stereotype? Though, honestly, she wouldn't have thought he would.

In the first place, Amandine couldn't have imagined in a million years that Eliot could ever have an affair. For nearly twenty years, excepting the last few months, he's always seemed so single-mindedly in love with her and their life together. While her colleagues often complain about their husbands' absentmindedness, general reluctance to do household tasks, or occasional offers to "help" with the kids, as if it somehow wasn't their job in the first place, Amandine has never had any such cause for complaint.

Eliot always used to bound upstairs the

moment he got in the front door, leaping into the bathroom to take over the twins' bathing, ushering Amandine out — washcloth still in hand — with instructions that she retire to the sofa with a good book and glass of red wine. He'd bathe the boys, cover their little bodies with moisturizing cream, pull on their pajamas, and tuck them into bed, while Amandine took off her shoes and curled up under the patchwork spread Héloïse had sewn for her thirty-fifth birthday. When she heard her husband's special soft reading voice floating down the stairs, Amandine would put down her book and creep up the steps. She'd stand in the corridor outside the twins' bedroom, peeking through the door to watch Bertie and Frankie snuggled up in Eliot's arms, gazing up at their daddy while he read as if they adored no one more in the whole wide world. When he turned out the light, Amandine would slip back downstairs and wait for Eliot to join her in the kitchen so they could cook dinner together. Since he was the better cook, Eliot would usually make the food while Amandine prepared vegetables and located pans as they talked about the ups and downs of their respective days. At least, that's how it had been, how Eliot had been, before everything changed so suddenly at the beginning of the year. When he started working long hours and being so distracted at the time, no doubt — Amandine knew now — thinking of Sylvia in every moment he wasn't with her.

Amandine's colleagues, in moments of jealousy or disbelief, would sometimes ask how she had such a happy marriage after so many years. And Amandine would tell them: *We say yes to each other, in all things, big and small, every day.* So, if she asked for a cup of tea, Eliot would make it, without question, without delay. If he asked her to take a right turn while they were out driving, she'd do it without first asking why. If either of them wanted sex or to take a trip or see a certain film or buy something slightly extravagant, then the other would agree and, of course, would be agreed to in their turn when the time came. And, when occasionally they lost their way and fell out of sync, they'd bicker — like everybody else — then talk until they found their way again. And this was how they became a true couple, who took care of each other completely, instead of two people with often opposing needs forced to fight to get them met. Amandine would tell her colleagues this and, of course, they wouldn't believe her. Well, she supposes, they'll have the last laugh now.

Amandine knows, as she stands in the corridor outside Eliot's office (she had bathed and put the boys to bed tonight, hearing the front door open and shut halfway through her third reading of *How to Catch a Star*), that she has to confront him tonight. She has to get it out in the open and either give him an ultimatum or insist he leave. She isn't yet sure which option she will go for; it might depend on how Eliot reacts. If he's contrite enough and begs her forgiveness on bended knee, then perhaps, just perhaps she can find it in her heart to forgive him. Amandine has never thought of herself as a woman who could forgive infidelity — although stupidly she's never even pictured the scenario with Eliot, so impossible had the idea seemed — but now that she's actually faced with it, she's embarrassed to admit that part of her wants to forgo confronting him at all. Part of her wishes she'd never found the note, wishes she was still ignorant, that she wasn't about to risk losing the only man she's ever loved. But, as she stands there, ready to knock, Amandine knows that she can't go back and she can't pretend. She has to face the hideous facts of her changed life and somehow, ultimately, make the best of them.

■ ■ ■ ■

"Come in!"

Amandine steps into Eliot's office, already knowing that she isn't wanted, that he wishes she wasn't there. She can feel his reluctance, so strong that it comes off him in waves, almost knocking the breath out of her body, almost knocking her off her feet. So, when Eliot turns around to face her and she sees the faraway look in his eye, she isn't surprised at all.

"I thought you might come and kiss the boys goodnight," she says. "It's been days since you've done it."

"I'm sorry," Eliot says, turning back to his desk. "I came in late, I didn't want to disturb you, I didn't want to excite them, if they were almost asleep."

"You're always home late nowadays," Amandine says, hating the sour, vinegar-sharp taste of the words in her mouth, but unable to stop herself spitting them out.

"I've told you," Eliot says, without turning around, "I'm working on a big case at the moment, it's taking up all my time."

"I know," Amandine snaps. "So you keep telling me."

"The boys are okay, they understand,"

Eliot says. "They won't be scarred for life because they don't see their old man every day for a few months."

"It's already been a couple of months," Amandine says. "And how much longer will it go on for?"

Eliot lets out a heavy sigh and Amandine's heart sinks. She wishes she could stop herself, could stop them both from going in this horrible direction, but she can't.

"You could support me a bit more," Eliot says. "You used to. It's not like I can say no to the partners, surely you can understand that."

"You used to support me more too," Amandine says, "but a lot's changed lately, hasn't it?"

"What's that supposed to mean?"

Amandine is silent. Now is the moment. Now is the moment to say it. But she's scared. Once she speaks the other woman's name she cannot take it back. Their life together will be forever changed. That is it. Amandine hesitates. Then she thinks of her mother, how Héloïse wouldn't have waited a second after she found the note to confront Eliot. She'd have chased down the first train to London, barged past his secretary, flung open his door, and shouted, demanding to know who Sylvia was.

"Never mind," Amandine says in a small, slight voice, one so desperate and sad she can hardly believe it's really hers. And then she turns to go.

After his wife leaves, Eliot sits in his study staring at the wall. He knows it can't go on like this. He'll have to tell her soon. He wishes he could tell her right now, this second. But he gave his word that he wouldn't, not just yet, not until the details are finalized. He knows their family will never be the same again. He can't bear it and yet that is how it is and there is nothing he can do about it. At three o'clock in the morning, Eliot gets up and creeps down the corridor, checking on his boys, before slipping into bed next to his wife.

CHAPTER ELEVEN

"I don't know what to do." Amandine sinks her head into her hands. "I don't know what to do."

Héloïse reaches across the table and gently squeezes her daughter's hand. Amandine looks up and gives her a tiny, hopeless smile. They're sitting in the booth in the back of Gustare, a plate of Cosima's chocolate and pistachio cream cupcakes between them. Héloïse has already eaten one, which is unusual since three or four would be her normal consumption. But, ever since she started jogging she has, funnily enough, felt far less hungry than before, which is a strange but pleasing phenomenon. In the past few days Héloïse has felt her body shifting, every day wobbling ever so slightly less than it did the day before.

"It will be okay, *ma petite*," Héloïse says. "No matter what happens, you will be okay."

Amandine gives her mother a quizzical look.

"Have you done something different with your hair?"

Héloïse touches her tangled gray bob. "No. I mean, I haven't cut it since . . . I suppose it's a bit of a mess."

"No, it's not." Amandine leans closer and squints. "It's like you've — it's not so gray anymore, it's almost glowing a little — have you tinted it blond?"

"Non!" Héloïse laughs. "If I dye it again, it'll be black."

Amandine studies her mother suspiciously. "You're a lot . . . happier. What's happened?" She frowns. "Did you meet someone?"

"No." Héloïse laughs again. "Of course not."

"Okay then, so what is it?"

Héloïse shrugs.

"Come on," Amandine says, "you're a lot . . . you're significantly less suicidal than you were last week."

Héloïse smiles. "I'll take that as a compliment. But nothing has happened. I'm just . . . I'm starting to come back to life a little, that's all. It's nothing more."

"It's not nothing," Amandine protests. "It's a bloody big deal. And I'm sorry I haven't noticed. I'm sorry I've been so pre-occupied with my own messed-up life not to see what's going on with you."

"Don't be sorry, my sweet, you should be preoccupied with your own life; you've spent enough time taking care of me and mine."

Amandine sighs. "Can you tell me what's going to happen? It'd make everything so much easier to deal with."

"Would it really?"

"No, I suppose not." Amandine shrugs. "But will you tell me anyway?"

Héloïse sips her cappuccino. "I wish I could help you, *chérie,* I wish I could assure you that everything will be all right, but I can't see it. I've looked and I can't — you know I haven't been able to see clearly since your father died."

Amandine reaches for her mother's hand. "It's a shame," she says, wanting to relieve her mother of the subject of her father. "I'm so worried about the boys. I just can't imagine —"

"I don't think he's having an affair," Héloïse interrupts. "This is Eliot, he's too . . . I just don't believe it, I don't." She swallows the last of her cappuccino. "But . . ."

"What?"

"I'm sorry, *chérie,* I didn't know what was

197

best. I didn't . . . I thought perhaps I shouldn't be involved. I didn't want to get between you. I —"

"Mother, what's going on? You're scaring me."

Héloïse takes a deep breath. "I felt something shift a few months ago. I don't know what. But it was the day you dropped the boys at my house, when your babysitter fell through. I'm afraid I didn't look after them well, they just watched television all —"

"Never mind that now," Amandine interrupts. "Do you remember what day that was? It might help me to figure out . . ."

Héloïse nods. "The eighth of March. That's when I felt it the first time."

Amandine frowns. "Why that day? What's special about that date?"

Héloïse shrugs. "I don't know."

"Did something happen?"

"You tell me."

"I don't know."

"Think about it."

"What day was it?" Amandine asks. "Lent term ended on the eleventh, so that must have been a Friday, so it was a Tuesday. I wasn't working in the afternoon. I took Frankie and Bertie to the park . . . before I got a call and I had to — oh."

"What?"

"Eliot received a letter that morning. Handwritten. I remember because our address was written in purple ink."

Héloïse, who had been reaching for a chocolate and pistachio cream cupcake, drops her hand to the table and stares straight at her daughter. "Purple?"

"Yes. It's unusual, I suppose, so I remembered it. I left the letter on Eliot's desk, and that night —"

"Purple?" Héloïse says softly, thinking of the green ink in her books, but trying to focus on Amandine's mysteries and not her own.

"He didn't come to bed. He slept in his study, that's what he told me, and I thought it was strange but I didn't want to make a big thing out of it. He told me it was nothing, that he was working on a case all night, and I believed him."

"*Bien,*" Héloïse says. "Then I suppose the thing to do now is to find the letter."

I'm having sex with your sister. I'm sleeping with your sister. I, okay . . . Hey, Kat, remember your sister? Well, I know it sounds crazy, but I think we might be trying to have a baby . . .

George hurries along King's Parade, toward Trinity College to track down Kat.

She's been avoiding him for days now and he can't let it continue. He's not exactly sure why she's so upset — can she really think he'd be a horrible match for her sister, that he's so unworthy of her? — but he's determined to get to the bottom of it. Kat is his best friend and he can't lose her over this. It'd be dreadful if he and Cosima married and Kat refused to speak to them. He'd hate to cause a family rift, to be the reason for displeasure and disharmony. He couldn't bear it. He'd rather give Cosima up altogether. Well . . . almost.

George crosses the road onto Trinity Street, glancing up at St. Mary's Church, wondering, as he does every time, whether he'll one day find the time to climb to the top along with all the tourists. Why is it so often true that, when something sits on your doorstep, you take it for granted? He slows his pace as he passes the Cambridge University Bookshop, looking in the window at the display of book sculptures. A three-dimensional Mad Hatter's Tea Party has been created from a single copy of *Alice in Wonderland.* George ponders it. Why, after all, is he rushing? He hates confrontation. If he didn't care so deeply for Kat he'd never be going to face her now, to ask why she's avoiding him. If he didn't need her so much, he'd just let her go, drop out of the book group and never see any of them again.

As he ambles along Trinity Street, images of silky white wedding dresses and giggling babies with chubby fingers they wrap around his thumb fill George's mind and he smiles. It seems strange to him now that he's never thought about these things before, never wanted them. How misguided he must have been. But now he's seen the light. He remembers how she looked at him, how she kissed him, unlike any way he's ever been looked at or kissed before. And every moment of time, every molecule of air, contained promise and possibility.

As he reaches the little courtyard of trees at the end of All Saints' Passage, about to turn left onto the cobbled path outside Trinity College, George closes his eyes and turns his face up to the sun, mumbling thanks to all the deities he knows of for his great good fortune. When he opens his eyes again, he's face-to-face with Kat.

She just stares at him, unable to hide her horror. His smile drops, all his joy draining away at how unhappy she is to see him.

"I was just — I'm heading into college. I'm late for a tutorial."

George looks at her. It doesn't take any of his limited magic to know that she's lying.

Since the moment they met he's been able to read her face and know her emotions as well as he knows his own.

"Have you got a few minutes? I was on my way to see you," George says, aware that he's begging. "You've been avoiding me."

"I haven't," Kat says. "I've been busy."

"You've been avoiding me," George says again. It's probably the most direct he's ever been with anyone in his life and he can already feel the skin on his neck starting to itch.

Kat bites her lip, avoiding his gaze.

"Please." George swallows. "I need to talk about this, I want to make it better again. I can't stand you not speaking to me. I'm not sure why you're so against the idea of me and Cosima, but —"

Kat rolls her eyes. "You and Cosima? What, did you get engaged over cupcakes? Are you getting married? Did you forget she's still married herself?"

"Hardly," George says. "He's having a baby with another woman."

Kat scowls.

"Look, this isn't just a fling for me," George says. "You don't have to worry about me hurting your sister. I'd never do that — I love her."

Kat laughs. "Love her? *Love* her? What

the hell are you talking about? Can you hear yourself? You don't love her. You can't. It's been, what, five minutes? Anyway, she doesn't love you, you know that, right? She might seem okay but she's still mourning the end of her marriage. You don't get over a husband in a month, even with magic, even . . ."

"Okay, okay," George says, "I seem to have made it worse. I thought it would be a good thing to say so. I thought it'd reassure you. I didn't mean —"

"You don't get it, do you?" Kat snaps.

George frowns. "Get what?"

Kat rolls her eyes.

"What?" George protests. "I don't understand. What —"

Kat shakes her head. "No. I'm not going to tell you. If it matters . . . if our friendship matters to you at all, you'll figure it out."

And with that, she turns and walks away, leaving George staring after her, wondering what just happened.

Noa has passed a glorious few days in a haze of delightful normalcy, engaging in carefree conversations with checkout girls, chatting about the weather with the college porters, discussing politics with other students.

Last night Santiago took her dancing.

They caught a late train to London and took a taxi to an area Noa had never been. Santiago greeted the doorman with a few incomprehensible words of Portuguese in his ear, upon which the door cracked open and a dim sliver of light shone out.

No one in the club spoke English and Noa drifted toward the bar on a wave of lyrical words, barely audible above the beat of drums and sensual song. It seemed to Noa that every man she saw was unusually beautiful: tall with dark hair, olive skin, enormous deep brown eyes, and brilliant smiles. The women were equally mesmerizing and every one extremely elegant. Noa had dressed up for the occasion but feared she stood out too starkly with her blond hair and blue eyes. The gorgeous Brazilians stared as she slipped past them and she tried to shrink herself a little smaller with every look.

"They are struck by your beauty," Santiago said with a smile. "You are a rare jewel."

Noa smiled; with him, she felt it.

"*É verdade!*" Santiago laughed, pulling her through the crowd and onto the dance floor. "Let me show you how beautiful you are."

As Noa flew across the floor, stepping and turning and dipping as if she were being blown by a perfect wind, she thought that Santiago must either be a dance maestro or a magician. She'd never moved so smoothly, so quickly, so gracefully. She'd never felt so in sync with her body and the world. Her heart beat in time with the drums, her breath swelled with the song, her feet skipped along the piano notes. It was as if Noa's skin was dissolving into the air until she was weightless, a spirit floating through the air.

"There," Santiago whispered into her ear as the song subsided, "see how beautiful you are."

Noa could only nod. She could only let him hold her as the music started again and dance and dance until she couldn't stand any more. Noa had once seen a film about a ballerina who found a pair of enchanted red ballet shoes. When she wore them she could dance without stopping, her feet at last able to match the joy of her heart and its desire to dance forever. Unfortunately, the ballerina couldn't control the shoes and died. Which is rather how Noa felt as she sank into Santiago, their bodies blending together, on the journey home.

Now Noa hurries along Bridge Street toward Magdalene College. She has another tutorial with Amandine, on Monet and the

French Impressionists, though she fears her essay won't be up to scratch, since she hasn't really slept in the last few days. When Noa reaches Amandine's office, she finds Kat standing at the door.

"Hi," Noa says, instantly a little embarrassed to remember how they last met. "I'm . . . I've got a tutorial with —"

"She's not in," Kat interrupts. "I don't know where she is."

"Oh, okay." Noa stands at the door. She scratches around her increasingly fuzzy brain for some useful words and, fortunately, finds something.

"So, um, how's the mathematical department?"

"Fine."

"How's . . . George?"

The second she says his name, Noa knows she's made a dreadful mistake. Unfortunately, these were the only two facts she knew about Kat: that she taught applied mathematics and she was in love with George. It left her conversational repertoire rather limited. She should have stuck to mathematics.

Kat starts to cry. Little stifled sobs escape as she bends over, head in hands, hiding her face. Torn between the urge to run and the need to be polite, Noa turns her own face to the floor and shuffles her feet.

"Sorry," Kat's voice is muffled. "I shouldn't, I shouldn't . . ."

"It's okay," Noa lies, finding a few more appropriate words. "Don't worry. I, um, I understand."

Kat looks up, brushing her hands across her cheeks. "You do?"

"Well, um, I, I mean . . ." Noa averts her eyes, racking her brain for something more sympathetic and comforting to say. "That is, I . . ."

"He says he's in love with my sister," Kat blurts out. "My *sister.*" She says this last word as if her sister was a creature worse than those inhabiting the seventh circle of hell. "And he shouldn't be, he can't be . . ." Kat bursts into sobs again.

"Oh" is all Noa can manage. "I didn't . . . Oh, dear."

"Too right." Kat screws up her eyes at Noa. "But then I'm sure you already knew about them, didn't you? Given your 'gift' for sneaking into other people's private thoughts?"

"Seeing their biggest secrets," Noa says, a little hurt. "But don't worry, I can't do that anymore. I . . . um," she trails off, suddenly unable to remember the name of that sexy Brazilian or any facts surrounding him.

"Well, anyway, something happened, but it's a relief really. It means people don't hate me anymore, which is nice."

"Yeah," Kat says, sniffing. "I suppose." She regards Noa curiously. "But don't you think it's a shame? Don't you miss your magic?"

"No," Noa lies again. "I like being normal."

"Really?" Kat says, as if she couldn't imagine anything worse than this in the world, except perhaps for her best friend being in love with her sister.

"Well . . . So, what will you do, about George and — ?"

Kat shrugs. "What can I do? It's done."

A little shiver runs through Noa and, all of a sudden, she can feel Santiago's voice in her head, his kiss on her lips, and his breath in her mouth.

"Well," she says, her voice as smooth as cachaça. "You could cast a spell."

Kat frowns. "What do you mean?"

When Noa smiles, it's *his* smile. When she speaks, they're his words. "What is the use of being a witch, after all, if you can't use a little magic?"

"Oh!" Kat says suddenly. "Oh, my God. Of course."

Noa frowns, suddenly herself again and

feeling a little foggy. "What?"

"Of course. Of course! How didn't I see it? She's enchanted him." Kat starts pacing up and down. "I know what she's doing. The stupid, foolish girl, she knows it's the last thing in the world she should do, she's risking her life."

"I'm afraid I . . ." Noa says, still a little lost.

"I've got to do something right now." Kat grabs Noa by the shoulders and starts shaking her. "I've got to save her — both of them — before it's too late."

Ever since her first vision of the man with the green pen, Héloïse has been doing everything she can to get another. Unfortunately, these peeks into past, present, or future have always been beyond her control. She's never been able to conjure them up at will, although there are circumstances that can encourage a little extra sight, so Héloïse has been focusing on doing what she can: long candlelit baths, walks in the Gwydir Street cemetery at twilight, afternoon naps in the hammock in her garden, drinking cups of cold almond milk and eating a pistachio croissant at Gustare for breakfast . . . Sadly, so far, none of these little tricks has worked, although Héloïse has certainly appreciated an excuse to try, and she's rather surprised by how she's starting to enjoy the little things in life again. It isn't much, but it is something.

She hasn't heard from François in nearly a week. She wonders if he's punishing her for taking her attention away, for trying to live again. She hopes not and, if he is, she hopes he'll forgive her for the second time. Not that, in all his pleadings for her not to let him go, François has ever blamed her for the circumstances surrounding his death; it's only Héloïse who's done that.

Today Héloïse is taking a big step: she's returning to her college. Not to teach, she doesn't know if she'll ever return to that. But she misses the library, the beautiful college library with its high ceilings, cream walls, dark wooden bookshelves, mosaic floors, and busts of famous alumni in alcoves under each enormous window. Apart from the two-year sabbatical, Héloïse has been researching the works of Simone de Beauvoir all her life. Her expertise is renowned throughout the university, so whenever a student was studying French literature of the early-to-mid-twentieth century, or feminism, they came to Héloïse. Before François died, Héloïse imagined that if she ever stopped reading she'd stop breathing too and, even after she semi-retired, she'd spent every afternoon of every day in the Newnham College library researching and writing and watching students come and go. She's always thought she'd rather die here than any place on earth and, as she hurries up the stone staircase leading to the library, Héloïse finds that she still does. She only hopes that when the time finally comes it'll be swift and sweet, like falling asleep on a Sunday afternoon in the sunshine, with her nose in a good book. If only it had been that way for poor François too.

"Je t'aime," she tells him, softly. *"Je vous aimerai toujours."*

Héloïse waits a moment for his echo and, when none comes, she pushes open the heavy wooden door, her heart quickening as she steps inside. She's grateful that the ancient librarian, Molly, is on her break as Héloïse isn't ready for consolations and chats just yet. She'd waited until eleven o'clock before coming, knowing that Molly usually had her cup of tea and biscuits around that time. Slowly crossing the mosaic floor, Héloïse finds her favorite reading desk overlooking the master's private garden. It's the only view of the walled garden in the college, and Héloïse can only see a little slice of it: the edge of a bench and half of an enormous red rose bush. It'd make a lovely reading spot on those rare rain-free days, she's sure. But Héloïse is content just to look from the window, to imagine and speculate what it might feel like to sit in the garden, though she will probably never know for certain.

Héloïse opens *A Moveable Feast,* hoping to find a clue or get another glimpse. As she turns the pages, she feels almost over-whelmed with desire to know the man whose words she loves to read, whose thoughts and feelings are so close to her own. Not that she expects anything to come of it, not really, but the very fact of being curious, of feeling adventurous, after so long of feeling nothing but grief and guilt, is wonderful enough. Héloïse simply wants to try and solve the mystery; anything that happens after that is a bonus.

Héloïse lays her hands on her open book and gazes out of the window again. The sun glints in through the window and flashes into her eyes. Héloïse blinks, then closes her eyes on the bench and the bush of red roses. It's in that moment that the vision comes to her: two men standing at the market stall surrounded by books. Ben smiles at the other man, who has his back to her, and talks animatedly, though Héloïse can't hear any sound. The other man carries a bag; he lifts it up and removes a pile of books. On the top is *A Moveable Feast.* It gives off a slight glow. The man hands the books to Ben, who smiles and says, "Thank you." Héloïse waits, hoping the man will turn so she can see his face, but he does not. And then the vision disappears.

Héloïse opens her eyes. Ben knows him. He knows the man with the green pen. It's a lead. She smiles. Her adventure is about to begin.

CHAPTER TWELVE

Héloïse has always believed that the world can be divided into two sorts of people: those who, once their wound has healed, rip off the Band-Aid quickly and those who pull it off slowly, bit by bit, prolonging the agony. Héloïse has always been a ripper. She has to wait two days before she can confront Ben about the man with the green pen, since he doesn't work on Wednesdays. On Thursday, after a gulped-down breakfast of milky coffee and crisp bread, she arrives at the market square to find him setting up his bookstall in the soft early morning sun.

"*Bonjour,* Ben."

Crouched over a box of books, he looks up, surprised.

"You're up early, Lou."

Héloïse nods, not wanting to waste time on chitchat.

"I have a question," she says.

"Yes?" Ben stands, brushing his hands off

on his T-shirt.

Héloïse dips inside her bag and brings out the two books she'd bought. Ben frowns when he sees them.

"You didn't like *The Old Man and the Sea?* Really?" he asks. "I'm sorry, I thought you would."

"No." Héloïse shakes her head, impatient. "It's not that. I loved it. I'm not here to return anything. I'd just like to know who sold them to you."

"Oh?"

"The books are full of marks," Héloïse explains, "in green pen. Thoughts and comments on the text . . ." She trails off, reluctant to go into greater detail. She may be direct in saying what she wants, but Héloïse is still of a generation that doesn't discuss private experiences with strangers. Ben isn't a stranger, but still. Héloïse hasn't even told her daughter about the man with the green pen.

"Ah, I see," Ben says. "I'm sorry about that, I can give you clean copies, I didn't realize —"

"Non," Héloïse says quickly, "it's not that. I don't want new copies."

"I don't understand."

"I want to know who sold them to you." She slips the books back into her bag and

215

fixes him with her most winning smile, the one that got Héloïse her first date with François and a lot of other lovely things over the years. She knows she's nearly sixty, and still a little haggard from two years of sleepless nights, but she hopes she still has it. "Are you allowed to? Or is there some sort of code? A book buyer to seller confidentiality, like a lawyer or doctor?"

Ben smiles in return. "No, of course not. It's just . . ."

"What?"

"They belonged to my father."

Héloïse's heart soars and plunges in the same instant. "*Mon Dieu,* I'm so sorry, I didn't realize he had passed away too, I —"

"No, no, he's not dead." Ben grins. "Far from it, crazy old goat. Last week he was on a boat in the Atlantic Ocean protesting whaling."

Héloïse widens her eyes and pulls her silk scarf a little tighter around her shoulders. "He was?"

Ben nods. "Yep, ever since he retired, Dad's been doing his best to save the world from rack and ruin. It's pretty amazing really, if a little worrying sometimes, the things he gets up to."

"*Alors!*" Héloïse says. "I had no idea."

"I know, crazy, huh?"

Héloïse smiles, then she's tentative, picking up a book from the pile already stacked on the table, turning it over in her hands as if she might be thinking of buying it. She doesn't look up. "And your mother, she doesn't mind?"

Ben shakes his head. "She died five years ago. That's when everything kicked off, actually. I think he wanted to do something special, to make a difference before he died . . ."

"Oh, I see." Héloïse wonders what to say next. How can she direct this conversation toward getting what she wants? What *does* she want? "And is he home now, or still on the Atlantic Ocean?"

Beginning to stack up new piles of books from his boxes, Ben laughs. "No, he's back, in one piece, thank God. Sleeping off all the protesting at home."

An idea strikes Héloïse. She should invite them both over for tea. Then she realizes she can't. It's one thing trying to track down a man with a green pen, it's quite another to serve him tea and cake in your kitchen. Whatever would François make of that? Not very much, she's sure.

"I'd love to see him sometime," Héloïse says, trying a different tack. "It's been so long. Perhaps . . ."

"Yes, he'd love that, I'm certain. You must visit him for tea. I'll give you his number."

Héloïse smiles, slightly surprised at how well that tactic worked. "That would be delightful," she says. "Do you think he might be free tomorrow?"

Amandine has arrived early. She sits on a turret at the north of Magdalene College chapel, directly above the nave. Amandine is happiest when the book group meets at her college because she times their meeting to coincide with Mass. Amandine would have loved to have sung in a choir, if only she wasn't as tone deaf as her mother. Even Bertie and Frankie tease her, giggling whenever she inadvertently bursts into song when a pop song comes on the radio. Her rendition of "Girls Just Wanna Have Fun" particularly amuses them. Occasionally, Amandine has thought of applying a little magic to smooth the sharp edges off her voice but it doesn't seem fair somehow to all the real singers who've worked so hard to hone theirs.

The moon hangs low and full in the sky. It's buttery yellow, heavy and rich. Amandine can feel its tug. She wraps her cardigan around her, not that she can really feel the cool breeze, but just to give her a little comfort. Over the past few days she's searched the house for Eliot's letter but found nothing. She's been through every drawer, every bookshelf, every cabinet. Nothing. For the next half hour, Amandine mentally scours her house, checking all the potential hiding places where the letter might be. Perhaps Eliot threw it out, so it'll never be found, but Amandine doubts it. Her husband is a hoarder. He keeps random receipts for years; he certainly wouldn't have thrown away something as important as a letter from his lover. Or whoever Sylvia might be.

Just as Amandine is beginning to wonder if she's being stood up tonight or if she somehow miscalculated the date, George pokes his head over the turret.

"Hello."

Amandine rests her copy of *Great Expectations* on the tiles and stands to help George onto the roof. He dusts himself off and nods at the book.

"He should have stuck with the original ending."

Amandine frowns. "The depressing one where Pip and Estella don't end up together? Why would you want that?"

George shrugs as he sits on the roof. "It's more realistic. I didn't believe in the Hollywood sunset. Didn't fit with the rest of the book."

Amandine sighs. "Realism's highly over-rated. I get enough of that from life, I don't need it from books as well."

George looks at her, a little concerned. He opens his mouth, then shuts it again and glances at his watch. "Oh, sorry I'm late."

Now Amandine shrugs. "At least you showed up. No one else has."

George glances about, as if some of the other witches might be hiding behind the turrets. "Ah, okay."

Amandine regards him quizzically. "Why are you relieved?"

George shakes his head. "No, I'm not, of course not." He pauses. "Well, yes, perhaps just a little."

"Why?" Amandine sits next to him. "What's going on? Is my mother — ?"

"It's not Héloïse, I haven't seen her since our last meeting." George takes a deep breath. "It's Kat."

Amandine frowns. She feels sadness, desperate confusion wafting about, so thick in the air it almost makes her queasy.

"What happened?"

"She hates me," George murmurs. "She absolutely hates me."

"Why?"

George shrugs. "I don't know. I don't, I think . . . maybe she thinks I'm not good enough for her sister. But I don't get it; if I've been good enough to be her best friend for this long, then why is she so upset by my dating her sister? I just, I don't —"

Amandine stares at him. "You're dating Cosima?"

George nods.

"Oh."

"What?" George scowls at Amandine. "Are you saying it's too soon? Are you saying you wouldn't want me dating your sister?"

Amandine frowns. "I don't have a sister."

"That's not the point," George snaps, his eyes filling with tears. "Am I really so hideous? Really? I'm a good man. I am. Does it matter that our babies will be short, fat, and bald? Most babies are anyway."

"Babies?"

George shrugs. "That's not the point. The point is that Kat's furious. We had a huge fight and she walked away. We haven't spoken since. That's never happened with us before, I don't understand it, I just don't understand."

Amandine looks at her friend, at his watery eyes behind thin gold-rimmed spectacles. She wants to help, to take his pain away, to offer him a sense of understanding and so, without thinking out the consequences, she does.

"She doesn't hate you," Amandine says. "She loves you."

"I don't think so," George says. "She used to, but she certainly doesn't seem to anymore. I only wish she did."

"No." Amandine shakes her head. "I mean, she *loves* you."

George stares at her, speechless.

Amandine nods, then shrugs.

"She *loves* me?" George whispers. "But . . . well, that explains why she doesn't want . . . but my God, I never, that's just — incredible."

"It's not that incredible. You're a lovely man. I'm not surprised."

George laughs. "I'm hardly an Adonis, am I?"

"I don't think most people are that shallow, do you?"

George fixes Amandine with a wry smile. "You're one to talk. Your husband — excuse me for saying so — is one of the most gorgeous men I've ever met."

Amandine's face clouds and her eyes fill with tears.

George steps toward her. "What? What's wrong? Is Eliot all right?"

Amandine nods. "See, this is why you're a catch. You're so bloody thoughtful, observant, sweet . . . If you had a wife I bet you'd notice whenever she'd had a haircut or was wearing a new dress. I bet you wouldn't cheat on her with your secretary."

"No, well, I don't have a secretary, but . . ." George trails off, staring at Amandine, openmouthed. "Is Eliot having an affair with his secretary?"

She sighs. "Yes. No. I don't know. I'm convinced he must be having an affair with someone, either his secretary or some beautiful barrister in a short skirt. It's really the only sensible explanation. *Maman* assures me he isn't, but I just don't know. I don't know what else it could be."

"Why?" George asks. "Why do you think so?"

"He's been so different, so distant. I've felt nothing from him, no love, not even a shadow of the adoration he's always had for the boys and me. He's numb. He's distracted, he's not with us, he's not loving us because he's thinking of her."

"Well" — George is tentative — "that doesn't mean . . . after all, it could be something else, he might have a big case on, or —"

"I found a letter."

"A letter?"

"Well, sort of. A piece of paper with her name all over it. Sylvia." Amandine spits out this last word as if it's poison. "Sylvia. A hundred times. In his handwriting."

"Oh."

"Yes. Exactly."

"It doesn't look good," George says, doing his best to focus, though he's still thinking of Kat. "I must admit."

"No, it doesn't, does it? There is a letter too. He received it when he started being weird with us."

"But you haven't read it?"

"No, of course not. Otherwise I'd know what the hell was going on, wouldn't I?"

"Yes," George admits. "Yes, I suppose so."

"I've spent the last three days searching the house, but I can't find it anywhere."

"Ah." George's eyes light up.

"What?"

"Well, if I did have a wife, but I wanted to hide a letter from her, I wouldn't keep it at home."

"You wouldn't?"

"No," George says with a smile, delighted, with all the agony he seems to be causing lately, to finally be of some help. "I'd keep it at work."

"Ah," Amandine exclaims. "Of course."

■ ■ ■ ■

Kat stands in her kitchen. It's been a long time since she's actually cast a baking spell. Her mother warned her so often against spells for one's own gain, and Kat desperately hopes this doesn't count. She's mainly doing it to save her sister from risking her life, and George from being stuck with something he doesn't want. That it will alleviate her own heartache a little is an incidental blessing.

Luckily, one thing Kat doesn't have to worry about is how to do the spell in the first place. Kat learned her method from her mother and has never changed it. Lucinda Rubens baked her spells into bread. Every Saturday morning (in addition to other times that arose spontaneously) she set up her kitchen for an early-morning bread baking session, bustling down the stairs while her husband slept, waking Kat on the way. Together they filled the little house with the smell of yeast and dough and happiness. Peter Rubens always woke with a smile on Saturday mornings. He'd whistle in the shower, bound down the stairs, spin Kat around the kitchen, then pretend to tango with his wife before dipping and kissing her full on the lips.

After breakfast, Kat would go around to the neighbors with her mother, carrying a basket of bread. During the week, they'd make inquiries to see who needed their help. They baked yarrow bread for those with broken hearts, sorrel bread for neglected children, stephanotis bread for couples who were fighting, pear blossom bread for anyone grieving, laurel bread for those needing financial help, and a simple sage bread for everyone else.

When Lucinda died, Kat was too busy taking care of the new, squalling, motherless baby to bake bread on a Saturday morning. And after that, her father stopped whistling in the shower or spinning her around the kitchen. When Cosima was old enough to learn the secrets of special bread making, Kat taught her all the techniques and skills she knew. Once again the house was filled with the smell of yeast, dough, and happiness. And once again their father began whistling in the shower. Sadly, at seventeen, Kat was now too big to spin around the kitchen although happily, for Cosima at least, she was still the perfect size.

As it turned out, Cosima had quite a flair for flavor. She created things that shocked Kat, who had only ever followed her mother's more mundane recipes. One Saturday, Cosima made rosemary, stilton, and walnut bread and their father ran up and down the street after breakfast, telling his neighbors he was training for a marathon. Another Saturday her bacon and brie bread caused Peter Rubens to quit his sales job and revisit a great passion for pottery and carpentry that he'd long before abandoned. Kat personally puts her father's remarriage down to the chocolate and chili bread Cosima made when she was six. Kat liked her stepmother and loved that she was finally free to leave her father and little sister and go out into the world to live her own life.

Usually, baking spells required that the intended recipient eat the bread. However, in this case it isn't possible for either Cosima (since she'd instantly know it was spell bread) or George (since Kat isn't speaking to him right now), so she will have to do something a little unconventional and eat it on their behalf. Kat isn't entirely sure whether this will work, and wishes she could ask her mother, but of course she can't.

This is the first time Kat has needed to invert one of her mother's beautiful, kind, sweet baking spells into something ugly, cruel, and sour. She's used a slight twist on the binominal theorem to capsize and corrupt the original spell.

$$(x + a)^n = \sum_{k=0}^{n} \binom{n}{k} x^k a^{n-k}$$

Once she'd calculated the weights and measures on her list of slightly sinister ingredients, Kat went shopping.

Now she unwraps the bouquet of dark red roses, begins ripping off the petals and adding them to the flour, salt, sugar, and water. She snips off thirteen thorns and sprinkles them into the mixture. Kat grinds in the black pepper, jasmine (separation), and basil (hate). Then, when she's kneaded the dough — pounding and slapping it on the bread board — until it's far too dense to be delicious, Kat adds the final touch: two pods of vanilla and three drops of her own blood. She doesn't let it rise, doesn't stroke or shape it, but slams it straight into the oven. Then she whispers a few words and sprinkles them with a few exquisite equations to ensure the perfect balance of the spell.

Nearly an hour later, when the bread is nicely burned and black, Kat cuts two slices: one for George and one for Cosima. She turns out all the lights, draws all the curtains, switches off all electrical equipment, and sits down at the kitchen table. A single candle flickers in front of the bread, casting shadows of broken promises and impossible futures. Kat bites into the first slice. It's dry and dense. It sticks to the roof of her mouth and catches in her throat so she has to swallow seven times before it'll go down.

It takes Kat thirty minutes to eat both slices of bread. In between every bite she mumbles an incantation: of love lost and forgotten, of friendship regained and illusions shattered. When her plate is empty, Kat blows out the candle and sits in the dark. Then she closes her eyes and prays that it's not already too late.

CHAPTER THIRTEEN

When George wakes the next morning he can instantly feel that something inside him has dramatically and fundamentally changed. Or rather, he's changed back to how he was before . . . At first he's not sure what it is and then, as he pulls himself up to sit and turns to see Cosima lying asleep next to him, he knows.

"Oh, shit."

She stirs.

Fuck. He freezes. *Fuck. Fuck. Fuck. How the hell did this happen?*

And then it all starts coming back to him. The café. The food. The pizza. The cannoli. The wine. The sex. The nonstop sex they've been having. Kat. Love.

Oh, fuck.

She must have drugged him, she must have — and then he remembers the baking spell. The fertility bread. George opens his mouth, but this time he's too stunned to even think anymore, let alone speak.

"Hey, you," Cosima half-opens her eyes and gazes happily up at him. "Morning."

"Morning," George mumbles.

Cosima frowns. "Are you okay?"

George nods. "Yeah, sure, of course. How are you?"

"Still a little knackered after last night," she says with a grin, "but happy."

Last night? Oh, fuck.

George nods. "Right, right. Yeah, me too."

Cosima sits up. "Are you sure you're okay? You look a little peaky. Shall I make you some tea? I've got special herbs that'll clear a cold up before it —"

"No!"

"What?"

"Sorry." He coughs. "I mean, no thank you, I'm fine."

George slides out of bed, scrambling around on the floor for his underwear while trying to maintain some semblance of decency.

"What are you doing?"

"I, um, I just remembered, I've got an early-morning tutorial, with that crazy chap, the one who likes to work at dawn, anyway . . ." George pulls on his trousers and looks around for his shirt.

Cosima laughs nervously. "Are you running out on me?"

"No, of course not," George says, "don't be silly." He steps quickly over to the bed, giving her a chaste kiss on the cheek. "Sorry, I've just got to go."

Héloïse stops outside 28 St. Barnabas Road, her hand hovering over the bell. It's like a Band-Aid, she thinks, just rip it off. Héloïse rings the bell, steps back, and waits.

"I'm sorry, *mon amour,*" she whispers. "I love you, I do. And —"

The door opens. Theo stands in the doorway, smiling. It's been a long time since Héloïse has seen him, and the first thing that strikes her is how little he's aged. The second thing that strikes her is just how handsome he is.

"Come in, come in," Theo says, stepping aside to let Héloïse enter. She watches the back of his head, his thick wavy white hair that curls at the nape of his neck. He's a full head taller than she, while François was the same height, and strolls while François always hurried. I wonder if it'll always be like this, Héloïse thinks, a constant stream of comparisons with the love of her life and every man she meets.

"It's lovely to see you again," Theo says, leading her into the kitchen, past endless shelves of books. "How long's it been? Feels like forever."

"I don't know," Héloïse says, though she's been trying to figure it out since yesterday. "When did you retire?"

"About a decade ago, when Maggie first got sick."

"I'm sorry to hear . . ."

"Thank you," Theo says. "I was sorry to hear about François too, of course, Ben told me."

The kitchen is as crammed with books as the corridor, though it hardly seems possible. A dozen shelves are screwed into the bright yellow wall, weighed down by about five hundred cookery books. Héloïse studies the titles as Theo opens the fridge.

"I'm afraid I can't bake anything decent," he says, pulling out a plate adorned with a large chocolate cake. "I'm okay to cook, but baking isn't my thing. Maggie loved it, so I was simply the happy recipient of her creations. This one's courtesy of the supermarket down the street."

"It looks perfectly yummy," Héloïse says, wondering if, one day, she'll be able to talk about François like this: with love and without sorrow. "Thank you."

"It's funny that we never had tea before," Theo says as he sets the cake down on the table and switches on the kettle. "We've always had so much to talk about, books and all that. Earl Grey or English Breakfast?"

"Earl Grey, please."

"Or would you prefer coffee?" Theo asks. "Sorry, it's an English arrogance, assuming that everyone always wants tea."

Héloïse smiles. "I've been here so long I think I'm an honorary British citizen," she says, glad that François can't hear her, since he was always far more patriotic than she, insisting they celebrate Bastille Day every year with champagne in bed and fireworks in the garden.

"Two Earl Greys it is, then," Theo says, pouring boiling water into their cups. "Milk? Sugar? Both? Neither?"

"Neither," Héloïse says, "so perhaps I am still a little French after all."

"I thought so," Theo says as he makes a detour to the fridge for milk and a cupboard for sugar. "You've always been far too glamorous to be British."

Héloïse feels herself blush. She tucks a curl of hair behind her ear and twirls her pearl earring between thumb and forefinger. When Theo sits down next to her and begins slicing the cake, they fall into silence. Héloïse wonders if it's an awkward silence, or if that's simply her interpretation, generated by nerves and secrets.

"I hear you're quite the adventurer."

"I get into my fair share of scrapes," Theo says, glancing up from the cake with a smile. "Or a little more than that, perhaps."

"I don't think I've ever done anything truly adventurous."

"That depends on your classification, I suppose."

Héloïse gives a little shrug. "I'd suggest that tracking down whaling boats on the Atlantic Ocean is significantly more adventurous than teaching the social and political theory of Simone de Beauvoir, in anybody's opinion. Wouldn't you?"

Theo smiles again. "I can't argue with that, I suppose. Cake?"

He slides the plate over to Héloïse.

"Merci."

"Your accent is marvelous," Theo says. "I could close my eyes and have you read the phone book aloud and listen for hours."

"Merci beaucoup," Héloïse says, softly, blushing again.

"Sorry," he says, "I didn't mean to make you self-conscious."

"Not at all," she says. "You didn't."

"I did."

"Okay." Héloïse smiles. "Maybe just a little."

Theo takes a large forkful of the cake and Héloïse follows suit with a smaller bite while he chews.

"What do you think?" Theo asks as he swallows.

"About what?"

Theo smiles. "Life, death, the universe, everything —"

"Oh, well, I don't —"

"No, sorry, I was just teasing, I meant the cake."

"*Alors,* well, it's rather . . ."

"Revolting."

Héloïse laughs. "I didn't want to be rude, but —"

"Don't worry," Theo says, "I'm sure the multimillion-pound supermarket can take the hit. However, since I've now let you down so significantly on the baking front, will you let me cook you dinner to make up for it?"

Héloïse starts to smile, then she remembers. *Non. No, I can't. It's too soon. I'm sorry.* Héloïse opens her mouth.

"Yes," she finds herself saying. "That would be lovely."

Noa hurries along Downing Street. She's a

little late for her date with Santiago, having fallen asleep while reading a book on Brazilian art. She's so tired lately (probably because she too often stays up late with Santiago) and often finds herself falling asleep in the middle of the afternoon. She finds him in the foyer of the Museum of Archaeology and Anthropology, studying a collection of Viking spears.

Noa stands behind him. "Sharp," she says.

Santiago turns, a soft smile on his lips. "You came."

"Sorry I'm late, I fell —"

"— asleep. It's no problem. I like being here. It gives me inspiration."

Noa stares at him. "How did you know?"

Santiago doesn't answer but takes her hand. "Follow me."

They walk up a narrow wooden staircase and come into another room full of artifacts enclosed in glass cases. An enormous totem pole stands in the center of the room, higher than any tree Noa's ever seen, carved with the faces of animals and birds. Next to it stands a vast wooden bear, his mouth roaring and his paws raised as if about to strike. Noa shivers and looks away.

"Have you ever been to Africa or South America?" Santiago asks as they cross the room, weaving between glass display cases.

"I've never been anywhere outside Europe."

"Oh," Santiago says, "then you must see this."

They pass a case of tribal masks. Bright white eyes stare out at Noa from dark wood, long white teeth, pierced noses and ears, framed with wild white hair made of feathers and wool.

"We have masks like this in my country too," Santiago says. "We have incredible festivals to celebrate the Catholic saints and Macumba spirits. We dance and drink all night, on the beach, under the stars." He laughs. "Most of us usually end up in the sea."

Noa glances over at him, realizing exactly what it is about him that so attracts her. It's not simply the way he looks, though he is exceptionally beautiful — his big brown eyes framed with long black lashes, a beauty spot under his right eye, flawless olive skin — or his talent as a painter; it's the way he is: self-confident and strong, someone without fear. This is what pulls Noa to him, because she feels that way when she's with him.

"Wow," she says. "That does sound incredible."

"Check these out." Santiago brings Noa to a glass case of tiny figures, brightly colored in various costumes.

"Sweet," Noa says, "like little dolls."

It's a moment before she notices that every figure is faceless, having a skull stripped of flesh and bare bones where their face and limbs should be.

"They're skeletons."

"Yes," Santiago says with a smile. "Aren't they fantastic? They're from Mexico, toys used to celebrate *El Dia de los Muertos.*"

"What?"

"The Day of the Dead."

"Gosh," Noa says, a thought of her own suddenly bursting forth, "how gruesome."

"No, not at all!" Santiago laughs. "It's a glorious festival. We celebrate it in Brazil too, though not as magnificently as they do in Mexico. They create altars in their homes, on the streets, in graveyards. They honor their dead, framing their photographs with bright yellow flowers, cooking their favorite foods and leaving the dishes as offerings. It's a time when the whole country comes together to remember those that others might otherwise have forgotten."

Noa listens, thinking she detects something else in Santiago's voice — a tinge of sorrow — suggesting he's lost someone he won't forget.

"Ah," she says. "Well, yes, that does sound

very . . . special."

Santiago turns to Noa, clasping her hands tightly.

"You're special," he says.

"I am?"

"Very. And you have absolutely no idea how powerful you are."

"Powerful?"

Santiago nods. "You've got the strength of a shaman running through your veins."

"I have?"

"Oh, yes." Santiago gazes at her. "Tell me what you want."

"What?"

"What do you want, right now, more than anything?"

Noa looks into Santiago's deep brown eyes, trying to figure out the answer he wants to hear but, although that's usually too easy, all she can think of right now is that night, the night he painted her, of being naked and beautiful and eating the sweetest honey she'd ever tasted.

"No, not that." Santiago gives a wry smile. "You can have that whenever you want. That's far too easy. What about your other dream?"

"The National Gallery?" Noa asks.

"Yes, exactly." Santiago nods. "But, in fact, I've been thinking of an alternative option . . . what about Sotheby's?"

Noa frowns. "Sotheby's?"

Santiago smiles. "Yes, wouldn't you like that?"

An odd sensation tickles the back of Noa's neck, but it's soft and insignificant. She shakes it off.

"Well, yes . . ." Noa says tentatively. "I suppose, yes, of course I would."

Santiago grins. "Well, that's wonderful, because I may just be able to help you with that."

Now Noa smiles, suddenly flushed with anticipation. "Really? Wow. Thank you. Thank you so much."

"You're welcome, my dear." Santiago's smile deepens. "You're so very welcome."

Noa sits cross-legged on Santiago's carpet, watching him collecting various objects from his shelves. She wants to ask what they are about to do, but she's a little nervous. His home seems slightly different from her memories, darker and denser somehow. The air is thick and heavy with the smoke of snuffed candles, even though all of the twenty-eight candles in the room are lit. The colors of Santiago's sunsets — dark reds, deep purples, and royal blues — on the walls are darker too and almost seem to be shifting and swaying, as if she's watching the night sky reflected in the sea. Some of the collection of mysterious foreign objects from around the world on the shelves are new too, she's sure: jars of dried herbs and flower petals, collections of feathers, bottles of liquids in various colors, and a bowl of overripe fruits. So now the room doesn't so much resemble an exotic antiques shop as a cornucopia of Chinese medicines.

Santiago carefully places everything he selects into a wooden box he carries in his left hand until finally he walks back to Noa and sits on the floor next to her. The candles flicker and sway as he sits, as if just blown by a gust of wind. Once more, Noa wants to ask what they are doing, at nearly two o'clock in the morning, but she's afraid he might actually tell her the truth, so she keeps her mouth shut.

Santiago picks a large dark red porcelain bowl from the floor and begins dropping pieces of his collection into it, while muttering a nearly unintelligible chant:

"Eu chamo aos espiritos das trevas do grande mar e das florestas. Peço-vos que venham e tirem a voz desta mulher, tirem o poder da sua vontade, o seu espirito e a façam subordinada a mim. Este é o meu pedido e por isto vos darei o meu sanque . . ."

Noa fixes her gaze on what goes into the bowl, reading the labels on the jars which are all in Latin: the tail feather of a white peacock, four drops of midnight rain, a pinch of *Pelargonium,* a snap of ginger root, nineteen cherry stones, three laurel leaves, a splash of a Parisian sunset, a dusting of dried pig's blood, six lobelia leaves, and a sprinkling of verbena oil.

Santiago holds out the bowl to Noa.

"Now you must say the words of what you want."

Oh, crap, Noa thinks. What am I getting myself into? But she does as he says.

As Noa's wish settles into the bowl, mixing with the strange set of ingredients, Santiago stands and walks slowly around the room, counterclockwise, blowing out each of the candles in turn, whispering the chant once more, then sits down next to Noa and kisses her cheek.

"Well done." Santiago smiles. "That is all. And now we must wait."

With the exception of the annual Christmas party, Amandine never visits Eliot's London offices. She's always so busy at college or with the boys that she rarely has time to run down to London at all. In the old days, when they were dating, they'd often take the train to Covent Garden to hang out at the markets, or to Bloomsbury to visit the British Museum. They'd spend endless hours — when time split so an hour passed in a second and a second was infinite — walking, hand in hand, and talking, about everything and nothing all at once.

Now Amandine visualizes Eliot doing all this with another woman, a younger, simpler, more beautiful woman. For, despite what Héloïse saw, Amandine finds it impossible to imagine anything else. Her teeth hurt at the idea of her husband holding hands with another woman. She can't even entertain the thought of anything more.

Amandine walks up and down Carnaby Street eleven times before she stops at Eliot's offices and pushes open the heavy glass doors. She can't procrastinate forever, since she's aimed her visit for lunchtime, since it will be the most likely time for Eliot to be out. If he's having an affair, he'll certainly be out for lunch, in a ridiculously expensive restaurant or . . . somewhere else.

Amandine takes the lift up to the four-teenth floor. She bites her lip. She walks across the thick cream carpet until she reaches Lauren at the reception desk. They'd met six months ago at the Christmas party. Lauren had known her name on sight, probably having been given a file of colleagues' spouses to commit to memory the week before.

"Mrs. Walker!" Lauren's already bright face illuminates at the sight of Amandine. "How perfectly lovely of you to visit us. Are you doing some shopping on Oxford Street?"

Amandine shakes her head. Lauren had been a possible candidate for the affair when Amandine was going through the roster of every female she knew who worked with Eliot, but now she scratches Lauren off the list. Although what she feels emanating from Lauren isn't genuine happiness at seeing her, it certainly isn't horrified shock or hatred.

"No," Amandine says, "no shopping. I'm just here to see Eliot. I can wait in his —"

"Ah, lovely," Lauren says, beaming underneath her slightly orange-tinted skin. "I'll call and let him know you're here."

"He's here?"

Lauren nods, picking up the phone. "He's in his office."

Amandine panics. She holds up her hand to stop Lauren putting the call through, but it's too late.

"Hello, Mr. Walker. I've got your wife waiting in reception." Lauren glances up at

Amandine, giving her a reassuring smile. "Yes, your wife. She just arrived."

In the everlasting minute that passes, Amandine half-considers mumbling an excuse and dashing out as fast as the heavy glass doors will allow her. This is it. She'll have to explain herself now. She'll have to confront him. There's no way around it. And then Eliot appears. He ushers her into his office without saying anything. When he closes his own heavy glass door behind them, he turns to his wife.

"Why are you here?"

"You're not pleased to see me," Amandine says. She turns. "I'll just go."

"No, sorry. It's not that, it's just . . . I'm busy. It's the middle of the day. I'm on a case, you know how it is."

Amandine shrugs. "Not really. I know you're never happy to see me anymore." This is it. Now or never.

"That's not true."

"It is. Let's not pretend anymore, okay? I can't stand it."

Eliot is silent. He walks behind his desk and sits in his chair.

"Please" — her voice is soft — "I need to know what's going on. I deserve to know."

Still Eliot is silent.

"Please."

Finally he nods. "Okay."

Amandine can feel a heady mixture of fear and relief wafting off her husband. It mixes with her own sudden rush of terror. Until this point, until he actually admitted it, she'd still been able to entertain a teeny tiny speck of hope, however false she knew it to be. Amandine's blood sinks to her feet and she sits, falling hard into the chair Eliot's clients usually occupy.

Eliot won't look at his wife. He shuffles papers on his desk, shifting them around and around. His phone rings. He doesn't pick it up. The sound echoes through the room, seeming to amplify with each ring, louder and louder with her silence. Amandine realizes that she'll have to be the one to begin.

"Tell me who Sylvia is."

Eliot pulls out a photograph from his desk drawer and slides it across the table. So she doesn't have to touch it, Amandine shuffles to the edge of her chair and peers at the picture.

"She's my daughter."

CHAPTER FOURTEEN

A girl with long blond hair stares back, with a slightly sullen look, her bright blue eyes so filled with sadness that Amandine can feel exactly what she feels.

Amandine looks up at her husband, utterly confused. Then, in the next horrific moment, she realizes what this means. The girl is his love child. Not only has he been having an affair, but this other woman he fucked got pregnant and gave birth to a baby girl. A daughter. Amandine is in such shock that she cannot even cry; her tear ducts have suddenly frozen, along with her heart. How long has he been seeing this woman, the mother of his other child? Was it a one-night stand? Or did it last for years? One thing Amandine is sure of is that Eliot has only just found out about the daughter, he hasn't known about her all this time.

Eliot finally looks up at his wife. Their eyes meet over the photograph, though neither of them looks down. He swallows, tears filling his eyes again and, despite herself, Amandine is moved.

"She's my daughter."

"Yes," Amandine fires the word at him. "I heard you. What I don't understand is why the hell you didn't tell me this as soon as you found out about it. You should have told me!"

"I'm so sorry," Eliot says, and Amandine can feel he is, he really and truly is. "I wanted to. Every day I wanted to. But I promised her mother, I gave her my word that I wouldn't tell you and the boys until I'd met Sylvia and —"

At the mention of their sons, Amandine winces and her frozen heart begins to crack. "Don't," she says softly, "don't mention them. Tell me when you started fucking this woman who's so special you'd keep a promise to her over your own wife?"

"Oh, God, is that what you think?" Eliot gasps. "I'm not having an affair. I was never having an affair. Sylvia's nearly fifteen. I knew her mother from school, I was only seeing her for a few . . . minutes. And then I met you."

Amandine glares at Eliot. But he's telling the truth. She can sense it. She can feel his turmoil of emotions: sorrow, regret, and confusion. If she couldn't, she'd never have believed him, not in a million years.

"A few *minutes*?" she asks.

Eliot nods, unable to meet her eye. "Yes, in fact, our relationship lasted a full fifteen minutes in the . . . um, toilet of the boys' refectory."

Despite herself, Amandine laughs. "How romantic."

Eliot gives her a halfhearted smile. "She never told me I had a daughter," he says. "I only found out a few months ago, on —"

"The eighth of March."

"How did you know that?" Eliot frowns. "Yes, her mother wrote to me, asking for money. I've been trying to figure out how to handle it, how to tell you and the boys. I didn't know what . . . I didn't know how to make it okay . . ." Eliot's beautiful face crumples and he cries, tears falling down his cheeks and onto his desk. "I couldn't undo it, I couldn't make it all right . . . I fucked up. I've fucked up our family and I can't do anything to make it better . . ."

Amandine stands, knocking the chair to the carpet, and dashes around the desk to her husband. She hugs him from behind, squeezing tight, resting her head against his. She feels his relief, his love, his pure adoration, his fear and confusion.

"It's all right," Amandine whispers. "It's okay."

Eliot whimpers in her arms, like a small boy, like a tiny, terrified little boy.

"It's okay," Amandine says again. "It'll be okay."

Although, right now, she doubts very much that it will be.

Eliot nods, still sobbing, mumbling something Amandine can't hear, and so she just closes her eyes and prays to Bes, Isis, Mama Quilla, Satī, Tsao Wang, Vár, all the gods and goddesses of marriage and family she knows of, for the protection and well-being of those she loves most in this world.

Kat paces up and down alongside her chalkboards. Her favorite PhD student, Hamish, watches her with an intrigued frown.

"What are you thinking about?"

Kat stops pacing. He's looking at her in the intense way he sometimes has, which makes her blush. She studies the piece of chalk she's holding.

"Nonlinear dynamics and numerical analysis, of course."

"You are not."

Kat smiles, her first smile since that awful afternoon. She shrugs, still wondering if her spell took effect. How will she know, since she's still avoiding them both?

"Okay, perhaps, not."

"Affairs of the heart." Hamish sits up. "Tell Uncle Hamish all about it."

Kat raises an eyebrow. "I hardly think that's appropriate."

"Why not? I'm not an undergraduate. We're virtually colleagues." Hamish crosses his legs. "Now, I know you're a lot younger than I am, but don't worry, I've got a very youthful mentality. I'm down with the kids. I'll understand."

Kat smiles.

"Let's go out for a drink," Hamish says, standing. "Alcohol does a glorious job of annihilating affairs of the heart, no matter how hideous."

"Really?"

"Oh, yeah." Hamish nods. "Many studies have been done, proper mathematical ones, with statistical analysis and everything."

Kat raises an eyebrow. "Oh, really?"

"But of course. I'm surprised you don't know them. A professor of your standing."

Kat lets slip a little smile. "All right then, fuck it. Let's go."

As they walk down Trinity Street toward the nearest pub, Kat thinks of the most significant drunken experience of her life:

the night she told George she loved him, the night he rejected her, the night he shattered her fragile heart. Hamish is right, the best thing — the only thing — to do right now is get completely, utterly, and outrageously drunk.

Héloïse has barely slept for the past week. She squints into the mirror, frowning at the bags under her eyes. Reaching for her concealer, she applies generous amounts to the shadows on her skin, then steps back for another look.

"Merde."

You are always beautiful to me, no matter what.

Héloïse almost jumps. And then bursts into tears. She slides down to the bathroom floor, presses her head to her knees, and sobs. It's several minutes before she can catch her breath.

"I thought you'd gone, I thought you'd gone forever."

Isn't that what you wanted?

"No," Héloïse gasps, "I, I just . . ."

She feels his touch on her cheek.

"I missed you," Héloïse whispers. "I've missed you so much."

So, stay with me, mon amour, don't leave me.

As Héloïse sits, her bare feet pressed to the cold bathroom floor, half-dressed in her silk slip for dinner with Theo, tearstains down her cheeks, she suddenly wants nothing more than to switch out all the lights, pull all the curtains closed, and fade away into François's arms. What was she thinking? She can't go out on what is essentially a date with another man. How could she? How can she forgive herself so quickly?

On her hands and knees, Héloïse crawls out of the bathroom and along the upstairs corridor, the soft skin of her knees scraping along the carpet. When she reaches her bedroom, she scrambles over the enormous pile of discarded clothes on the floor in front of her mirror. Reaching her bedside table, Héloïse lifts the receiver off the phone. It rings five times before he answers.

"Theo? It's Héloïse."

She can almost hear him smile and, for a moment — holding life in her hand and death in her heart — she wavers. But her heart wins.

"I'm sorry, Theo, I can't come. I, I'm . . . Something's come up. An emergency. I'm really sorry."

"Oh, God, what's wrong?" The genuine concern in his voice twists her conscience. "Can I help? I can be there — Magrath

Avenue, right? — in ten minutes. Less if I speed a little."

"No, no, it's okay, it's nothing," Héloïse protests. "Please, don't come. I just need to stay at home. I'm sorry. I'm so sorry to put you out like this."

"Don't worry," Theo says softly, "don't worry about me. Take care of yourself. And, if there's anything I can do, please call. Okay?"

Héloïse nods, before realizing he can't see her.

"Yes," she lies. "I will. I will."

When Héloïse slips the receiver back into its cradle, she rests her head against the side of the bed and starts to sob again.

While Kat drowns her sorrows in her third pint of Guinness, Hamish sneaks a few admiring glances from beneath the rim of his own glass. He's been hiding his heart — brimming over with love and adoration — from his supervisor for nearly three years. The first time he saw her, the moment he stepped into the room covered with chalk-boards, he was knocked sideways. Mathematical equations were scrawled and scratched along every inch of the room; they twisted and turned through the air like strings of Christmas lights, bobbing along to the precise beat of an invisible metronome. And there, in the center of it all, was the most beguiling woman he'd ever seen. Hamish had known girls before, fellow math students he'd shared a few clumsy fumbling hours with, but he'd never known a *real* woman before: one clearly as clever as she was beautiful, one who loved mathematics as much as he and who surpassed him in her brilliance with numbers at every turn.

Hamish had fallen for Kat, befuddled head over clumsy heels, in that moment and his adoration had only deepened as the years passed. Of course, he knew she could never share his feelings as surely as he knew that $E = mc^2$. How could a goddess like Kat fall for a silly kid like him? But this knowledge didn't dull his adoration by the smallest fraction or the slightest decimal place. Hamish is not a man of great emotional ambition. Professionally, he dreams of being as acclaimed as Johannes Kepler or Joseph Fourier. Academically, as far as his head is concerned, he longs for life-changing things. But for his heart, Hamish has fairly modest aspirations. For his heart, Hamish is content with physical proximity and mathematical conversation.

Finally sitting with Kat in a pub and skirting personal subjects (even if they seem to suggest she has feelings for another man) makes Hamish happier than he could have dreamed possible.

Kat glances up from her now empty glass. "Another one?"

"Always," Hamish says, scrambling to his feet and hurries off in the direction of the bar, downing the rest of his own beer on the way. When he returns with two more pints of Guinness, Hamish slides into the seat next to Kat. If she notices his swift change of place, she doesn't show it.

"So," Hamish says, "are you going to tell Uncle Hamish all about this nasty cad who broke your heart?"

Kat sighs. "He's not a cad, actually. He's a very sweet man. He just doesn't love me. At least, not in the way I want him to."

"Much as I hate to disagree with you, my most eminent professor," Hamish says, "I'm afraid I must. If the man doesn't thank his lucky stars for you every day, if he doesn't court you with roses and champagne and sing ballads under your balcony every night, then the man is a cad. And an ungrateful git, to boot."

Kat giggles. "I don't have a balcony."

"Well, perhaps that's the problem. Maybe you should have one built. It's sure to bring out the inner Romeo in every man who passes by."

Kat takes another gulp of Guinness, then gazes up at Hamish. "You're sweet," she says, slurring the last word so it sounds more like *sweep.*

"Oh, no," Hamish says, with a theatrical sigh. "Please, I'd rather be a cad."

Kat giggles again. "Okay, sorry. But, you know, I've always thought Romeo was highly overrated. I mean, he was so fickle. First declaring his undying devotion for — what was her name? — Rosaline? Then suddenly he meets Juliet and he's all over her. Who's to say, if he hadn't killed himself, he wouldn't have been in love with a different girl before the week was out?"

Hamish smiles. "So you're saying the man had no consistency?"

"Exactly." She sighs. "No staying power. There are those of us who give our hearts to someone and stay faithful for years — despite all common sense to the contrary — we're steadfast, committed, loyal, dependable, constant —"

"— fools." Hamish gives her a wry smile.

For a moment Kat is silent, her eyes welling up, and Hamish is suddenly terrified he's made a huge mistake, stepped too far over the line. Then Kat bursts out laughing and grabs hold of Hamish's knee. Sparks of shock and delight fire up his spine and he sits completely still, waiting to see what she might do next. It would be too much to hope for, surely, that she might . . .

"You're right," Kat says, gasping to catch her breath. "You're absolutely right. I've been a fool. A total, complete, and utter fool. Giving the best years of my life to, to — a fantasy."

Hamish, emboldened by far too much alcohol, very slowly and very gently slips his arms over Kat's shoulders and gives her a little squeeze. She lifts her head toward him and gazes up into Hamish's eyes. He holds his breath. And then, with their lips only inches apart, just as he thinks it might actually happen — the thing he hasn't even dared to imagine possible, except when he's alone in the privacy of his own bathroom — Kat suddenly puts her hand over her mouth, whispers "oh, no," and promptly throws up.

Héloïse wakes. Her vision is blurred and her head aches. She lifts her head off the bed and rubs her eyes. Then she hears the knocking on the door. It stops, then starts again.

"*Foutre.*" Héloïse pulls herself up and stumbles across the room. Catching a glance of herself in the mirror, she curses again. As she staggers down the stairs, pull-ing her fingers through her hair, Héloïse wonders who the hell is calling on her uninvited. Amandine would have phoned first. It's only when she opens the door and sees Theo on her doorstep that she realizes she's still wearing her silk slip. Héloïse steps back and hides her body behind the door, then, remembering how hideous she looks, hides her head as well.

"I'm sorry for surprising you," Theo says, "but you sounded so distressed on the phone. I waited awhile and I couldn't stop worrying, I was scared that maybe you might have . . ."

Héloïse thinks of the paracetamol in the bathroom cabinet and her promise to Aman-dine.

"Can I come in?"

"No!" Héloïse calls out from behind the door. "I mean, I'm a mess . . . You don't need to worry, anyway, I'm fine, really."

"You don't look fine," Theo says, still standing on the doorway. "That is, you — you're still beautiful, of course, but —"

Héloïse can't help but smile. She glances behind her at the coat rack, pulls off a long black cashmere coat, and wraps it tightly around her. Taking the front door key off the hallway table, she pats her hair once more, then slips out the front door and shuts it behind her. Now standing only a few inches from Theo, Héloïse looks up at him.

"Can we sit in your car?"

Theo smiles. "Of course. It's this one here."

He points to a small white car a few feet away, then steps up and opens the passenger door.

"*Merci,*" Héloïse says as she slides inside the car.

Theo shuts the door softly. Moments later, when he's sitting beside her, Héloïse glances at him.

"Nice car. Very clean."

"Thank you. It's electric."

"*Pardon?*"

"It doesn't use fuel. It runs on batteries," Theo says. "It's better for the environment."

"Oh, I see."

Theo smiles again. "I'm not very good at small talk. I — Maggie and I were married for so long, we were virtually telepathic. I sort of lost the knack."

Héloïse glances over and catches Theo's eye. She returns his smile. "Yes, me too."

"We're like two teenagers."

Héloïse nods, then she thinks of what teenagers get up to in parked cars and shakes her head. Theo reaches out his hand, then retracts it.

"Don't worry," Theo says. "I remember."

"Pardon?"

"I know how you're feeling. I was a complete wreck when Maggie died, for years afterward. I could barely leave the house for months. I wanted to die; for a long, long time I dreamed of dying. I didn't do anything, because of Ben, but I wanted to. That was all I wanted to do."

Héloïse nods. She can feel tears at the edges of her eyes and blinks them back.

"I would love for us to be friends," Theo says. "I would love for us to be more than friends, or at least test that out . . . But I know it might be a long time before you're ready to even think about anything like —"

"How did you do it?" Héloïse blurts out. "How did you become normal again?"

Theo is silent for a while. "Little by little, day by day, bit by bit. And then, one day you wake up and you want to be alive again. It sneaks up on you, I suppose. But you can't force it to happen any faster than it will."

"I thought I was," Héloïse says softly, "I thought I was getting better and then . . ."

"You get setbacks, it's all part of the process," Theo says. "Be gentle with yourself. You lost the love of your life. Some days it's all you can do just to keep on breathing."

Héloïse nods again, tears slipping down her cheeks. She glances down at her hands clutched together in her lap. The fingers of her right hand twitch and she slowly reaches out across the car for Theo. He wraps his fingers around hers — the same fingers she saw in her vision — and holds her gently.

"Thank you," Héloïse whispers, "thank you."

"What if she hates me?"

"She won't hate you."

"She might."

Eliot hugs his wife and kisses her on the cheek.

"She'll love you just like I do."

Amandine smiles. "Not just like you do, I expect."

"Well, yes, maybe not."

Eliot and Amandine are sitting at a table for four in Gustare. It's nearly half past twelve on a Saturday afternoon. Héloïse is at the playground with Bertie and Frankie, while Eliot and Amandine wait for Sylvia and her mother.

"I don't think they're coming," Amandine says.

"They will."

"They're already half an hour late."

"Yes, well, Tina has never been the best timekeeper, I must admit. But she usually turns up in the end."

"Usually?" Amandine sighs. "We should have gone to London, we should have met them there."

Without taking his eyes off the door, Eliot reaches for his wife's hand and squeezes her fingers.

"Don't worry, they'll be here."

"Do you want another espresso?" Amandine pushes her chair back from the table and stands. "I'm having another espresso. Maybe two."

She walks around the table but, just as she steps toward the counter, Eliot grabs for her hand again and pulls her back.

"They're here," he hisses, "they're here."

Amandine looks up to see the sullen teenager, along with an older, thinner, blonder version of her, pushing her way through the door.

"Oh," Amandine exclaims, falling back into her chair as quickly as she can. She pats down her hair, smoothing her fingers through it for the fiftieth time that hour, then straightens her silk shirt and adjusts her long cotton skirt. Neither Sylvia nor

Tina, Amandine notices, has made a similar effort with her wardrobe. Not that it matters, since both mother and daughter are quite stunningly beautiful. Amandine watches Tina cross the café floor as if it's a catwalk, the delicate feet of her long, thin, denim-clad legs sashaying between the table, her elegant fingers brushing through a river of endless blond hair, her enormous blue eyes blinking, narrowing with distaste as she surveys the tiny café. She slides into the chair opposite Amandine, who now feels like a fat, bald dwarf and would have preferred that Eliot's ex-girlfriend had sat a little farther away.

"It's a pleasure to meet you," Amandine lies, extending her hand toward Tina, who shakes her head.

"Dirty taxi fingers," she sniffs, wiggling them to showcase the dirty germs swarming all over her fingertips. "Is there a toilet in this place?"

Eliot and Amandine exchange a look.

"It's just downstairs," Amandine says, trying to blank out the image of teenage copulation that's just flashed up in her mind, "at the back, on the right."

Tina sighs, standing again. She casts a glance at Eliot as she sashays toward the stairs. "Double espresso." She nods at Sylvia. "And no caffeine for her, no matter how much she begs. No pastries either."

Sylvia, who still hasn't sat down, watches her mother go. As Tina disappears, Eliot stands and hugs his daughter, who stiffens slightly.

"Thank you so much for coming," he says, "it means a great deal to us. What would you like to drink? Orange juice? Apple?"

"If she's having a double espresso, I'll have one too."

Eliot looks stricken. "I'm sorry, sweetheart, but your mother said no. I agree with her too, you're a little young. How about a cup of tea?"

Sylvia rolls her eyes. "I suppose. And a slice of pizza."

Eliot nods and hurries off to the counter. Amandine watches him chatting with Cosima as she flicks on the cappuccino machine and stacks up a generous pile of almond biscuits onto a plate. Partly to pretend she isn't feeling great big crashing waves of pure hatred rolling off Sylvia in her direction, Amandine focuses her gaze on her husband's back and Cosima's face. She's too far away to feel exactly what Kat's sister is feeling, but by the look on her face she'd swear it was love, pure love. Almost maternal. Strange. Very strange.

"So," Sylvia snaps. "You're the woman my dad's shagging now."

Amandine turns to Sylvia. "I'm sorry?"

"You heard me."

"Yes," Amandine says carefully. "I did."

"He'll dump you too, you know, just like he dumped my mum. Men always do."

"I, um," Amandine hesitates. "I'm not sure that's true."

Sylvia rolls her eyes again. "Shows how much you know."

"Well, I suppose I haven't had very much experience. Your father was my first boyfriend, really."

"Oh, jeez," Sylvia says, eyes widening, "that's so pathetic."

"Really? I thought it was rather —"

And then, to Amandine's undying relief, Eliot arrives with a tray full of food and drink. Amandine helps him unload it. Sylvia crosses her arms.

"They only had pizza with red peppers and mushrooms," Eliot says. "Is that okay?"

Sylvia shrugs. "I'll pick them off, I s'pose." She snatches the cup of tea off the tray and then begins picking at the pizza.

A small but high-pitched shriek sounds from across the café. "Put down that pizza! Right now, young lady, don't make me slap you!"

Eliot and Amandine look up at Tina striding toward them. Sylvia doesn't look up but just rolls her eyes, taking a huge bite of pizza before dropping it onto the plate. Another angry squeal emanates from Tina as she reaches the table. She holds her open palm above her daughter's head and, for one horrible moment, Amandine thinks she might actually carry out her threat. Instead, she takes her other hand to squeeze open Sylvia's mouth, then scoops out the masticated pizza with her fingers and drops it onto the table.

"Gross."

"It's your own fault, missy," Tina snaps. "I told you no carbs except on Sundays. How do you expect to lose weight when you never stop gobbling?"

Amandine wants, more than anything, to tell this woman not to speak to her daughter like this. She wants to nudge Eliot and tell him to say something. But she doesn't. She just gives Sylvia a look of great sympathy and bites her tongue. But when the girl's eyes fill with tears, Amandine can't stop herself.

"I'm sure she doesn't need to lose weight," Amandine says softly. "She's already so thin, and very beautiful."

Tina snorts. "Well, she won't stay that way

unless I do something about it. She'll be"
— Tina casts a disapproving eye over Amandine — "fat and frumpy before you know it."

"I doubt that," Amandine says. "I don't think it'd be possible."

Ignoring her, Tina eyeballs her daughter. "Right, missy, get up. We're going to find you some healthy food, grilled chicken and a Diet Coke. And we" — this time she eyeballs Eliot, and throws a meaningful glance in Amandine's direction — "will have to lay some ground rules if you're gonna have visitation rights, okay?"

Eliot looks at her, then at his daughter, then nods.

Tina takes Sylvia's hand and begins pulling her out of the café. She turns around to her ex and Amandine. "We'll be back in a bit, when you've finished scoffing all those buttery biscuits, then we can talk some more, okay?"

Amandine gives a short nod and Eliot manages a half smile. They sit in forced silence until Tina and Sylvia are out of the café and halfway down the street.

"I hate Tina," Amandine whispers.

"I know. Me too."

"I feel so sorry for Sylvia."

"Me too." Eliot sighs.

Amandine reaches for a biscuit. "Sylvia hates me."

"She doesn't."

"She does, she really does."

Eliot takes a biscuit. "Well, okay, but it won't last. You'll win her over, you'll see."

Amandine gives her husband a reassuring nod. "Yes, I suppose so," she says. "One day." But she's never been less sure of anything in her life.

Noa is sitting on her aunt Heather's sofa with a bag of ice on her head, hoping to alleviate the migraine that hasn't lifted since that last night with Santiago, when she gets the call. The woman says she's calling from Sotheby's, and Noa nearly bursts out laughing but remembers Santiago and his spell just in time. When the woman says they're offering her a position as one of their junior acquisition buyers to start next week, Noa wonders if it really could have been Santiago's spell that did it, or if, as is more likely, he actually just bribed several people. Either way, she can't quite believe how lovely he is and how lucky she is.

"You want me to start next week? On Monday?"

"Yes, certainly, if that will suit your schedule, Ms. Sparrow."

"Of course, absolutely. It's just . . ."

"Yes?"

"Well, I'm still . . . I haven't completed my studies yet."

"We understood that you have a first in art history from Magdalene College, Cambridge."

This is the moment. A crossroads opens up in front of Noa and she stands at the center, knowing which turn she should take but hesitating. It might not be the specific dream of her life, just yet, but it is the opportunity of a lifetime and — if she does well, blessed by Santiago's particular magic — it's likely to lead her there. She could have experiences so rare and unique, so beyond the realm of normal possibility, that she would be mad to pass up the chance, however immorally obtained it was. She could go back to her crappy little life, or she could step into this magnificent new one. All she has to do is say one word.

And then, as her own voice hovers on her tongue, she tastes something — sharp and sweet — and swallows it down. And her voice when she speaks now is tinged with cachaça and the trace of a Brazilian accent.

"Yes," Noa says. "Yes, that's correct. I do."

CHAPTER FIFTEEN

How is he going to tell her? How is he going to tell her that he's not in love with her, that he never has been? Well, perhaps he'll omit that last piece of information. Although, since she clearly cast a spell on him, she shouldn't really be surprised, should she? She's the one in the wrong, she's the one who should be sorry, not him. And yet, George simply can't bring himself to be angry. Perhaps it's the way Cosima looks at him, with such fresh happiness, optimism, and hope. He can't let her down; he can't shatter all her expectations.

At least he's managed to avoid having sex again, feigning various sore throats and headaches. Although he knows he won't be able to keep it up for much longer. She's already getting suspicious. Especially given the fact that he turns down all her offers of herbal cures. He has to tell her. He has to let her down gently, but soon. George remembers something Héloïse once said about ripping off Band-Aids — the faster you do it, the less it hurts. Perhaps George is a coward, but he's never been able to do it that way. Even though he knows he should, he still ends up taking the corner and pulling it slowly, tearing the little hairs out of his skin. So it is with Band-Aids, so it is with life. But not this time; this time he must be firm. He must.

And, after that, he'll have to address the small matter of his best friend being in love with him. Oh, God.

"You must be very excited."

Noa nods. "Yes."

Santiago smiles, wide and bright, his teeth brilliant against his olive skin. Noa feels the flush of desire she always does when he smiles. "I'm glad. I'm glad I could help make one of your dreams come true."

Noa smiles, soft and small.

"Forgive me, my sweet," Santiago says, "but you don't seem quite as delirious with delight as I'd expected."

Noa shakes her head. "No, of course, I am. I'm sorry, I don't . . . I'm just not feeling myself lately. I'm getting headaches and I'm feeling . . . fuzzy. It's probably flu."

Santiago reaches across the table and

takes her hand in his. He smiles again and raises one wicked eyebrow. "I can give you something to take care of that."

Noa smiles. "Oh, you can, can you?"

"Yes, I've heard that Brazilian honey and Brazilian kisses can work miracles when it comes to colds and suchlike." Santiago lifts Noa's hand and presses her skin softly against his lips.

Noa shivers.

"Feel better?"

Noa nods. "Than I've ever felt before."

"Good." Santiago grins. "And that's only a preview of coming attractions. By midnight you'll be on top of the world, I promise. I'll make it my personal mission."

"Well, thank you," Noa says. "I suppose I'll be forever in your debt."

"Oh, really?" Santiago raises his wicked eyebrow even higher. "I like the sound of that."

Noa gives his cheek a playful pat. "Cheeky bugger. Anyway, I'm already in your debt, aren't I? So I'd better be careful, or you'll end up owning my soul."

Santiago laughs, deep and long. Noa hears the rush of the Amazon River in his voice, the joy of the Rio Carnival, the power of the Atlantic Ocean.

"You must be relieved to be done with all

that studying," he says.

"Well, yes, I . . ." Noa trails off, wondering why — now that the excited shock of the job offer isn't quite as startlingly bright — she's starting to feel something else, something rather . . . she isn't quite sure what: as if she's missing a part of herself she never knew she had. The strange feeling lingers on the edge of her consciousness: a dark shore on a lake of gold.

Santiago leans back in his chair, sliding both delicate hands through his thick black hair. "Analyzing art only entertains your brain and closes your heart to the true beauty. You would have ruined yourself. You would have tainted the sweet innocence of your precious soul."

Noa looks at Santiago as he speaks, the strength of his sentiments silencing her own thoughts. As he waits for her to reply, Noa finds that her own words hover just beyond her reach and she can only find those that echo his.

"Yes," she says, "I suppose the experience of art is most . . . transformational when one doesn't have an opinion on it. I still experience it, when I see something new . . . I feel I'm looking at life for the first time and everything is magical." Noa glances up at him. "It's how I feel when I look at your paintings."

Santiago smiles. "Darling girl," he says, leaning over the table and kissing her. And, with that, everything else is forgotten.

Héloïse sits with Theo on the bench in the Botanic Garden she shared with François. When they began their walk earlier that afternoon, wandering in and out of streets as they talked, she had no idea where they'd end up, until her feet walked them to the gates of the gardens. After they crossed the lawns Héloïse showed Theo the little lake with the curtains of willow trees, the river, the path of woodchips, and the hothouses. Occasionally, their hands brushed together and, once or twice, their fingers somehow entwined. When she stopped at the bench, Héloïse sat in the middle, so Theo could only sit close to her.

"This was mine and Frankie's bench."

Theo smiled. "Then I'm honored to be here."

Héloïse nods. They sit in silence for a while, watching the ducks floating past on the pond, dipping their heads into the water and turning themselves upside down, tail feathers pointing to the sky.

"How did your husband die?" Theo speaks slowly, each word a tentative step. "You don't have to tell me, of course, I just . . ."

Héloïse is silent, gazing out at the ducks as if she hadn't heard him at all.

"Maggie died of cancer. She had a double mastectomy, nearly ten years ago. She was in remission for almost five years. Then it spread. She died twelve weeks after we found out . . ."

"Oh, you poor, dear thing." Héloïse turns to Theo. "It must have been hell."

"It was."

"Frankie died instantly," Héloïse says softly. "One moment he was here, the next he was not. I often thought, which would be worse, to lose someone quickly or slowly. But how can I know?"

"I hope we'll never have the chance to compare, to know both ways and decide for ourselves."

"Yes," Héloïse says, "of course."

"Tell me your happiest time," Theo says, "the happiest moment you shared."

"Amandine's birth," says Héloïse instantly. Then she pauses. "Well, actually, it was a moment of great joy, certainly, but it was also many hours of great pain. And, when she was finally born, I remember I wept with relief. I confess all that agony took some shine from the joy, at least at first."

"Yes, I imagine it might. Maggie was in

277

labor with Ben for nearly two days." Theo smiles. "That's why we stopped at one."

Héloïse drops her voice to a whisper. "We tried to have another. We couldn't. I had five miscarriages before Frankie persuaded me to let go, to stop trying."

Theo rests his hand on her arm. "I'm so sorry."

"Thank you."

"Do you want to tell me . . . ?"

Héloïse shakes her head. "No, not yet. Later. Let's talk of something else."

"Okay. Of course," Theo says, quickly racking his mind for another — distinctly different — topic. "Do you miss teaching?"

"Yes." Héloïse stops, surprised by her answer. The books she'd missed, certainly; she hadn't realized she'd missed the teaching too.

"Do you think you might go back?"

"I . . . I never thought about it before. But yes, perhaps I'd like to do that. One day. I don't know . . ."

"I bet your students loved you. I bet you're a wonderful teacher."

Héloïse smiles. "How do you know?"

Theo smiles again. "Intuition. Magic. Some things you just know."

Héloïse gives him a sideways glance. For a moment she wonders if, somehow, he does know, if he possibly shares her gift. But, if he did, then wouldn't she realize it? It's strange, and Héloïse can't explain it, that although she kept her own gifts a secret from François for all the years of their life together, she can — for this moment, at least — imagine telling Theo. Why? Then, with a twist of guilt, her heart constricts and Héloïse throws the idea into the little pond to be eaten by the ducks.

"So, you've brought me to François's bench," Theo is saying while Héloïse is still shaking off her guilt. "Will you let me return the honor?"

She looks up at him. *"Pardon?"*

"I'd like to take you to mine and Maggie's favorite place. If you'd like to come?"

"Bien sûr." Héloïse smiles. "I'd be honored."

Cosima and George stroll along King's Parade. They pass the art galleries and boutique shops: collections of pretty dresses, sparkling jewelery, gourmet chocolates. The sun is setting behind King's College, casting a shadow of spires and turrets across the pavement. As Cosima chats about a particular pretty dress she wants to buy, George remembers one Christmas when, at Kat's suggestion, the book group met above

King's College chapel to listen to the choir singing Christmas carols. It was snowing. The four of them sat around a tiny floating fire, cradling cups of hot chocolate, watching the snowflakes fall above them and listening to the beautiful music rise up below them. It was — and still is, despite all his recent adventures — one of the happiest nights of George's life. The memory of it injects him with a little shot of courage.

"I've got to tell you something," George says. "I need to —"

"Yes, absolutely," Cosima says, excitement dripping from her words. "But can I tell my news first? I've been wanting all day to tell you. I've just been waiting for the right time, but maybe that's now."

"Oh, okay, sure," he says, happy to postpone the agony of rejection a few moments longer. "What is it?"

Cosima stops walking. She turns to him and smiles, her face lit up, radiant. And George knows: before she speaks aloud the fact that will change his life forever, he already knows.

Noa stands outside Amandine's office door. She could be a coward about this, she could just send a letter to the administrator, informing the university of her intentions, and leave it at that. Then, when she didn't turn up to her tutorial on Tuesday, Amandine would make a few calls and find out what happened. But, despite the fact that she can feel her heart getting harder, Noa can't quite bring herself to do this. Amandine was kind to her, she offered her forgiveness and friendship, and Noa, even though memories of her past are starting to get a little hazy, still holds a soft spot for her teacher.

"Come in!"

Noa pushes open the door and steps inside Amandine's office. The first thing she notices is that *The Kiss* has been hung back on the wall. For a moment she wishes she could still see people's secrets. She'd like to know what's happening if, as she suspects, things are getting better in Amandine's marriage.

"Oh," Amandine says, as she sees Noa. "I thought we didn't have a tutorial till Tuesday."

"We don't," Noa says. "We didn't. I've come to tell you . . ." For a second Noa hesitates. Even though she's already done it, even though she's taken the left turn and walked too far to see the crossroads now, telling her teacher feels so final, so irreversible.

"What?" Amandine sits up. "Are you okay?"

"I . . . I . . ." Her hands are shaking, her palms are sweaty, her head is throbbing. But, just as Noa is about to shake her head, to confess to her teacher that she isn't okay, not at all, she tastes cachaça on her tongue. Noa licks her lips, fear and indecision instantly evaporating. She feels Santiago's breath on her cheek, his voice in her head.

"I'm good, I'm great." Noa smiles. "Actually, I've come to tell you I'm leaving."

Amandine frowns. "You're leaving? What do you mean?"

"I've been offered a job. As an acquisitions assistant at Sotheby's. I start on Monday."

Amandine smiles. "I'm sorry? I don't understand. Is this a joke?"

Noa licks her lips again. Suddenly, she's never felt so powerful, so determined. "No, I'm serious."

"But that's . . . it's not possible. You haven't even got your degree yet. How did this happen?"

Again, Noa hears his voice in her head. She speaks the words he whispers. "My uncle's best friend is head of acquisitions there," Noa says with a nonchalant shrug. "I guess nepotism isn't so bad when it's in your favor."

Amandine raises her eyebrows. "Yes, I suppose so. But to just give you a position like that . . . ? Won't you do an internship first? Perhaps during the summer, while you finish your degree?"

Noa shakes her head. "I did one last summer." Her lie is effortless, easy. She feels Santiago's presence so strongly she almost turns to look for him. "I've got enough experience for them and for me. I don't need any more and I don't need to finish my degree. I was doing a degree to get a job like this and, even then, I never thought I'd get *this* job. So I'm not going to give up the chance now."

Amandine considers. "I see what you're saying, but it seems an awful shame. I mean, I thought you were studying art history because you loved it, because you wanted to learn, not simply to get a job afterward."

For a second Santiago's grip loosens as Amandine's words momentarily eclipse his in Noa's head. She frowns, confused.

"Well, yes, I did," Noa admits, her own words rising up at last, "but I don't really . . . I don't love studying so much anymore. I want to get out there and start living. I'm bored with reading books all the time. I want some real life experience, I —"

"Yes, I understand that," Amandine interrupts, scared that she's about to lose one of her best students, and her favorite. "But can't you just wait a year? What's a year, after all?"

For a moment it seems as if Noa hesitates again. And then the spirit that infused her as she walked into the room overtakes her again. Noa shakes her head and stands so straight she seems to gain ten inches.

"No. I'm sorry. I can't," she says. "My mind's made up."

CHAPTER SIXTEEN

Héloïse sits in the car next to Theo. They've been driving for nearly an hour and, not being much of a driver herself, Héloïse has completely lost track of her internal navigation.

"Where are we going?"

Theo smiles. "That's the seven hundred and fifty-third time you've asked me that and my answer is still the same: it's a secret. I'll tell you when we get there."

"I hope I'll know by then, unless you're taking me to another world."

"Sort of, well, a perfect world, at least." Theo turns the car left along yet another tiny country lane edged with squat walls made of stone and canopied with oak and chestnut trees.

"Even better."

When they reach the end of the road Theo turns left again and stops at the edge of a field.

"The sea!" Héloïse cries.

"Southwold beach," Theo says. "Our favorite beach. We came here every weekend during the summer when Ben was little."

He opens the car door and Héloïse opens her door too. Together they walk along the path across the field and toward the sea. The air is nearly warm, but not quite warm enough for Héloïse to slip her cardigan off her shoulders. When they reach the beach, Héloïse slides off her high heels and carries them. As her toes sink into the sand, she remembers the soft, wet dirt of the Botanic Garden and smiles.

Theo reaches the edge of the sea first. He stops on the hard, wet sand as the water laps at his feet. He reaches out his hand to Héloïse, beckoning her forward, and she comes, stopping when they stand side by side, but she doesn't take his hand.

"I just remembered another time," she says. "With François, on a beach. Not this beach. I don't recall which. Perhaps in France. We were sitting on deckchairs. Amandine was four or five, sitting at our feet building tunnels in the sand and filling them up with seawater. François had packed a picnic and he gave me a — *quel est le mot?* — thermos of hot coffee. He kissed my hand as I took it and I remember thinking:

286

This is it. It doesn't get any better than this. Happiness. Joy. All the way up and through. I felt so grateful, so suddenly, I started to cry." Héloïse smiles. "François didn't understand. I had to reassure him that everything was okay, more than okay. Perfect."

Theo reaches for Héloïse's hand, but stops and drops his by his side again. "I had so many perfect moments on this beach," he says. "I . . . I couldn't come here for years after Maggie died. The first time I did all those moments came crashing down on me and I sobbed and sobbed." He smiles. "This old German couple found me and helped me back to the car. We sat together as the sun set. They couldn't speak a word of English and had no idea what was going on."

"That's so sweet," Héloïse says.

"Yes, I was very touched. It was a big turning point for me."

"Oh?"

Theo grins. "Yep, that's when I started trying to save the world."

"In the Atlantic Ocean?"

Theo laughs. "Well, yes, that and other things."

"What things?"

Theo ponders. "I plant trees, pick up litter, protest against crazy government laws . . . I sign petitions, support charities, anything I can, really, to help heal this beautiful, messed-up, neglected planet."

"*C'est magnifique,*" Héloïse says. "You are one of these wonderful people who is so good and makes the rest of us feel guilty."

"Oh, I hope not," Theo says, glancing at Héloïse's hand, his fingers twitching. "I hope I inspire people to help too; it would be a great shame if I did the opposite."

"*Alors,* no, that's not what I mean, not at all. I think it's wonderful what you do; this is the sort of thing that gives meaning to life."

"Well, the way I see it, if everyone did a little thing every day for the world, it'd be enough to sustain it."

"I never thought of it that way," Héloïse says.

"No, nor did I," Theo says, "until I did. Most people don't, they just hope someone else will take care of everything. I suppose governments should, but they don't."

"*C'est vrai.*"

Theo nods. "It's crazy that people think, because they don't own the wider world — the highways, forests, and fields — because it doesn't belong to them that they don't need to take care of it. So they take care of their own little patch and leave the rest to rot." Theo smiles. "Sorry, I started to rant, I didn't mean to, I just get a bit passionate about this sort of thing."

"*Non,* don't apologize," Héloïse says. "Passion, *c'est fantastique,* always."

"Thank you," Theo says. "Well, okay, then. So, now we've been back to both our pasts, how about we — well, how about you let me take you out to dinner?"

Héloïse takes his hand across the sand and in front of the sea. Theo squeezes her hand and smiles a special, secret smile.

"*Oui.*" She smiles. "Thank you. I would love that."

Noa passes her probationary period at Sotheby's in a breathless blur. Although she really has no idea what she's doing, she makes it through with lots of nodding and smiling and saying yes to everything asked of her. All the while, even though Noa knows she should be having the time of her life, she can't shake her migraine, or the feeling that something is very, very wrong. Noa finds a shared flat in South Kensington, again courtesy of Santiago, who was thrilled to hear of her turn in fortune and refused to confirm his greater involvement in obtaining Noa's position. "Magic luck" was all he said.

He visits her at his friend's flat on Friday nights and they all go out drinking in various clubs. One night Santiago brings his extremely beautiful cousin, Claudia, and the three of them go out to dance (*foró*) and drink (cachaça).

"How are you loving your new job?" Santiago asks, yelling over the drumming that reverberates through the walls and Noa's chest.

"Yes," she shrieks instead. "It's . . . incredible! I still can't believe — thank you."

"Nâo problemo," Santiago says. "Didn't I tell you, it's so much better to live with art, to see it, touch it, smell and taste it, instead of merely studying it?"

Noa nods vigorously. "I can't believe, yesterday I was helping to catalog a Renoir and a Rothko. And on Monday a *Monet* sold for one hundred and seven million dollars. And I touched it an hour before it sold. Unbelievable."

Claudia slips her hand onto Santiago's thigh. Noa watches, wishing once more that she could see any secrets between them. She never thought she'd miss her curse, and she doesn't, not really, but it certainly had proved useful sometimes. Now she's just like everyone else, left to guess at what's going on, always at risk of being betrayed or shocked by something.

"It all sounds so glamorous," Claudia says. "So sexy."

Noa's eyes widen. "I suppose so, I . . ."

"One day you must sell Santiago's paintings," she continues. "I'm sure they will sell for a fortune."

Santiago laughs. "In time, *minha linda,* in time. Let's give little Noa a few months to get settled in before we discuss any of that."

Noa glances from one to the other, sensing something between them, a code woven in between their words that she can't see or understand. She doesn't know what to say, so she says nothing.

"I'm bored with talking, let's move, come on." Claudia stands and holds out her hands. "You too, little Noa."

With great effort of will, Noa shakes her head. "You go, I'll sit this one out." She wants to collect her thoughts. For, although the months have been a magnificent, majestic, magical whirlwind, she's also felt a little adrift and alone, unmoored in a world that doesn't quite make sense. It doesn't help that her compass (albeit a cursed compass) was taken away before she set sail. Noa has to remind herself that if she still had the truth-telling Tourette syndrome, she'd never be able to live this new life.

"No?" Claudia laughs. "Don't think, just dance. Now!"

Noa looks up at this extremely beautiful woman who, with her enormous eyes, long black hair, and imposing — intimidating — gaze, reminds Noa of Elizabeth Taylor as Cleopatra. She certainly can't say no to her.

"Okay," she says and stands to be pulled onto the dance floor by both of them.

The air is thick with heat and sweat, the music so loud it blows all the thoughts out of Noa's head, the drumming beating through her body, the floor sticky with splashed drinks. Santiago pulls Noa and Claudia close to him, twisting his hips, pressing his chest to their chests, snaking his shoulders to the beat of the drums.

Noa wakes up the next morning alone in the flat, wondering why, since she'd barely touched any alcohol last night, her head feels so heavy, her brain so fuzzy, her vision is so blurry, and she can't remember anything that happened at all.

After three months of supervised visits, and with his agreement to fund Sylvia's private education at Cheltenham Ladies' College next September, Eliot is at last permitted a private meeting with his daughter, without her mother. He brings Amandine along for

292

moral support, although she suggests it'd be better if she waits elsewhere in order to give father and daughter some time alone together.

"Okay," Eliot says, "but don't go far, so you can come quickly if anything goes wrong."

"All right," Amandine says, laughing, "you find a nice café and I'll find another one around the corner, okay?"

"Or you could just sit at the other side of the café."

"I can't, sweetie, I didn't bring my dark glasses and newspaper to hide behind, sorry."

"Shut up." Eliot smiles. "I'm just scared, that's all."

"I thought things were going well?"

"Better than that total disaster in Cambridge does not mean well; it just means it wasn't a complete disaster."

"It'll take time." Amandine takes her husband's hand. "She's had nearly fifteen years without you, fifteen years with that mad lunatic of a mother — sorry — but it's no surprise that Sylvia's a little . . . highly strung."

Eliot sighs. "I wish, I just hope we can have a positive influence on her, that we can help her to be happier, you know?"

"I'm sure we can," Amandine says, though in truth being a role model to her husband's daughter, who still hates her as much as she ever did, is not something Amandine either believes she can do or is sure she wants to.

"Okay, we're here."

They stand together outside Tina's front door.

"Are you going to knock?"

Eliot shakes his head. "I'm just waiting to see if they can feel my presence first."

"Chicken," Amandine says, knocking.

The door opens immediately. Sylvia stares back at them from across the threshold. She clutches the door so it's still half-closed.

"You came," she says.

"Of course we did."

Sylvia narrows her eyes at Amandine. "She's not coming too, is she?"

"Hey, Sylvie," Eliot says gently, "don't be rude to your —"

"My what? What is she to me? She's nothing to me."

"She's my wife," Eliot says. "And I'd like for you to be nice to her, please."

Sylvia rolls her eyes.

"Shall we come in and say hello to your mother?" Eliot asks.

Sylvia shakes her head. "Don't bother, she hates her" — she nods at Amandine —

"anyway."

"It's okay." Amandine shifts forward again. "Let us in, sweetie, we just want to check everything's okay."

"No, go away." Sylvia clutches the door frame, her knuckles white. "I don't want you here. Go away, go away!"

Eliot frowns. "Why are you being like this, Sylvia? What made you so angry? It's not —"

Amandine shakes her head, looking straight at Sylvia. "She's not angry. She's scared."

"Scared?"

"Yes. Aren't you, sweetie?"

Sylvia scowls. "I'm not scared, you're stupid."

"What is it?" Amandine steps closer and Sylvia shrinks back into the gap between the door and the wall. "Is it your mum? Is she okay?"

"Go away," Sylvia shouts. "You're not part of my family. You're nothing to me."

"Sylvia!" Eliot snaps.

Sylvia narrows her eyes and screams, "Fuck off!" then slams the door.

Amandine and Eliot stand on the doorstep, staring at each other in shock. For a moment everything is silent. Then they hear

Sylvia suddenly burst into sobs behind the door.

"Sylvia, darling, let us in." Eliot pounds his fist against the door.

"Sylvia, please, we can help you," Amandine says softly, wishing Kat was with them and could cast a spell to loosen the lock.

And then, slowly, the door opens. Eliot quickly steps inside and pulls his daughter into him, holding her close to his chest while she sobs. Amandine slides through the gap and into the house. She hurries down the corridor, glancing into the open rooms as she goes. Pushing through the kitchen door, Amandine backtracks into the living room, having caught sight of something. When she steps inside Amandine sees Tina lying across the sofa, her arms flopped to the floor, a bottle of vodka standing upright on the coffee table.

"Eliot!" Amandine calls out as she strides across the plush cream carpet to the sofa. "Eliot. Come here!" She hears him behind her as she's checking Tina's pulse. Sylvia's sobbing gets louder.

"Has she taken anything?" Eliot asks his daughter. "Any pills?"

"I don't know," Sylvia gulps, "she's always taking pills."

"She's unconscious," Amandine says. "I'm

calling an ambulance."

"No!" Sylvia cries. "Don't! I did it once, she nearly killed me. I just let her sleep it off. She'll be okay. She's always okay."

"We can't take that risk." Amandine pulls her phone out of her pocket and presses 999. "We can't be sure she'll be okay."

"No!" Sylvia screams, hurling herself toward Amandine and hitting her. "Stop! Stop!"

Eliot jumps into the room and grabs his daughter, holding her tight while Amandine talks into the phone.

"It's all right, sweetheart," Eliot whispers. "I've got you now, I won't let you go, I promise, I won't let you go."

For the last few weeks Noa has felt awful. Her head is heavy as lead, her vision blurred by dust motes that float in and out, her fingers trembling so she's constantly dropping things. Today, given the task of setting up a viewing gallery for the Rothko auction, Noa is having trouble seeing the colors.

She steps back from a large red and blue canvas and squints her eyes, but the colors are muted and fading and sliding into each other.

"What's going on?" Noa whispers, her hands sticky with panic, her heart racing in

her chest. The pounding of her heart spreads to her head and Noa wonders if she's about to have a brain aneurysm or some sort of mild stroke.

Stumbling toward a marble bench in the gallery, Noa collapses, shoulders hunched, head down on her knees. A swell of nausea overcomes her. Shaking, Noa starts to sob, mumbling prayers that no one will walk in and see her. *What's happening? What the hell is happening to me?*

When Noa takes a deep breath and looks up, she's staring straight at herself: naked and smiling a little self-consciously, a huge canvas framed on the wall. Noa stares. There's something strange about the painting and she can't initially put her finger on it. Then, gazing up at her own eyes, she realizes. It's as if Noa is staring into her own soul, as if her spirit has been captured so completely on canvas that it's stronger, brighter, more alive than when she looks into the mirror, at least lately. Ever since Santiago painted her damn portrait.

Noa squeezes her eyes shut, desperately hoping it will be gone and back to normal when she looks again. But, when Noa opens her eyes the painting hasn't changed and now every Rothko has disappeared, replaced by more of Santiago's naked women, their eyes all as bright as hers, as if he's somehow snatched up their spirits and trapped them in oils.

And then there is Santiago standing in front of her.

Noa stumbles back.

"*Olá,* beautiful," he says, stepping toward her. "Are you feeling a little under the weather? Shall I give you a kiss, make you feel all better?"

Noa stares at him, her heart nearly stopped by shock.

"Go away," she mutters. "Leave me alone."

"Aw, now, why would you say that?" Santiago gives her a dejected look, placing a thin hand to his chest. "You'd wound my feelings, you'd hurt my heart . . ." He grins. "If I had a heart, of course."

"What have you done to me?" Noa cries. "What have you done?"

"Oh, nothing much," Santiago says. "I've only caught a piece of your soul, that's all." He holds his thumb and forefinger apart an inch. "Just a tiny little piece. I'm surprised you've noticed it at all."

Noa screams, pressing her hands hard over her eyes, her heart pounding, her skin wet with sweat. And when she looks again Santiago and his paintings have disappeared.

When Kat sees her sister walking toward her along King's Parade, she almost turns and runs the other way. But, just as she's about to, Cosima spots her and waves.

"Sis!" She hurries along the pavement until, a little breathless, she reaches Kat. "Sis, it's been forever. Where've you been? You haven't been into the café in ages. Are you avoiding me?"

Kat scowls at her sister. "Are you still going to pretend you're not doing any baking spells?"

Cosima glances down at her feet. "I didn't tell you because I knew you wouldn't approve."

"You say that like I'm some sort of stick-in-the-mud," Kat hisses, "like you're getting stoned and I'm calling the police, but it's not —"

Cosima smiles. "You actually did that once, remember?"

"Cosi! That was nothing compared with this. You're messing around with something extremely dangerous. This isn't simply breakup brownies, this is really serious. Forget about everything else, about poor duped George, and stupid ex-Tommy, and all that. If you get pregnant, you're risking your life."

A guilty look flits over Cosima's face. "I'm not hurting George, he's happy, he wants —"

"He's not in love with you, Cosi, you've cast a spell on him. That isn't love and I . . ."

"Shut up!" Cosima shouts suddenly. "Just shut up!"

Kat looks at her sister, shocked.

Cosima's face falls. "Look, it's too late, okay? It's too late. I've already done it."

"Done what?"

But Cosima doesn't have a chance to say anything before Kat understands. "Oh, God. It's done, isn't it? You're — you're already pregnant."

Cosima nods. Slowly.

"Hell, Cosi, what were you thinking?" Kat snaps. "I don't believe, I can't believe . . . You can't keep it, you can't risk your life for something like that, you can't —"

"*Something like that?* That's my baby you're talking about, not some sort of . . . meaningless mathematical equation."

"That's, that's not what I meant."

Cosima shakes her head. "Yes, it was. You don't get it, you've got no idea how I feel. You don't know what it's like to want something so desperately and be denied it. You're so smart and amazing and you've always gotten everything you've ever wanted, just like that, well —"

"I haven't." Kat's eyes fill with tears. "I haven't."

Cosima reaches out to her sister, their fight instantly forgotten. "What is it? What's wrong?"

"Nothing," Kat mumbles, "it's not important, not right now" — she nods at Cosima's belly — "not compared to this."

"I'm sorry, sis, I know . . . I just . . ."

"No, Cosi, you don't know. You're risking your life, it's insane — have you told Tommy?"

Cosima nods. "I called him. He said he was still sad about what he'd done, and sorry, but he was happy for me and his . . . she gave birth a month ago. So he's already a father — Lily Rose, that's his daughter's name." Cosima laughs, though her eyes fill with tears. "Hey, maybe our girls can play together, maybe they'll be best friends, how crazy would that be?"

Kat rests her hand on her sister's shoulder. "I'm sorry, Cosi, I really am. It's horrible, what you've been through. But what about George? Don't you care what he feels, what he wants — you didn't think, Cosi, you just didn't think it through at all."

"Hey," Cosima protests, "I did think

about him, of course I did — and it was an accident. I didn't mean to enchant him, I only meant to . . . anyway, it's not the end of the world, he wants kids and I'll sort out the spell thing. I'm still working on it, but I'll figure it out. Then I'll be able to explain everything to him. He's a wonderful man and he'll be a wonderful father. It'll be . . ." Tears fill Cosima's eyes. "Please let me do this, please. Don't take her away, I couldn't live if you . . . I can't live without her now, not anymore."

"Her?"

Cosima nods, then smiles, wiping her eyes. "Yes." She places her hand on the small swell of her stomach. "I'm sure."

Kat sighs, knowing she'd already lost the battle before she even began. "But what about you, about the risks, what are you going to do? No doctor will support you in going through with . . ."

"It's okay," Cosima says, "don't worry, I'm managing it. Herbs, spells, all that . . . you don't have to worry about me."

Kat looks at her sister and her eyes fill with tears again. "But I do, I do worry about you, I always have. And, your daughter, you'll always worry about her too, that's what being a mother means."

"Oh, sis," Cosima says, and starts to cry.

■ ■ ■ ■

When Cosima returns to the café that evening she bakes a spell to heal her sister's heart, to help her find love. If Cosima doesn't make it through this pregnancy after all, if Kat's fears are founded, then Cosima wants to be sure her sister is taken care of. She wants to be certain that Kat will find true love one day — sooner rather than later. And there is only one cake that will take care of that: a special one of her own creation.

Cosima lines up all her little jars of dried herbs and flowers, then carefully picks the ones she needs.

"Acacia, for secret love. Celandine, for joys to come. Bluebell," she whispers, "for constancy. Bougainvillea, for passion. And chrysanthemum, for truth."

She finds her special ceramic baking bowl and begins to add the usual ingredients: flour, sugar, butter, and eggs.

"And the only flavor strong enough to mask the flowers." Cosima opens the cupboard above her head and takes down two bars of the finest dark chocolate she's ever tasted. "Ninety-nine percent. Perfect."

After she's grated in a beetroot, for moisture, and added vanilla pods, for extra flavor, Cosima pours the dark, thick mixture into a small baking tin and slips it into the oven. An hour later, she cools the cake, then glazes its black (with a tint of purple) surface with a chocolate icing seasoned with a little dust of daffodil, passionflower, and cosmos: new beginnings, faith, joy in love and life. Then she places it gently in a bright red tin and walks with it to Kat's house. Just as she's about to ring the bell, Kat opens the door.

"Hey," Cosima says. She holds out the tin to her sister.

Kat eyes her suspiciously. "You expect me to eat that?"

Cosima nods. "Please. Trust me. You won't regret it."

"I won't?"

Cosima smiles. "I promise."

"A little lower, lower, lower — that's it. Stop."

Noa stands on a ladder holding aloft a very valuable painting. It's to appear in an exhibition by a modestly famous artist who creates vivid reproductions of bloody carcasses being devoured by vultures and lions. Noa has an inkling, deep in the recesses of her memory, that she didn't used to like this artist's work, but now she finds herself admiring the paintings. When her boss comments on the brilliant originality and searing realism of the art, Noa agrees wholeheartedly.

"Next."

With great relief, Noa steps down off the ladder. She's been feeling dizzy lately and not simply when she's standing up high. She selects the next painting and takes a few deep breaths before slowly ascending the ladder again.

"This is going to be a major auction," her boss says. "We're anticipating seven figures for that one."

Facing the wall, Noa frowns. "That's . . . incredible," she ventures, "though I'm not surprised."

"Yes, indeed, exactly," he says. "It's what we should expect. Lower on the left, a little more, that's it. Stop."

With a small sigh, Noa climbs down again. As they walk together to the next piece, Noa carrying the ladder in both arms, she glances over at him: highly polished shoes striding, bespoke-suited arms swinging by his sides. She wants to ask him something, something important, but she can't think what. Noa focuses intently, squeezing one eye shut, trying to catch hold of the feeling and envision the words, her own words, deep down in her murky soul. And then, like the carcass of a dead dolphin washing up on a beach of black sand, something pops to the surface.

"All right then," he says, "let's get on with it."

As Noa nods and sets down the ladder again, the tide sweeps in and pulls the body back into the depths of the ocean again. She picks up the painting and steps onto the first rung of the ladder. As she places her foot on the next step, she tastes the tang of cachaça at the back of her throat.

"Rupert?"

"Yes?"

She smiles, savoring the taste, curling her tongue around his voice. "I know an amazing artist you should meet."

"I'm not interested unless I've heard of him."

"You haven't yet, but you will," she says, each word silver-smooth with heat and liquor and sex. "His name is Santiago Costa."

Chapter Seventeen

They don't meet at Gustare but in a little café close to Trinity College, a scruffy place frequented by students. They sit in a booth at the back in a darkened corner. It's a long time before either speaks. Finally, George lets go of the coffee cup he'd been hugging to his chest and looks up. Kat stares down into her cup.

"Thank you for coming," he says softly. "It means . . . I'm so happy to see you. We've missed . . . I've missed you."

Kat doesn't look up. She taps a finger against her cup. Since eating six slices of her sister's cake — quite the most delicious thing she's ever eaten in her life — Kat has been feeling better, lighter and more . . . hopeful. She doesn't know what Cosima put in the cake but she guesses it was good and powerful. Without it, she couldn't be sitting with George right now.

"I know how hard this must be for you,"

George says. "It means the world to me that you came."

"I still think you're making a huge mistake," Kat says. "I know you want me to be happy about this, but Cosi is risking her life and you, well . . ."

"I'm sorry," George says, "I wish I could make it better, I wish I could give you what you want, I —"

"Me? Give me what *I* want? This isn't about what I want, this has got nothing to do with me, it's . . ."

"Wait," George says, softly. "I know why you were so upset about me and Cosima — before the baby, I mean — Amandine told me."

Kat frowns. "Told you what?"

"About you, about your . . . feelings for . . ."

Kat freezes. It's a few moments before she finds words. And when she does, it's surprisingly easy to forget about herself and her own personal humiliation and focus instead on her friend. Kat looks him straight in the eye. "Are you really okay with this? Do you really want a baby?"

George nods, deeply relieved that they've sidestepped the frightfully awkward subject of Kat's feelings for him. "I do. And don't worry, it'll be okay. A little unconventional, true. But it'll be wonderful, in its own way, I'm certain."

"That's what Cosi keeps saying," Kat says. And then — all of a sudden — she sees something she hadn't noticed a moment ago. She smiles. "It worked."

George frowns. "What worked?"

"It doesn't matter — but . . . you know what she did and you don't mind?"

George shakes his head.

"Jesus." Kat sighs. "You must be a saint. Well, actually, she didn't mean to enchant you. I warned her about baking spells, silly girl, they're notoriously unpredictable. But, anyway, what does that matter now?"

George reaches across the table and takes Kat's hand.

"I'm sorry," he says softly. "I'm so sorry I couldn't love you back."

Kat nods slightly, her eyes swelling with tears.

"But you know I care for you, deeply, virtually more than anyone else in the world, don't you?"

Kat's tears start to fall.

"Can we be friends again, please?" George says. "I miss you so much."

Kat closes her eyes. "I'm not sure I'm quite — I need to finish the rest of Cosi's cake — just give me time, okay?"

George nods, disappointed. Then he frowns. "Cosi's cake?"

But Kat doesn't respond. She lets go of his hand, then stands and walks away.

"We have to do something."

They're in the kitchen, Amandine chopping tomatoes and Eliot frying onions, while Bertie and Frankie watch TV in the living room.

"What can we do?"

"We can't just leave her there," Eliot says. "We have to help her. Jarvis would represent me. He's a snake but I don't think he's ever lost a custody case."

"Custody?"

Eliot nods. "We could sue for full custody. We'd stand a fairly good chance. After all, it's not as if I abandoned Sylvia. I never knew, and we've got a good home to bring her into, we've —"

Amandine stops chopping. "Have you already spoken to Jarvis about this?"

"Yes."

She puts down her knife. "Why didn't you tell me?"

"I just wanted to see if we stood a chance first, that's all."

"What about the boys?"

"What about them?"

"They don't even know about Sylvia yet, and you're talking about moving her in so we'll all be one big happy family."

"You don't want her?"

"I'm not saying that." Amandine feels a flash of panic in her chest. "But there's a lot to think about. We can't take her away from her mother just like that. It wouldn't be right, and she'd hate us for it. Have you talked to her about all this?"

"No, not yet," Eliot says. "I wanted to talk to you first, before —"

"And Jarvis before me."

Eliot steps away from the stove, walks over to his wife, stands behind her, and wraps his arms around her waist.

"You don't want her here?"

"She still hates me," Amandine says softly.

"She doesn't hate you, my love. It's just — you're not her mother, that's all."

She does hate me, Amandine wants to say. *I can feel it every time we see her, hatred crashing off her in huge waves.* But, of course, explaining exactly how she knows that would involve many further explanations.

"I don't think Sylvia would be happy here, I don't think —"

"Could we at least offer her the chance?" Eliot pleads. "Could we ask and see what

312

she says?"

Noa is staring at Santiago. Somehow, she knows she's dreaming, but she can't make herself wake up. She wants to run from him but her feet are rooted to the spot. Noa glares at him, trying not to show the fear rippling through her. "What did you do to me that night?"

Santiago laughs, deep and thick like swallowing molasses or plunging into the ocean. "Whatever do you mean?"

"You know exactly what I mean. You used your dirty magic on me."

Santiago shakes his head. "I didn't have to, darling. The delicious combination of my innate charms and your desire was quite enough to —"

"Liar!"

Santiago smiles. "You don't remember? We were sitting on the sofa, drinking tea, talking about art. You said something startlingly complimentary, and extremely accurate, about one of my paintings and I kissed you."

Noa scowls. "Yes, of course I remember. But . . ."

"Then we finished our tea and I took you on a tour of my collection. That was when you asked if I wanted to paint you. Naturally, I said yes."

"What collection? You never showed me a —"

"Didn't I?" Santiago grins. "I didn't show you my nudes? How remiss of me."

Noa catches the scream rising in her throat. "Exactly how many women have you painted naked?"

Santiago shrugs. "I'm not sure, *exactly.*"

"Then" — Noa speaks through gritted teeth — "give me an approximate number."

Santiago closes his eyes for a moment, his mouth moving as he counts. "Approximately fourteen hundred and seventy-six."

Noa gasps. "What the f— ? How is that — have you been doing nothing else in your life but painting naked women?"

Santiago shrugs. "Not all of them were alone. I've painted a few pairs, even a group here and there."

Noa stares at him, openmouthed. "How do you . . . ? How do you get so many women to take off their clothes for you?"

"I don't have to make them," Santiago says. "They all volunteered. Just like you did."

Noa laughs, a bitter laugh that burns her throat. "I can't believe it. I can't believe so many women would be willing — would want to be seen like . . ."

"Oh, every woman wants to be seen as beautiful. Every woman wants to hold a man's attention, to be looked at, to feel — even if only for a few hours — as if she's the most beautiful woman in the world."

"And how many of them have you slept with?" Noa asks.

Before he answers, she wakes, sweating. She glances at her alarm clock: 3:33 A.M. The same time as last night and the night before. She's had the same nightmare now for five nights in a row: she's standing at the auction podium, gazing out at a crowd of eager bidders, chanting and heckling and waving their numbered paddles. She glances behind her at the lot she's supposed to be selling: lot 36, *Storm over Bahia.* The dark canvas, great splashes of royal blue on black, deep purple seas beneath deep red skies. Now, as Noa looks more closely, she can see the dark gray fins of the sharks swimming beneath the purple seas and the big black wings of the crows cawing through the red skies.

She turns back to the heckling audience to see Santiago striding down the center aisle toward her, fury on his face. A flood of fear overtakes her. She wants to run, but she can't move. When Santiago reaches the podium, the bidders are booing and jeering so loudly that she can't hear what he's shouting at her. Silently, she prays desperately to be given her curse back, so she'll know his secrets, so she'll know what to expect, so she can be better prepared to escape.

When he reaches her, Santiago grabs her arms and presses her face down onto the wood. He forces his foot in between her feet, pushing her legs apart. Then she wakes.

Héloïse walks slowly across town. The restaurant Theo suggested is two miles from home. She didn't want to take the car, it would have been too quick. At least walking gives her time to calm her nerves. This will be their first official date. Theo offered to pick Héloïse up, but she declined, since that would make it even more scary and official. She'd also persuaded him to have lunch instead of dinner, on the basis that it'd be less like a date, thus a little less scary. What a mistake that was. She couldn't be more nervous if she was sitting her Cambridge entrance exam again.

As she clip-clops along Trinity Street in blue suede heels, she isn't finding the forty-minute walk any more calming than driving would have been. She's still more nervous than she's ever been in her life. More than on her wedding night, the birth of Amandine, or the dreaded day she turned fifty. They'd been nerve-racking moments at the time, but were nothing compared to this. It's only a first date, for goodness' sake, a first date. What's so scary about that? Héloïse talks to herself as she walks, trying to calm down, to not scream out loud. We've known each other for months, years! And yet, she feels completely different than she did before.

Thirty-eight years ago, getting ready for her first date with François, Héloïse hadn't been nervous at all. Finding François had been like opening a Christmas present to discover the most comfortable pair of slippers ever made: stitched with silk and lined with fur. She'd slipped them on straightaway, sinking into their soft, kind, attentive soles, never taking them off again. Until one day — in an instant — they disappeared. With François, love had been like sitting in your mother's lap while she read your favorite stories and let you eat chocolate biscuits and drop crumbs all over the sofa. Héloïse felt so taken care of, so safe. With Theo she feels a lot of things, but safe isn't one of them. Just standing near him makes her shiver. And the thought of touching or, God forbid, kissing him brings her close to having a heart attack.

When Héloïse at last arrives at the restaurant, she looks through the windows at the art deco décor, the black wood and cream walls, linen tablecloths and crystal glasses, until she sees him. Theo sits at the back of the bright white room in a dark leather booth. A bottle of water is on the table and he sips from a glass, watching the waiters gliding past, now and then glancing at the gold-framed posters of Noël Coward's plays on the walls: *Private Lives, Present Laughter, Blithe Spirit . . .*

"*Alors,* what am I thinking?" Héloïse mumbles.

Then he sees her and waves. Héloïse lifts her hand halfway. There's no backing out now. She inhales deeply, holds her breath, and pushes open the glass door. The scent of orchids swirls in the foyer as she surrenders her coat to the maître d'. He's dressed like Bertie Wooster, in a cream suit, plus fours, and a boater, which makes her smile. Thirty years ago she'd read P. G. Wodehouse to François in the evenings, his head in her lap, after putting Amandine to bed. Héloïse pushes the memory away as she crosses the restaurant floor, feigning an air of nonchalance. Theo stands as she reaches him, a delighted grin puffing out his cheeks.

"A beautiful restaurant," Héloïse says.

"I must admit I'm more of a pie and chips man, myself," Theo says. "But I thought you'd appreciate a little sophistication."

Héloïse smiles and sits opposite Theo. She glances up at the posters on the walls.

"I love Noël Coward. François and I saw them all. *Easy Virtue* was my favorite," Héloïse says. "He liked *Present Laughter,* but I found it too frenetic. I liked *Private Lives* a lot, very funny if a little contrived. So, what —"

Héloïse's nervous chatter is cut off by a waiter sweeping in and filling her water glass.

"Ah, thank you."

"So what do you fancy?" Theo asks. "Do you like fish? The waiter says it's their specialty. Apparently the sea bass in white wine sauce will melt in your mouth."

"I've only been with one man," Héloïse blurts out. "And I was with him for thirty-five years, and I never thought I'd ever be with anyone else."

Theo nods. Without saying anything, he pours her a large glass of the red wine that's just appeared on the table. Héloïse takes a sip. It's delicious. She takes another sip. Then another. The warmth of the wine spreads to her skin and, little by little, Héloïse begins to relax, her nervousness evaporating into the air, mixing with the scent of orchids.

"I can't believe we're going to see her at last."

George forces a smile, desperately trying not to look as terrified as he feels. "How can you be so sure she's a she?"

"Because I wished for her."

George squeezes Cosima's hand, the buoyancy of her happiness keeping him afloat. The months have been a whirlwind of hormones and pistachio cream croissants — strangely, the only thing that Cosima had been able to stomach during her first three turbulent months of pregnancy. As they walk along the hospital corridor, Cosima gazing out of the window, placing one hand on her belly, George thinks of the last time he saw Kat, ten weeks ago.

"She'll come around," Cosima had promised. "She'll come around eventually; if not now, then when she sees the baby. I promise."

Kat hasn't seen or spoken to either of them in over two months. And, according to Amandine, Kat hasn't contacted the other witches either. Amandine and Héloïse suggested the book group could still meet, just the three of them, but George thought it too disloyal and suggested the group be disbanded until, if, or when, Kat came back. For his part, he still calls her every day, but she never answers. Sometimes she sends him the odd text, telling him to give her a little more time. He doesn't know if she's called Cosi or not.

"Perhaps we could call the baby Kat," George suggests, "in honor of her aunt. What do you think?"

"That's a lovely idea." Cosima smiles. "It can be her middle name, since her name is Aura. I had a dream last night and — oh, I'll tell you later. We're here."

She stops outside a door. Above it a sign in large white letters announces:

Foetal Scan Department

Cosima lets go of George's hand and pushes the door open. George takes a deep breath and follows her inside. Thirty minutes later they are in a small dark room with an extremely enthusiastic nurse.

"Make yourself comfortable, Ms. Rubens," she says. "I'm about to squeeze some cold sticky stuff onto your tummy so we can get a quick peep at your little miracle."

Cosima snuggles down on the examination table before beaming up at the nurse. "We're ready."

The nurse turns to George. "Are you ready, Daddy?"

George blinks. No one has asked him this before, no one, certainly not Cosima. He hasn't even asked himself. *No, not at all. I don't know how this happened. I don't know what I'm doing.*

He looks up at the nurse and smiles. "Absolutely. I can't wait."

The nurse beams ever brighter. "That's what I like to hear, Dad. So, let's get started."

The nurse squeezes the sticky stuff onto Cosima's exposed stomach and all eyes turn to the screen of the fetal scanner. At first all they can see is static, then a mess of fuzzy movement and then . . . a head, belly, arms, and legs. A baby, kicking and flailing, with a tiny racing heart.

"Oh," Cosima gasps. "Oh, my girl."

George stares at the screen. How can it be? Cosima's stomach hasn't expanded much and yet he can now see that, contained within her womb, is a whole being, moving, growing, living. George has seen magic in his time, he's even seen miracles, but this is beyond any spell he's ever cast, beyond anything he's ever conjured up in his imagination. He stares.

The nurse laughs. "I think someone's had a little shock."

Cosima glances over at George. "Are you okay?"

Without looking at her, George nods, though it's not true at all. As a descriptive word *okay* is so far from what he's feeling right now that it's not even in the same language. He needs new words, words he doesn't even know, probably in languages he doesn't even speak, to say how he feels at seeing this new life, this new spirit and soul he has helped to create.

The baby turns and kicks and flips.

"You've got a feisty one." The nurse laughs. "You're going to have your hands full of mischief."

She gives Cosima a wink and, while the two women look at each other, George just keeps staring at the screen, whispering the same incantation: of new love and desperate hope, over and over again.

"Why did you open this café?" George leans against the kitchen counter, watching Cosima baking. When she walks past him to turn on the oven, he catches a whiff of cinnamon sugar. He breathes it in and smiles.

"I love getting up before dawn and filling the kitchen with the scents of pistachio croissants, lavender cookies, and chocolate cakes . . . I like feeding people with the most delicious food I can possibly make." Cosima smiles. "Sometimes with a little sprinkle of enchanted sugar or a dusting of charmed flour . . . But I just like giving people pleasure," she says, returning to the counter. She sprinkles a pinch of purple rose petals into a bowl of flour and stirs it until little white puffs burst over the bowl. "And delicious food is the easiest way to do that."

"I suppose so." George smiles. "We'll have to be careful though, that Aura doesn't become as round as she will be tall."

Cosima laughs. "Yes, you'll have to monitor me. You'll have to limit the amount of cakes I offer our little girl, or I might get a bit carried away."

Cosima picks a bottle of dried honeysuckle flowers off the shelf and adds a dash to her mix. She whispers a quick wish for her sister, of love and luck for her dear Kat. Then she adds a few heaped spoonfuls of amaranth, and an extra one for luck.

"I've been thinking . . ." George ventures.

"Yes?"

"That perhaps we don't need to move in together, to raise Aura, I mean. Not just yet, anyway. What do you think?"

Cosima looks up from her baking. The spoon keeps stirring her mix and the scent of chocolate and vanilla floats through the air. "You want to stay at your flat?"

George nods. "Of course, I'll be here whenever you need me. More often, in fact. You won't be able to keep me away. But I love my home, I . . . don't want to leave it, not just yet."

Cosima nods. "You can do whatever you want, George. It's fine by me. You can come and go as much as you please. It's totally up to you."

"Really?"

"Of course. You've given me the greatest gift in the world." Cosima grins. "Now I'll spend the rest of my life giving you anything else you ask for."

George steps forward, flooded with relief, grinning with delight. "Anything?"

Cosima steps back, holding her wooden spoon out between them. "Well, within rea-son . . ."

"How about a batch of your chocolate and sour cherry cupcakes?"

Cosima smiles. "Absolutely."

"A lifetime supply of vanilla and orange oil cannoli?"

"I think I can manage that."

"Your secret recipe for pistachio cream."

Cosima grins. "No way. Never. Not happening."

Hamish paces up and down the living room of his tiny student flat. As the weeks have passed he's been feeling more optimistic, almost hopeful, that some sort of relationship with Kat might be possible after all. Nothing has happened, not specifically, to suggest it. But he holds on to the moment in the pub when he'd definitely felt a spark of something — before she'd vomited all over them both. He wonders, of course, if he was just kidding himself. Some days he's racked with self-doubt. Others he's high on hope. He's tempted just to ask her outright, in one of their tutorials, but directness isn't his style. Despite his well-honed light and breezy manner with her, he'd prefer to wait three years then drop a few hints and cross his fingers — less risky that way.

"What's wrong with me?" Hamish moans. He stops pacing and flops onto his sofa. "I'm a coward, a bloody shameful coward." He sighs, crossing his long legs. "I should go to the pub and drown my sorrow and shame in too many pints." Then, suddenly, he stands again. "No! I should do what they do in those silly, soppy romantic films. I should buy a bunch of roses, a dozen, then chase her to the airport, or at least turn up uninvited at her office. Not quite so romantic, but the message is basically the same."

Before he can change his mind, Hamish strides across the room, picks up his jacket, wallet, and keys. Then opens his front door, steps outside, and slams it shut. It bounces open again. Hamish tries again. Same result.

"Bugger," Hamish mutters. "I can't even slam a bloody door shut. This does not bode well." Pulling it into place, he hurries off down the street toward the supermarket to find a bouquet of roses.

Two hours and six shops later, Hamish has settled for a slightly wilted bunch of pink carnations. His swift step has slowed to a reluctant shuffle as he makes his way along Trinity Street. When he walks through the college gates, Hamish feels his stomach plummet to the ground. What is he doing? What the hell is he doing? Is he a glutton for punishment and humiliation? He's an idiot, that's for certain, on his way to confess his love to a woman who's already told him she's in love with someone else. What is he thinking?

Just before he reaches Kat's office, Hamish turns on his heel and starts striding swiftly across the quad, back toward the street. He's got his pace up to a near canter, when he bumps into Kat coming out of the porter's lodge.

"Hey, Ham," she says, grinning up at him. "Where are you running off to?"

Hamish snaps his handful of flowers behind his back.

"Hey, Prof. Nowhere, I just, I . . ."

"We didn't have a meeting today, did we?"

Hamish shakes his head. "Nope, next Monday."

"Ah, okay, great," Kat says. "Well, I'll see you then."

"Yep." Hamish nods.

The snapped head of a carnation drops to the floor between Hamish's legs. Kat picks it up and hands it to him with a quizzical look. Hamish sighs, taking it, and revealing the rest of the bunch.

"Who's the lucky lady?" Kat asks with a grin.

"I, um, well, actually, I bought them for —" Hamish takes a deep breath of courage, filling his lungs with strength and power and madcap haste. "— my mother."

"Oh," Kat says. "What a sweet son you are."

Hamish regards her, horrified. *No, not sweet!* He wants to shout. *I'm manly, courageous, virile, daring, bold, plucky, macho. Oh, who am I kidding?*

"Thanks," Hamish mutters. "See you on Monday."

Then he turns and hurries away.

It's early Friday morning and Noa sits on a train bound for Cambridge. She hasn't slept in nearly forty-eight hours, being too scared of falling back into that dreadful dream again. She feels herself being dragged into a swamp and it's taking all her effort of will to keep her grip on reality. She's meeting Santiago at his home to pick the paintings they'll sell at Sotheby's. For some astonishing reason, Rupert has given her carte blanche to choose five paintings and, if they do well, she'll return again to select ten more.

"Come in, darling girl," Santiago says as he opens his front door. "Don't you look absolutely gorgeous? Come in, come in."

Noa smiles, despite herself. She knows for a fact that she looks shocking.

"Thanks." She steps over the threshold and follows him into the kitchen. She has to tell him about the nightmares and the hideous headaches; she has to ask him about her future, about the possibility of returning to university. But it can wait. Right now Noa — as always whenever she sees him in the flesh — is too starstruck to focus. Seeing Santiago is like stumbling on a film star in the supermarket and it always takes her several long moments to recover.

"Tea?"

Noa shakes her head.

Santiago smiles. "Come on, you know we always have a good time after you drink my tea."

Feeling her resolve weakening, Noa swallows a smile. "Well, maybe later."

In response, Santiago steps forward and kisses her, long and hard. For a few moments afterward, Noa forgets why she's there at all. Then he pulls back.

"Okay," Santiago says as he steps into the living room, "you want to take care of business first and save pleasure for later? I can respect that."

"Yes, um, exactly," Noa says, tasting sea salt and Sambuca on her tongue, her thoughts drowned out by waves crashing against the shore.

"Follow me then, my love." Santiago takes Noa's hand and leads her into the living room. Stacks of paintings lean against every available space, making the dark room feel more like a cave than ever. Noa is reminded of the catacombs beneath a twelfth-century church she saw in the south of France. She'd loved the frescos of the Catholic saints on the walls but had felt an irrational fear of being trapped there for eternity, her image and soul caught to be seen by future generations of art lovers.

Noa walks slowly toward the closest stack of paintings and runs her fingers along the frames. She glances up at the dozens of shelves lined with hundreds of strange objects. Her eye settles again on the little statue of the naked boy, the birth baby.

"Of course, I know the choice is yours for the paintings," Santiago says. "But I've selected the five that I think you should take. I'm sure you'll —"

Noa looks up as he steps across the room. "Wait."

Santiago turns around. "What is it?"

"I've, I've got to ask you something, some things . . ." Noa says, pacing along the carpet between the sofa and the shelves. "I've been thinking — I haven't been sleeping, I'm having these hideous nightmares, I'm feeling awful and . . ."

In a second, Santiago is at Noa's side, tucking his arm around her waist and gently lifting her over to the sofa. He kisses her lightly, stroking her hair.

"What's wrong, my love? Why didn't you tell me? I can help you —"

Noa fixes her gaze on her hands curled tightly in her lap. "Well, actually, I mean . . . that's what I wanted to ask you about, that is . . ."

"What, *querida,* what is it?"

Noa drops her voice to a whisper. "You mentioned, the first time I was here, that your mother had to, had to . . ."

She glances up to see the concern in Santiago's eyes. "Yes?" he prompts. "What?"

Noa speaks so softly she can hardly hear herself. "Protect you from black magic."

Santiago nods. "Yes, she did."

"And . . ." Noa stares back at her hands again. "Did she ever . . . ?"

"What?" Santiago gently lifts Noa's chin and fixes his soft gaze on her. "Tell me, it's okay, I won't be offended, don't worry."

Noa takes a deep breath. "Did you ever do it yourself? Black magic? Did you practice . . . ?"

Santiago leans back, breaking their eye contact. "What are you asking, Noa? Are you suggesting I did something . . . untoward with you?"

Noa shrugs. "Well, it — the Sotheby's job — was hardly obtained through the most official, moral channels, was it? You —"

"We," Santiago says. "I might have set it up for you, but you went along with it every step of the way, so I'd be careful before —"

"I'm not blaming you, I'm grateful for what you did, for everything. But I've been thinking . . ."

"What?"

Noa frowns at the sudden snap in Santiago's voice.

"Just that, maybe I stepped . . . maybe I shouldn't have said yes to it all so quickly, maybe I should take a little break . . . it might stop the —"

"What?"

"I'm not saying I'm going to quit, or anything like that," Noa says softly. "But at this rate I'll have a nervous breakdown and be off sick for six m—"

"Don't be silly," Santiago says, his voice smooth as cachaça again. "I can help you with the nightmares, headaches, or whatever. It'll only take a sprinkling of a spell to sort all that out."

Noa shakes her head. "No," she mumbles. "No. I don't want to do any more" — she mouths the word — "magic."

Santiago frowns. "Whyever not?"

"Because, it's got me . . . it's too unpredictable. I'm suffering hideously from the side effects of the last spell you cast and —"

Suddenly, Santiago stands. He looks down at her, his eyes narrow, his lips thin, his teeth clenched.

"You. Ungrateful. Bitch."

Noa's eyes widen with shock. "What? I, no, that's not it at all, I'm not —"

"Shut up. I've had enough of your whining. I've done nothing but be good to you, more than good. I gave you the two things you wanted most of all, and this, *this* is how you react?"

"No, please, I didn't mean to sound ungrateful, not at all, that's the last thing I want." Noa reaches up to Santiago but he shrugs her off. "I'm so, so grateful for everything you've done, I couldn't be more — this isn't about you, anyway, you don't need me to promote your paintings, you're far too talented for that, I'm only —"

Santiago takes a deep breath. Slowly, he squats down in front of her until they are face-to-face. His voice, when he speaks, is as cold as the fingers pressing into her knees and as dark as the eyes scratching into her soul.

"You will not take a break from Sotheby's. You will stay and see that my paintings sell for the fortune that they deserve. You will stay until my name is on the lips of every art collector in the country. You will stay until I tell you that you may leave. Do you understand?"

Noa just stares at him, still as stone.

"I won't ask you again."

Noa nods, quickly.

"Say the words."

"Yes," Noa says. "Yes, of course, I understand."

Santiago stands and smiles. "Good," he says, as bright and light as if absolutely nothing had happened. "I'm glad we've got that clear. Now, let's get back to business. I'll show you the paintings I think are best for the first show. I'm sure you'll agree."

Noa nods again. She keeps nodding when Santiago shows the pictures he's selected, she nods when he tells her the prices at which to sell them, she nods when he tells her what to do next. She nods for the final time when he hugs her and tells her he loves her. And then, as soon as she's out of his house and halfway down the road, Noa starts to run and doesn't stop until she reaches Amandine's office.

CHAPTER EIGHTEEN

Amandine has convened an emergency meeting of the Cambridge University Society of Literature and Witchcraft on the rooftop of King's College. They sit in a circle (not hovering this time, the severity of the situation having sucked the buoyancy out of them) with Noa, pale-faced and clutching her knees to her chest, in the middle. Amandine sits cross-legged between Kat and George. Cosima is next to George and Héloïse sits on a little stool between Cosima and Kat.

Kat leans close to Amandine, whispering, "Why did you ask Cosi to come? She should be taking it easy, not sitting up on rooftops about to do goodness knows what."

"I know, I'm sorry," Amandine says, "but tonight we need all the help we can get."

"I'm fine, sis," Cosima pipes up. "Stop worrying."

Kat sighs. "Okay, okay. Anyway, what's

going on?" Kat says, this time loudly enough for everyone to hear. "Why are we here? Why is the kid here?"

"Black magic," Amandine says, "from what I can tell. We need to lift a spell that took her gift away. He's been able to seep into her mind and corrupt her heart. We've got to get her strength back."

"Who did it?" Cosima asks.

"Never mind that," Amandine says. "Let's focus on what we need to do now."

"And what are we supposed to do?" George sits forward, looking ever so slightly terrified. "We don't do black magic. I can hardly even do regular magic. So, I don't think —"

"Don't underestimate yourself," Cosima says.

"Exactly," Amandine says. "We can't afford any self-doubt and low self-esteem, not right now."

"Do you have a plan?" Héloïse asks.

"I have an idea. We'll try it out and hope it works. After that, I don't have a clue."

"Shit," Cosima says, looking at Noa, who's turning grayer every second, has a cold sweat, and is shivering so hard her teeth chatter. "I hope it works too, 'cause that girl is in trouble."

"She's trying to fight it off," Amandine

337

says, "but it's too strong, she's got no strength left." She stands. "We'd better get started."

The other witches stand too, Kat jumping up, George tentative, Héloïse and Cosima easing themselves up slowly.

"I've prepared an incantation," Amandine says. "We'll all speak together and hopefully our combined strength will be enough to support Noa in dispelling the hold he has over her." She glances down at the girl — for now Noa looks just like a scared little girl, almost a baby, as if she's regressing to infancy and incapacity with every second — and feels the sickening wrench of Noa's fear in her heart.

"Now," Amandine says. "Follow me."

The four witches nod, waiting, ears open and ready to pounce.

"*Dī, tē perdant,*" Amandine begins softly. "*Tē malēdicō.*" She repeats it three times, then nods to the others to join in. As the witches chant, the breeze gathers, circling around them until it's a wind so strong that Cosima clutches George's hand to steady herself. Their hair whips across their faces; their clothes twist around their bodies, flapping like untethered flags. Noa presses her head into her knees and moans, long and loud. And then it starts to rain. Not the usual light drizzle of a Cambridgeshire night but a hard sleet that hammers down and stings their eyes. Still, the witches don't stop chanting. Noa's moan becomes a high-pitched wail, so they shout above her, above the rain and the wind, until the five of them are screaming into the sky.

"Dī, tē perdant. Tē malēdicō."

"Dī, tē perdant. Tē malēdicō."

"Dī, tē perdant. Tē malēdicō."

For nearly half an hour they scream, heads tipped back, soaking-wet faces turned to the bright, butter yellow moon, throats throbbing and scratched by the force of their cries. When the golden clock on the highest turret of King's College begins to chime the twelve strokes of midnight, so low and loud that it reverberates through all their chests, the rain and wind stop so suddenly that the witches' screams are stopped by shock.

"It's not working," Héloïse calls out.

"I know." Amandine sighs. "I know."

"I knew it wouldn't," George says. "We're not strong enough to combat black —"

"So," Kat interrupts him, "what are we going to do now?"

Noa starts to sob. She shakes so hard and her teeth chatter so loudly that everyone standing in the circle around her can hear.

The sound is like fingernails on chalkboard.

"I don't know," Amandine admits. She breaks the circle, crouching down next to Noa and hugging her tight. "I don't know."

Without the wind and the rain, without their words, the air is so still and quiet that, when a thick cloud floats over the moon, the darkness suddenly becomes something menacing, as if the black sky were actually a hundred thousand black crows waiting to swoop down and tear out their eyes.

"I know what to do," George says softly.

Amandine, still holding Noa tight, looks up. "You do?" She can't keep the surprise out of her voice, since she'd been underestimating him too.

"I think so," he says. "At least, I have another idea we could try."

"What is it?" Cosima asks.

"Well . . . I think," George begins, "I think we need to — sort of — let Noa give us strength, so we can give it back to her. Then she can reclaim her gift and reclaim herself."

Héloïse frowns. "What do you mean?"

"Okay. Do you remember the first time we met her? When she joined the book group and told the truth and shook everything up a little?"

"Yes." Kat, Héloïse, and Amandine speak in unison, some with slightly more bitterness than others.

Cosima looks blank.

"Well, what if we did that again?"

"But we can't," Amandine says. "Noa's not able —"

"I know," George says. "Not her. Us."

"Us?" Héloïse asks.

"Yes. After all, black magic sucks its power from lies and deception, doesn't it? And Noa loves art because it tells the truth," George says. "So I think, if we can start speaking the truth, telling each other what we really think and how we really feel, then we might become powerful enough to —"

"Seriously?" Kat asks. "You really think that's wise? With the secrets yo—"

Amandine gives Kat a sharp look. "Let's try it," she says. "We've got nothing to lose."

Noa begins to moan again, scratching hard at the skin of her scalp. Amandine tries to stop her, tries to grasp her hands, but Noa fights back, clawing at both their faces.

"Let's try it now," Amandine shouts. "We've not got long until she's just a shadow of herself, until we've lost her forever."

The witches glance around at one another, waiting for someone to speak first.

"Come on!" Amandine calls out. "Don't be such a bunch of cowards!"

341

"You go first then," Kat snaps, "if you're so bloody brave."

Amandine takes a deep breath. "All right. Okay. So, I hate my stepdaughter. She's awful to me. And I know she's suffering, I know her life is horrible, but I . . . I hate her and I pretend to Eliot that everything's okay, but it's not, I dread every time she visits and now Eliot wants to get full custody and I don't know what to do."

The other witches stare at Amandine.

"Wow," Kat says. "You don't do things by halves, do you?"

Amandine takes a deep breath and exhales loudly. "Bloody hell. Wow. Gosh, I sound awful, don't I?" But she's surprised by how relieved she feels to have said aloud the thing she's been most scared to. "Now you go."

Kat shakes her head. "Someone else. I'll go last."

"*Maman,* help, please!" Amandine shouts. "We can't waste time, go!"

"I'm falling in love," Héloïse says softly.

All the witches stare at her in shock. Amandine is openmouthed.

"What?"

"He's called Theo." Héloïse smiles. "He used to own the bookstall in the market square. We've not kissed yet, but I'm nearly ready and . . ."

"Maman," Amandine regains her composure. "Why didn't you tell me?"

Héloïse gives a little shrug. "You had all your own worries to think about, I wasn't sure how you'd feel. Your father . . . He's taking it rather well, I believe."

Kat, Cosima, and George all look confused.

"You're still talking to him?" Amandine asks.

Héloïse shakes her head. "Not lately. He hasn't spoken to me in a while. I think it's his way of giving his silent blessing. At least, that's what I'm choosing to believe."

"Well, in that case, *Maman,* I'm very happy for you."

Héloïse steps over to her daughter and hugs her tight. *"Merci beaucoup, ma petite chérie,"* she whispers into her shoulder. Then she looks up again at the other witches. "Okay, next!"

"My turn," Cosima says. She turns to George. "I'm sorry I . . . I tricked you, into all this." She nods down at her belly. "I didn't mean to, really, I didn't. The spell went a little wrong, but, but I know I shouldn't have gone along with it." She drops her voice to a whisper. "I'm really sorry. I hope you can forgive me."

343

The witches all stare at her. George reaches for her hand.

"I know what you did," he says, "and, yes, of course I forgive you. It doesn't matter. I love our baby. I can't wait to be a dad. And that's all that matters, okay?"

Cosima exhales. "You are simply the sweetest, kindest, loveliest man I've ever met. And you're going to be the most amazing father, I know it, and I'm going to follow your example in every way."

Kat sighs, shaking her head.

"Okay," Cosima says, "now it's your turn."

Kat glances at Noa, still in Amandine's arms. There is nothing she wants to do less right now, than endure any more truth, but she can see that, with each word spoken, Noa seems a little more alive. She glances from Cosima to George and back. Then she fixes her gaze on her sister.

"I was so happy before you came along. Then you took Mama away and Dad and then George." Kat's eyes fill and her voice drops. "And I hate you for all that. I know I shouldn't but I do. And this" — Kat nods at Cosima's belly — "this is the icing on the cake. I wish, sometimes I wish . . ."

Cosima steps forward toward her sister. "What?"

Kat begins to cry. "I wish, sometimes, that

you'd never been born."

Cosima steps forward and reaches her hands out to Kat, but Kat just stares at her feet, tears dropping onto her shoes. Cosima picks up her sister's hands and holds them tight.

"I'm sorry," she whispers. "I'm sorry, sorry, I'm sorry . . ."

She dips her head into Kat's shoulder, mumbling the same words over and over again. Suddenly, Kat lets go of her sister's hands and wraps her arms around Cosima and holds her tight and sobs.

"I love you, sis," Cosima mumbles into Kat's shoulders, "I love, love, love you . . ."

Suddenly, George stands up.

"Okay," he says. "I'm, I'm . . ." He takes a deep breath. "I am gay."

The other witches stop and look at him. Kat and Cosima let go of each other. Kat wipes her eyes, her mouth open.

Héloïse smiles. "You hid that well, *mon ami.* I never — you're clearly more powerful, a better spell caster, than you think."

Amandine raises her eyebrows. "That explains a lot."

Kat steps forward. "It certainly bloody does."

George holds up his hands. "I'm sorry, Kat, I'm sorry I've never told you. I just, I

345

just . . . We've never talked about that sort of — anyway, I'm not, I don't like . . ."

For a moment Kat is absolutely furious, then hurt, then relieved. She hurtles through these emotions as if she were on a roller coaster on a Blackpool pier. And only when she reaches the end does she realize that this is the best news she's ever heard. It wasn't that George didn't find her attractive. It wasn't that he didn't like her that way. It wasn't that she was somehow unlovable. All these years she'd thought there was something wrong with her, something missing (and there was, though not something she could do anything about), but that wasn't it. She was fine, she was perfect. She just wasn't a man.

"Oh, why didn't you tell me? You stupid, stupid . . ." Kat grabs George and hugs him tight, her words dissolving into sobs.

"I'm sorry, I'm sorry," George mumbles into her shoulder.

Kat pulls back, wiping her eyes. "Don't be daft," she says. "It's not that. It's just, if I'd known that twenty years ago it might have saved me a fair amount of unrequited heartache, that's all."

"What?" George asks, startled.

Kat smiles. "Oh, don't worry about it. It's my own silly fault. I should have told you years ago. And, honestly, I'm starting to think the whole crush had more to do with my own romantic insecurities than you, anyway."

"Oh, okay," George says. "Well, that's good — I guess."

"Hey," Cosima bursts out. "Sorry to interrupt all this emotional growth, but she needs our help."

Everyone looks to the ground at Noa, who's begun softly groaning.

Kat reaches for her sister's hand and squeezes it. "You're going to be a wonderful, wonderful mother." Then she kneels on the ground next to Noa.

"Dī, tē perdant. Tē malēdicō. Dī, tē perdant. Tē malēdicō . . ."

Cosima joins in, then Amandine and Héloïse and George. Finally, between soft groans, Noa begins to chant too — her words are broken and her voice jagged, but she doesn't stop. Gradually their voices grow louder and louder, until all the witches are shouting into the sky. In a second the heavens seem to open. A gale tears through the witches, so they all drop to their knees. Clouds of hail pelt their bent shoulders. Shattering claps of thunder sound so close that they all press their hands into their folded arms. Silver forks of lightning splinter the sky, so close to the roof they are blinded by light. But still the witches keep chanting. Their voices rise and fall, separating and uniting, dancing together and always strong. Then, suddenly, the air is still again.

The witches fall silent.

Gradually, Noa uncurls and tips her head slightly so she's looking up. Slowly, she smiles at each witch in turn — a little curl of her bloody, chapped lips — a small smile of triumph, gratitude, and relief.

"Thank you," Noa says softly, her words still bruised, but no longer broken. "Thank you."

CHAPTER NINETEEN

Cosima glances over at her sister standing at the counter, folding pink paper napkins. She's shut Gustare for the afternoon for the baby shower. Every table is sprinkled with rose petal confetti; every place is set with a single chocolate and rosewater cupcake with swirls of pink icing, each of them topped with a frosted cinquefoil (beloved daughter) flower. Pink balloons bounce and bob against the ceiling and a vast array of cakes of every variety crowd the counter: chocolate and pistachio cream, vanilla and elderflower, red velvet, passion fruit and pear, white frosted layer cake.

Cosima has been up all night baking, having taken a little morning power nap for a few hours. The sisters have been decorating in silence since ten o'clock. The other witches, invited a few hours before all the other guests, are due at lunchtime. Cosima sits at the other end of the counter, blowing up pink and white balloons.

She stops and sighs. "I don't have enough puff for these. I need help."

Kat puts down a pink napkin, then picks up the unfolded pile and brings them over to her sister. She sets them down and takes a balloon. "Let's swap."

Cosima smiles. "Thanks."

Kat stretches the balloon, pulling it taut. "So, how are you and —"

"Good. Really good, actually," Cosima says as she begins to fold. "I honestly think it's worked out in the best way of all."

Kat raises an eyebrow at her sister. "You're saying that raising your baby with a gay man is the best possible scenario for parenthood."

Cosima giggles. "Well, not the ideal perhaps, but in the absence of Tom — a nice committed heterosexual husband — then yes, I'd say that George will be the best partner and, most important, the best dad ever."

"Well, I suppose . . ." Kat stretches the balloon until it's about to snap. "But I still think —"

"I know," Cosima says softly. "But life isn't like a perfectly balanced equation, Kat. It's messy and muddled and you just have to go with it. And it's all going to be okay,

okay? I promise. George is excited. He's virtually as excited as I am." She places her hand on the large bump of her belly. "And I'm taking care of us, the best care. We're getting regular scans and my blood is being monitored like crazy. They'll induce me at the end of next month, two and a half weeks before I'm due, just to be on the safe side, and —"

"I'm still terrified," Kat says, stretching her balloon to the breaking point.

"Careful," Cosima says, gently relieving Kat of the balloon. "Anyway, how are you and George?"

"We're fine. We're good." Kat sits at the counter. "We're on the way to being friends again. I've come to my senses." She raises an eyebrow. "It must be that cake you gave me. Won't you tell me what was in it?"

"Nope," Cosima says. "But I can tell you, you're going to be . . ."

"I know, I know." Kat smiles. "I'm going to be okay. You're going to be okay. We're all going to be okay."

Noa sits in the breakfast nook of her aunt Heather's kitchen. Her aunt stands at the stove, stirring hot milk for their coffee, still steeping in a cafetière. Noa bites her thumbnail and gazes absently at her aunt.

"A chocolate cake for your thoughts," Heather says.

Noa focuses. "Cake?"

"I bought one from that café. I know you like them."

"Gustare," Noa says. "I've missed you."

Heather smiles. "I missed you too."

Noa lets out a little sigh.

"What?" Heather pours the coffee.

"I was just wondering," Noa says.

"Wondering what?"

"What I should do now."

"Well," Heather says, "that all depends on what you want to do."

"No, I meant, how am I going to live with this 'gift' of mine, without alienating everyone I ever meet?"

Pouring hot foaming milk into their cups, Heather considers. "Well, what about those witches? They like you, don't they?"

"I suppose so, yes, they saved my life."

"There you go, see," Heather says. "Some people have courage, and they are able to see and speak the truth, and some people are cowards and they have to hide their fear in lies. You just have to search the world for the brave. There are fewer of them, of course. But friendship is always about quality over quantity, don't you think?"

Noa nods. "And what about love?"

"Ah." Heather smiles. "Well, love's easy. In that case, you only have to find one."

"That's not easy," Noa says. "It's not easy finding one person to love you if you're not very easy to love."

Heather hands her niece a cup of coffee, then kisses her on the cheek. "My dear girl, you have no idea. You've a lot to learn about love. What you hate quickly becomes ferocious. You hit it for long enough, it'll hit you back. But what you love soon becomes beautiful. So it is with any trait, any personality quirk. When you embrace something you don't like, really and truly accept it as a slice of who you are, when you stop seeing it as obnoxious, it won't be obnoxious anymore."

Noa sips her coffee. "That sounds pretty damn difficult to do."

"Perhaps," Heather admits. "It takes practice, certainly. But of everything in life, it's the part most worth mastering."

"Yes," Noa says, momentarily imagining an entire lifetime of self-loathing, "I expect it is."

"How's your mum?"

Sylvia shrugs. "Okay."

"I meant —"

"Yeah, I know. She's still sober, okay?

Sixteen days."

"That's great," Amandine says, squeezing the steering wheel. "That's a great start."

Sylvia shrugs. "I guess. She's still a bit of a bitch though. But at least it's better than before."

"It'll get better too, every day," Amandine says as she pulls the car alongside the curb outside Sylvia's school. "I'm sure."

"Bullshit," Sylvia says, her fingers on the door handle. "Don't say things like that when you've got no clue."

Amandine tenses, about to object, but then she nods. "Yes, you're right but I hope so, I hope it'll get better, for you both."

Sylvia sniffs, pushing open the door. She mutters something before stepping out onto the pavement and slamming the door shut.

Amandine opens her own door, gets out of the car, and hurries around to the pavement.

"I'm not a kid, you know," Sylvia says. "You don't have to walk me to the front gate."

"I know," Amandine says, "I just enjoy your company."

"Liar. Why are grownups so full of shit?"

Amandine's eyes widen. She's lost for words and then, she thinks of Noa. "You know what?" Amandine says, stopping in

354

the middle of the pavement. "You're right. I was full of shit. I don't enjoy being with you when you're rude to me. I don't enjoy feeling how much you hate me. I don't enjoy trying so hard to befriend you and having everything, every time, thrown back in my face."

Sylvia stops walking and regards Amandine with a look of openmouthed astonishment and muted admiration.

"I don't hate you," she mutters. "I just wish . . ."

"What?"

Sylvia shrugs.

"What?" Amandine asks again. "Please."

"I . . ." Sylvia trails off, glowering up at her stepmother. "Look, if you weren't with my dad, you wouldn't give a shit about me, so don't —"

"That's not true," Amandine says. She's surprised to feel a sudden shift in Sylvia's emotions, from violently angry to lonely and scared. "I think you're amazing. Hey, you're Eliot's daughter, I know you must be amazing. And I'd like to get to know you, if you'll let me, I really would."

Sylvia bites her lip and shrugs again. And, for the very first time, Amandine feels a tentative rush of affection coming off her stepdaughter and is so overcome with gratitude, relief, and tenderness that she offers Sylvia a secret.

"You know, I can teach you some rather cool things, if you'd like."

Sylvia looks skeptical. "What things?"

"Special things, things most people can't do."

"Yeah?"

Sylvia is deadpan, but Amandine feels her curiosity and excitement rising. Out of the corner of her eye, Amandine sees a teenage boy lingering by the school gates. He's tall and lanky with floppy black hair and stares at his shoes as if they contain coded messages he's trying to decipher.

Amandine nods over to him. "Who's that?"

"Oliver Greene."

"Well, I believe he rather likes you."

Sylvia eyes Amandine suspiciously. "No, he doesn't."

"He does. I promise. I can tell."

Sylvia squints. "How do you know?"

Amandine smiles. "It's one of my gifts."

"That was delicious," Héloïse says. "Thank you."

They sit on the sofa in Theo's living room after a dinner of coq au vin. A cafetière of coffee and a plate of dark chocolates sit on the table in front of them. Héloïse wonders what will happen after coffee. They've been on three more dates — to the cinema, to the park, and to Gustare — since the posh restaurant. They still haven't kissed and, now that she's sure it's about to happen tonight, she's ever so slightly scared. How will it be? How will she feel? How would François feel?

"You're very welcome," Theo says. "And cooking isn't even my specialty."

A little shiver runs through Héloïse. Is he suggesting sex? She hopes not; she really isn't ready for that. A kiss, perhaps, but nothing more than that. Not yet. But she can't be certain that's what he means anyway. There was no flirtation with François; they were always totally transparent and matter-of-fact in their affections, going straight from meeting to falling in love, marriage, and parenthood. This is a whole new world and Héloïse is absolutely out of her depth.

Theo pours the coffee into two cups.

"Milk? Sugar? Neither? Both?"

"Red wine."

Theo laughs. "Okay."

He stands, leaves the living room, and returns a few minutes later with two large glasses of red wine. Héloïse takes a big gulp

357

of hers. If this evening is going to develop in any sort of sexual direction, then she's going to need the assistance of alcohol. A lot of alcohol.

"So," Theo says, sitting back on the sofa. "Tell me everything."

"Pardon?"

"I want to hear about your hopes and dreams . . . the things you've always wanted to do but have never done."

"Oh," Héloïse says, surprised. No one has ever asked her this question before. Not even François, although, to be fair, he probably assumed that her work and their life together was everything she'd ever wanted. "I don't really know. I suppose I've done everything now . . . But I saw the Dean at Newnham a few days ago. She offered me my position again, if I wanted it."

"That's wonderful."

"Yes." Héloïse smiles. "It rather is."

Theo sits forward, his fingers brushing hers. Héloïse flinches.

"Sorry," she says softly. "It's not . . ."

She glances down at Theo's hand again, then back at his face, his mouth, his lips. Suddenly, she's so overcome with the desire to kiss him that it terrifies her.

"It's all right," Theo says. "I'll only touch you if you really want me to."

"No," Héloïse says, "I mean, yes, I do. It's not, it's just . . . it's been a long time. A very long time."

Theo nods but says nothing. Instead he watches Héloïse, his eyes soft and kind, waiting to see what she wants to do. They sit in silence as Héloïse gradually calms her heart. Then, very slowly and carefully, she picks up Theo's hand, lifts it to her mouth, and kisses his fingers.

"Thank you," Theo says. Then he leans forward until their noses are only an inch apart. And he waits, looking into Héloïse's eyes until, at last, she closes her eyes and kisses him.

They sleep entwined, their bodies folded together, their breath encircling until two o'clock in the morning when Héloïse wakes with a start. She sits up in bed, blinking back tears in the dark, her heart beating hard in her chest. The nightmare is still slick on her skin and pulsing through her veins. It was a nightmare of blood and screaming, of grief and weeping, of birth and death.

Kat sits at her desk, fiddling with her pencils, staring absently at the infinite equations on her chalkboards, imagining what it will be like to hold her niece, the closest she'll ever come to holding her own daughter. She's often thought about adopting, but kept waiting in the hope that she might meet a man first, one who wanted to do it with her. Sometimes Kat wonders if it was the loss of their mother that made her and Cosi so keen to become mothers themselves, or if it's simply biological. Of course, it was worse for Cosi, since at least Kat had her mother for twelve years, while Cosi didn't have her at all.

There's a knock at the door. Kat swears. She'd forgotten about her fortnightly thesis meetings with Hamish. He pushes his way through the door before she invites him in, as he always does.

"Hiya, Prof, what's up?" Hamish asks, voice light and breezy as ever. The day of the carnation debacle, he decided to revert to the waiting and hoping method of seduction. "Ready to discuss the finer points of complex calculus?"

He flops down in his usual chair, long thin legs flung over the arm, feet sticking into the air, arms tucked behind his head in a way that isn't quite as nonchalant as it was before.

Kat sighs. If it were any other student, she'd pull herself together, suppress her feelings for an hour, and get on with the business of teaching. But Kat has always considered Hamish as much of a friend as a student. And, as such, she does him the honor of telling him the truth.

"I'm afraid the finer points of calculus are pretty much the last thing on my mind at the moment."

Hamish swings his legs to the floor and sits up, elbows on his knees, chin in his hands. "What's up, Prof? Tell me all."

"I'm going to be an aunt."

"Hey." Hamish grins. "That's great. Congrats."

Kat smiles, her spirits suddenly lifted by his infectious smile. "Thank you."

"Boy or girl?"

"Girl. She'll be called Aura."

"Cute."

"Yeah, it's lovely."

Hamish frowns. "Then why am I sensing a 'but' coming?"

Kat sighs again. For a moment she holds back, a little nervous to share such intimate details with someone who is still, technically, her student. Then, Kat finds that she doesn't care. She wants to talk with someone about how she really feels. She's sick of pretending with George and Cosi that everything's okay, that she's happy for them. But it isn't okay, it's horrible, heart-wrenchingly horrible.

"I can't . . . I wanted kids too, but I've got a . . . condition. And, well, for a while — quite a long while — I was sort of in love with, well, um . . . the gay man who'll be my niece's father."

"Bloody hell," Hamish gasps, simultaneously horrified by her confession while delighted at her use of the past tense. "That's a bit fucked up."

There's something in the way he says it, so simple and matter-of-fact, without telling her that everything will be okay. It's refreshing to have someone be honest and direct, without frills. It's a relief.

"Yes," Kat says, the edge of a smile on her lips. "Yes, it is. Well and truly fucked up."

Hamish nods. His favorite equation floats into his head:

$$f(x) = a_0 + \sum_{n=1}^{\infty} \left(a_n \cos \frac{n\pi x}{L} + b_n \sin \frac{n\pi x}{L} \right)$$

It's his safety blanket and he holds on tight. Then, with great effort, Hamish pushes it aside and musters all his strength. *It's now or never. It's your moment. Are you a man, or a mouse? Come on, you bloody coward, just do it!* Suddenly, Hamish leaps

362

up from his chair, strides over to Kat's desk, claps her cheeks between his palms, and kisses her full on the lips. When he pulls away, finally and reluctantly, Kat stares up at him in shock.

"What? What did you — why?"

Hamish shrugs, hoping that he doesn't pass out right in front of her. "Well, I've wanted to do that ever since I met you. I was never sure if you'd appreciate it, but since there's nothing I can do to help you out of your heartache right now, I thought I'd at least provide you with a little distraction."

Kat smiles.

"There you go," Hamish says, wiping his sweaty palms on his jeans and trying to calm his racing heart. "I didn't do too bad."

It's a moment before Kat can reply. "I always thought you were just a little bit crazy."

"Completely and utterly." Hamish nods. "Mad as a hatter."

The phone on Kat's desk rings. They both ignore it.

"Madder."

"But . . . it was okay?" Hamish ventures. "You didn't mind too much?"

"No, actually . . ." she says, her words

tinged with surprise. "I really rather liked it."

"You did?" Needing to hold on to something solid, Hamish leans against the chair. "You did?"

Kat smiles and steps toward him. "Yes, I really did."

The phone rings on.

"Maybe I should get that," Kat says.

Hamish gives her a shrug and a smile.

"Hold on a sec," she says, reaching across her desk to pick up. "Hello."

"Kat? It's George. I, oh . . . thank God you're here."

"I'm here," Kat says, a flash of panic flaring in her chest. "What's wrong?"

"She collapsed."

The words catch in Kat's throat. All she can hear is the blood thumping through her ears.

"We're at the hospital now. Will you — ?"

CHAPTER TWENTY

The funeral is held a week later, with all the witches in attendance, all wearing white, as had been Cosima's wish. They sit, in a dilapidated row, in front of the coffin covered with lilies, dozens of white petals already floating to the floor before the service begins, as if in mourning along with the congregation.

Sitting next to Kat, Amandine slides her hand behind her friend's shoulders, moving her fingers in tiny counterclockwise circles of eight, and mouths an incantation for the relief of grief. Next to Kat sits George, his eyes flitting around the church, looking everywhere except at the coffin and the vicar as he speaks about death and resurrection and hope.

"And now," the vicar says, "George Benett, the father of Cosima's daughter, will say a few words."

Kat glances over at George, who's staring

at a row of flickering prayer candles, oblivious to the vicar's words and everything else around him. She nudges him but he doesn't respond. Kat glances over at Amandine.

"Why don't you say something?" Amandine whispers.

Kat looks momentarily horrified, then nods. She stands and walks up to the pulpit. The vicar gives her a perplexed frown, but says nothing as Kat steps up.

"Hello everyone," Kat says. She coughs. "Sorry, I don't know what I'm going to say, but I'll try to think of something . . . I'm Cosi's sister." Kat glances down at the pew beneath her, checking on George, but he's still gazing into the candle flames. Héloïse nods, an encouraging little smile on her lips. Amandine gazes at her and Noa gives Kat a thumbs-up.

"I spent most of my childhood resenting my sister, wishing she'd never been born," Kat begins. "And then, one day, just recently, actually, I realized I loved her more than anyone in the world. I needed her. She balanced me. She was my, my . . . sister."

Kat looks out at the pews full of people sitting in rows in front of her. She wonders if she should sit back down. But then she realizes she doesn't want to.

"Cosi loved to feed people," Kat goes on.

"When she was a little girl, I taught her how to bake. She filled our house with the smell of hope . . . and new life. She brought my — our — dad back from — back to life after Mum died. Cosi's café was cherished by so many people. I'm guessing you all went — most of you were probably regular customers. She put so much love and magic into her baking. I bet you all had your favorite —" Kat tries to swallow her tears but she can't.

"Pistachio cream croissants!" Noa shouts out.

Kat blinks, scanning the crowd for the perpetrator and sees Noa looking up at her, grinning.

Kat nods. "My favorite too."

She looks out at the congregation again, blinking back her tears.

"Zucchini and caramelized onion pizza!" someone else shouts.

Kat sniffs, wiping her eyes with the back of her hand.

"Tiramisu cheesecake!"

"Vanilla and elderflower brownies!"

"Cinnamon and nutmeg biscuits!"

"Spiced chocolate cake!"

Kat starts to smile. She looks out at the congregation, at their happy, memory-filled faces, the taste of Cosima's baking still on their tongues, and feels her heart begin to lift.

"Passion fruit and pear cannoli!"

"Chocolate and pistachio cream cupcakes!" shouts Amandine.

"Dough twists dipped in Nutella!" Héloïse calls out.

Kat glances at George to see that he's looking back at her, the tiny quiver of a smile on his lips.

Héloïse sits up in Theo's bed, wearing his shirt. For ten minutes they've sat in silence, Héloïse overcome with shyness and almost unable to believe what's just happened. She's been with another man. Fourteen days and ten hours after she first kissed him, almost forty years after they first met. And it was beautiful. Not terrifying, embarrassing, or awkward, but absolutely, completely, and utterly beautiful. And electric, full of sparks and excitement. She'd swear she has little marks all over her body where Theo's fingerprints have been. Héloïse rubs the cuff of Theo's shirt between her fingers. François had a similar shirt, soft cotton, striped blue and white. A tear runs down her cheek and Héloïse bites her lip.

"Are you all right?" Theo asks, his hand resting gently on her thigh.

Héloïse nods.

"Is it something I did?"

Héloïse shakes her head, then nods.

"Yes," she admits, "I suppose it is."

"So, tell me what's wrong," Theo says, "and I'll fix it."

"Oh no," Héloïse turns to him. "You didn't do anything wrong. It's just . . . It's been over two years since . . . and I never thought I'd do this again. I never thought I'd be kissed and touched and . . ."

Theo opens his arms and, after a moment's hesitation, she curls into him, snug against the warmth of his chest.

"He was hit by a car," Héloïse says, so softly that Theo has to cock his head to hear her. "He was walking to the post box, with a letter of mine. I asked him to go because I wanted it to arrive the next day."

"Is that why you blame yourself?" Theo asks gently.

Héloïse shakes her head. "Perhaps, that too, but no, it's because . . ."

"You don't have to tell me."

"*Non,* I want to. I'm just afraid you won't believe me."

Theo smiles. "Try me."

"Or you'll think I'm *loufoque.*"

Theo laughs. "What's that?"

"Crazy. Mad. Insane. Barmy. Nutty. Lunatic."

"I doubt that," Theo says. "I doubt that very much."

Héloïse takes a deep breath. "Okay, then, we'll see."

Theo waits.

"I can see things."

"What things? Ghosts? Aliens? The Loch Ness Monster?"

"Non." Héloïse slaps him gently. "Shut up and let me finish."

"Okay, sorry, go ahead."

"Merci. I can see things before they happen. At least, I could before François died."

"You could?" Theo asks, seeming to genuinely consider this.

Héloïse nods. "When I was little, I knew my family would lose its fortune in the stock market crash of 1963. I saw that Frankie would develop diabetes if he didn't stop eating pastries at breakfast, lunch, and dinner. Sadly, neither of them heeded my warnings."

"Wow," Theo says. "Well, that's pretty incredible."

"You believe me?"

"Of course I do, why wouldn't I?"

Héloïse smiles. "I don't know, I just thought . . ."

"If you tell me something, then I will believe you," Theo says. "But I don't understand how you blame yourself for your husband's death."

"Because . . . because I didn't see it coming. I saw so many things, big things, stupid little things, and I didn't see that. I didn't see that."

"Oh, my dear." Theo wraps his arms around Héloïse and holds her tight. "You poor, sweet thing, carrying that all this time."

"I'm a mess," Héloïse whispers into his arms. "I'm a hideous, crazy mess."

"No, no, no," Theo says. "You are, you are . . ."

"Oh, God, see, you can't even —"

"You are . . . you are the woman I love."

To that, Héloïse has no reply. So, gently, Theo traces his finger across her skin, stroking her breasts, her belly. He tucks her gray hair behind her ears and presses his hand to her cheek. Then he starts to kiss her neck and Héloïse smiles, a smile that goes deep down to her toes, because she knows he won't stop, he'll keep kissing her until she's laughing and gasping and sighing with the deepest, most delicious pleasure.

George paces up and down his living room,

holding his little girl who's red-faced and screaming. All around him is an explosion of baby paraphernalia: bags of diapers, cloths, wipes, bottles, powders, creams, fluffy toys, cotton wool, towels . . . Aura is still tiny, too small to be alive, it seems, and yet she is. George has been in sole charge of his new daughter for less than twelve hours and he thinks she hasn't stopped crying in all that time. He's done everything the midwives instructed him to do: feeding, burping, washing, rocking . . . and yet still she cries. He's even tried magic, muttering a few incantations now and then, but none of his words seem to alleviate the squalling even for a moment. Why is he so weak, so ineffectual? All the other witches can do useful and powerful things with their magic, but he can't. He couldn't save Cosima; he can't even get a baby to stop crying.

George curses himself, then tries talking to his daughter in soft and gentle tones, asking what she wants, what he can possibly do to make her life a little better.

"You miss your mama, don't you? I know, my love, I know. I'm so sorry you've been left with me instead. I know I'm useless, I wish it wasn't like this, I'll learn more. As soon as you fall asleep, I'll read lots of books on raising babies, I promise." George goes on, pacing up and down, hoping somehow to soothe her even as he feels fresh blooms of panic in his own chest. "Do you miss the midwives, my love, is that it? Do you want a woman to hold you? Oh God, I wish I could give you your mama back. I'd swap me for her in a heartbeat, if it were possible, I would, I would, I would . . ."

George sees the splashes on Aura's tiny cheeks, terrified for a split-second, before he realizes that he's the source. He sits down on the sofa, wiping her wet cheeks with his little finger, then holds his screaming daughter against his bare chest. He gazes down at her blotched face, the little quiff of black hair, eyes squeezed shut, squashed nose, toothless, bloodred mouth wide open and screaming.

"What do I do, baby girl? Tell me what to do. I need help. I need you to show me. Please. Please. Please."

And then, as he pleads, all at once, George has an idea. He can't bring Cosima back, not her body, not her milk, her voice, or her smell, but he can bring back what she created, the atmosphere that Aura was brought to life in, the sounds and smells of the café. That, at least, would be something.

George stands.

"Okay, baby girl," he says, newly invigorated by his idea, even though he hasn't slept for more than a minute in at least twenty-four hours. "Let's take a walk."

An hour later (although Gustare is only a fifteen-minute walk from his home, he's never done the trip, or indeed any trip, with a newborn before), George and Aura arrive at the café. It's been closed for nearly two months and George has to force the door open over an enormous pile of mail. He kicks dozens of envelopes, mostly junk mail and bills, aside and pushes the pram into the tiny café. Mercifully, Aura has fallen asleep in the pram — George makes a mental note regarding the effectiveness of midnight walks through town to induce sleep — and so he settles her carefully by the counter while he picks up the mail.

"This was your mama's café, baby girl. And now it's yours. Though goodness knows how I'll keep it open for you. I can barely make beans on toast, let alone chocolate and pistachio cream cupcakes. You've got to taste those someday, though, they really are out of this world."

George sighs. He slips the stack of mail next to the till, then starts opening cupboards, looking for recipe books. "At least they were when your mum made them. I'm afraid it's unlikely I'll be able to create the same effect."

George searches for half an hour before he finds Cosima's own recipe book hidden in a cupboard under the till. It's another ten minutes, sitting and staring at the book, before he can bring himself to open it. Very slowly and very carefully, George turns the pages, running his fingers over Cosima's handwriting, the crossings-out and corrections, imagining Cosima bent over the book, biting her lip in concentration, absently brushing a hand over her flour-dusted cheek.

"What shall I try to make for you, baby girl? What would you like? How about something easy to start with, something very easy indeed." George stops on a page with the corner turned over:

Very Simple Sicilian Biscuits
100G GROUND ALMONDS
100G SELF-RISING FLOUR
25G GOLDEN CASTER SUGAR
25G SALTED BUTTER
1 EGG
1 PINCH POWDERED AMARANTH
2 PINCHES DRIED HONEYSUCKLE FLOW-
ERS

Mix all ingredients together. Roll out dough to about 1/2 inch thick. Cut into squares. Bake for 12 minutes at 220°C.

"Okay then." George takes a deep breath. "Let's give it a go."

Within half an hour, George has created more mess in Cosima's kitchen than he currently has in his own living room, though this time the chaos is culinary. Sweat drips off his nose and his head aches from tiredness and concentration, but he has a doughy batch of biscuits which look passable, if a little soggy, and Aura — perhaps lulled by the warmth of the kitchen and the smells — is mercifully still asleep in her pram. While the biscuits bake, George sits in a chair next to Aura, resting his chin on the curved edge of the pram, and watches her.

George is woken by a piercing scream. His eyes snap open, but the sound isn't coming from Aura, who's just been woken up herself and is starting to whimper. It's a moment before George realizes it's the wail of the smoke alarm. He jumps up, dashing past the counter into the kitchen, grabbing a towel, and pulling the burned biscuits out of the oven.

"Ow!" George drops the blackened biscuits to the floor, the tin tray clattering on the stone tile, the charred squares scattering. George sucks his sore thumb as Aura's cry crescendos, hitting the pitch of the alarm. Suddenly, George starts to scream himself, head flung back, eyes squeezed shut, as loud as his lungs will let him.

He screams for help. He screams for answers. He screams for revenge and retribution. He screams for forgiveness and strength. Then he stops. He flicks on the extractor fan above the cooker, nips back into the café, picks his daughter out of her pram, holds her close to his chest, pushes open the door, and steps out onto the street. In the fresh silence and the crisp night air, with the pull of the full shining moon, George hears a whisper on the wind and then he knows what to do.

CHAPTER TWENTY-ONE

George is hurrying along King's Parade, on his way to a lecture, when he sees him. George isn't entirely sure how he knows Santiago by sight, having never set eyes on the man before, but his certainty is immediate and deep.

George slows down, watching the swagger of the man, the cocksure air he inhabits, the way he wears his beauty like a glittering trap, ready to snare the spirit of the next woman he meets. A sudden spark of fury flares up inside George, one third fury at Santiago's unpunished cruelty but two thirds fury at his own inability to do anything about it. It's another moment before George sees that Santiago is following someone: Noa.

"Oh, God," George mutters to himself. "Help."

But since there is no one else to call on, without knowing what else to do, he starts following Santiago. Five minutes later, Santiago steps into the open entrance of a little art gallery opposite King's College. George speeds up and hurries in after him. He takes a few seconds to get his bearings among the paintings until he sees Santiago striding toward the back of the gallery, where Noa is standing in front of a large canvas of dark skies and purple seas.

Just as Santiago steps up behind Noa, she turns to see him. A few feet away, George feels waves of hunger and hate wafting off Santiago's skin.

"What the hell are you doing here?" Noa snaps.

Santiago smiles. "I thought you couldn't give me up so easily," he says. "Still admiring my paintings, I see."

Noa narrows her eyes. "Hardly. You think I don't know that you've been spying on me? I'm not stupid. I'm not here to admire your paintings — you're here because I want *my* painting back."

Santiago laughs. The sound is as dark and stormy as the painting behind him.

George shivers. He wants to turn and hurry away; he wants to return to the safety of his daughter and his café.

"You may be of no use to me anymore," Santiago says, bending toward Noa, "but you're here because I don't leave loose ends."

Noa doesn't move, though her hands are shaking. "You think I'm scared of you?"

"If you're not," Santiago says, "then you're stupider than I thought."

George steps forward. Noa looks at him in shock. Santiago regards him with contempt.

"Leave her alone," George says softly.

A soft smile licks the edges of Santiago's lips. "Oh, this is good. So, you've come to save her?"

George nods.

Santiago laughs, a low, slithering snicker that makes George feel as if he's just been licked by a snake. Santiago turns away from Noa to fully face him, then opens his arms wide, baring the breadth of his chest and the powerful muscles that pull his T-shirt tight across his skin. Inadvertently, George sucks in his belly and takes a little step back. Noa watches him, wide-eyed.

"Well then," Santiago says, grinning. "What are you waiting for, fatty?"

With every fiber of his being George wants to run from the gallery and not stop running until he reaches the café. So, careful to keep the fear from his eyes and the fire in his belly, George steps forward. He has one chance, he knows, one chance to catch Santiago off guard, one chance to pit the pathetic force of his power against the great, dark strength of Santiago's.

As he steps forward, George reaches out to press his fingers over Santiago's black heart and whisper the incantation, soft and low so Santiago can't hear the words:

Coniungere vires ad de iustitia, et cum fata vindictam.

Mando tibi, et in die graviter redempti.

When the words have lifted off his tongue, George shuts his eyes, waiting for the blow he knows is coming. And yet, nothing happens. The air around him feels still, silent, and bright. George opens his eyes. He's standing alone in front of the canvas of dark skies and purple seas. He opens his mouth. And then he sees something, a flicker of movement in the picture. George leans in and peers at the canvas. He squints, for the painting appears to be moving — ever so slightly — and nearly lost amid the crashing purple waves is a little bloodred boat being tossed among the spray, and clutching the helm is the tiny figure of Santiago, his face fixed in a scream.

Noa bursts out clapping. "Oh, George. I don't believe it. I don't bloody believe it."

George just stares, speechless. And then,

at the edge of his vision he sees a wisp of black hair, the flash of a smile, and, with his next breath, he inhales the scent of cinnamon sugar.

George smiles. "Thank you, thank you."

Cosima's voice floats through the air. *That wasn't me. That was all you.*

George frowns. "But . . . how?"

She laughs. *Sometimes we don't know our strength until we need to use it.*

Noa sits in the library, a pile of books on Monet on the long communal desk in front of her. She scribbles references and notes for her next tutorial. Every so often she stops to chew the cap of her pen. At the bottom of the pile is *Ulysses,* Amandine's pick for this month's book group. Noa hasn't started reading it yet, slightly put off by the sheer size of the thing. She fingers the edge of its spine. Fiction would be a lot more fun, she thinks, if the words were accompanied by pictures.

Just then, another student drops a pile of books onto the desk a few feet away. Noa looks up and frowns. He's dressed all in black with huge spiked boots, ripped skinny jeans, and a T-shirt emblazoned with an image of a bloody, severed head. He has matted, messy black hair, tattoos winding up his arms, heavily kohled eyes, two silver rings through his nose, and several more through both ears. Noa raises an eyebrow. He glowers at her and sits. Noa bites her tongue, then, unable to stop herself, leans toward him.

"It's a good disguise," she says softly.

He frowns. "What?"

"All this," Noa says, gesturing at him. "Your elaborate costume, all smoke and mirrors so people — your parents — won't see your secrets."

At first he looks at her, stunned. And then he laughs.

"You're hilarious. And delightfully bizarre."

Noa shrugs. "And your father will understand that you don't want to be an engineer. He might take a bit of convincing that you want to be a rock star, but I bet he'll come around eventually."

He stares at her. "Who the hell *are* you?"

"Noa."

He holds out his hand.

"Claude. It's fucking awesome to meet you."

"Thanks." Noa smiles. "And swearing doesn't make you more interesting. You do it to distract people too, so they won't see you. But, if you let them, they'll like you."

"Wow. You're pretty direct, aren't you?" Claude says. He eyes her and grins. "I think you might just be my new favorite person in the world."

"Oh," Noa says, a little taken aback.

Claude stands, slapping the engineering textbook on the top of the pile firmly. "So, since I won't be needing these anymore, let's split this joint and go find something fun. Failing that, we could drown our sorrows in copious amounts of caffeine. What d'ya think?"

Noa nods, concealing a little smile.

To love and be loved, she thinks, is perhaps not so impossible after all.

It's Sunday morning. Héloïse and Theo stroll along Market Street together on their way toward pistachio cream croissants and Italian coffee for breakfast at Gustare. Theo has a newspaper tucked under his arm, ready to share the book review section while they eat. As they walk, not talking for a while, Héloïse enjoys the silence, the fact that they can be together, not needing to say anything, simply being together. And she's still surprised, even after a year, by how easy it is, by how they seem to fit together without any effort or question. As they turn the corner into the market square,

Héloïse stumbles over a discarded Coke can. Without thinking, she bends down to pick it up, then walks on and drops it in the bin. As her fingers let the can go, Héloïse has a sudden flash of memory to the bottle of paracetamol that still sits in her bathroom cabinet. If I weren't here right now, she thinks, that can would still be lying on the pavement. Héloïse smiles.

Theo glances over at her. "I can hear you smiling."

"I was just thinking about the little things," she says, "about how it's just all a matter of perspective."

"Yes."

"Theo, I've got something to tell you. Something else."

"What?"

"It's about Hemingway."

"Oh?" Theo asks. "Great, I love Hemingway."

Héloïse smiles. "Yes, I know you do."

"You do?"

Héloïse nods. "A year ago I bought your books."

"What books?"

"*A Moveable Feast* and *The Old Man and the Sea.*"

"My favorites."

"You'd written all over them, in green pen

— annotations, comments, thoughts and feelings. I read them and I . . . I shared every opinion. I didn't realize it was you then, of course." Héloïse smiles. "But that's how I found you, I found you because of those books, because of what you'd written."

Theo fixes his gaze on her, a smile of private delight on his lips.

"What?" Héloïse asks. "What?"

"Those were my books —"

"Yes, I know . . ."

"But I didn't write in them."

Héloïse stares at him. "You didn't?"

Theo shakes his head. "Maggie did."

"Oh," Héloïse gasps. *"Mon dieu."*

"Yes." His smile deepens. "She drove me crazy, writing her thoughts in all my favorite books. When I'd go back to reread them I'd find all these essays in green pen." Theo laughs. "I had to keep buying extra copies so I could read them without getting distracted. Until Mags got to them too."

For a moment, Héloïse is knocked sideways, not knowing what to think or feel. Then Theo reaches for her hand.

"Maggie was my angel," he says. "And she gave me one last gift: she brought me you."

Héloïse sighs. She squeezes his hand. And then, for the first time since François died,

Héloïse sees a glimpse of the future. She smiles.

"Add dried azalea leaves to the list," Kat calls. "Oh, and we're nearly out of fennel flowers, so let's get more of them too."

George steps into the kitchen, notebook in hand. "Anything else?"

"Nope," Kat says. "Not right now."

"Aura wants you to see her drumming skills, when you're done."

Kat smiles. "I'll just pop the breakfast bread in the oven. Marcello'll be here in a few minutes, then I'm free."

"She's banging spoons on the tables and giggling maniacally. She'd be at it with the knives too, if I let her." He smiles. "That nurse was right, she's several handfuls of mischief."

"Just like her mum," Kat says, kneading an extra pinch of salt into her dough, "so we know she'll turn out all right in the end."

George nods, grinning. "See you in a sec."

"Yep."

When Kat comes out of the kitchen, wiping flour-dusted hands on her apron, and steps into the café, she sees her niece sitting on a tabletop with a spoon clenched tightly in each chubby hand, banging them against the wood. George sits at the table, drinking a cup of coffee, watching his daughter. Next to his cup sits a copy of *Winnie-the-Pooh* and one of *Ulysses*.

"How are you getting on with that?" Kat asks, nodding at the books.

Aura gives her aunt a toothless grin. "Amma!"

"Hello, kitten." Kat sits, holding out an espresso cup. "I've brought you your favorite, frothy milk."

"*Ulysses* is a walk in the park," George says. "*Winnie-the-Pooh,* on the other hand, is a little more complex . . ."

Kat blows on the milk to cool it. "I've been on page five for the last three days. I don't know what Amandine was thinking."

"Perhaps she thought we needed a challenge."

"Life's a challenge," Kat says. "I like to keep my literature simple."

George looks at her, then at his daughter. "Life's lovely," he says.

"Yes," Kat says. "Yes, I suppose it is."

She sets the cup down on the table in front of Aura. "Here you are, kitten. Drink slowly."

Squealing with delight, Aura grasps the cup in her chubby hands, then sets it down on the tabletop and drops one of her teaspoons into the cup. A little milk splashes up and Aura giggles.

The café door opens then and Marcello walks inside, bringing a gust of wind with him, along with Hamish.

"Ciao a tutti!" Marcello gallops over to Aura and squeezes her until she squeals with delight. Then he glances at George and winks. George blushes and gives him a little grin.

"Morning, all," Hamish says, stepping over to Kat and giving her a quick but rather passionate kiss. "You ready for *Relations Between Banach Space Theory and Geometric Measure Theory?*"

"Does *E* equal *mc* squared?" Kat smiles. "Unless you want to stay for pistachio cream croissants and coffee?"

"Too right," Hamish says. He follows Marcello into the kitchen.

Kat places a hand on her best friend's shoulder and George looks up at her. "You're right," Kat says. "It's lovely indeed." Then she nods in the direction of the kitchen. "And I think it's about to get even lovelier."

While they talk about George and Marcello's second date they don't see the teaspoon in Aura's cup slowly turn itself, stirring her milk. The little girl looks up, grinning her toothless grin. The scent of cinnamon sugar wafts through the air with a sprinkle of laughter.

"Ma-ma," Aura whispers. "Ma-ma!"

Amandine sits next to Eliot on a bench overlooking a lake in the Botanic Garden. The sun is slipping behind the trees and the shadows are long on the grass. Frankie and Bertie run across the lawn, their little legs dashing, their blond heads a blur, weaving in and out of the trees, giggling and screaming as Sylvia chases them. Eliot reaches for his wife's hand and laces his fingers between hers.

"Do you remember the first time we met?" Eliot asks.

"Of course. I look at the poster of that painting every day in my office. It's still my favorite."

"I've got a confession to make," he says.

Amandine stiffens. "Now I'm nervous."

"No, it's not a bad thing," Eliot says. "At least, I hope you don't think so."

"What is it?"

"The day we met, it wasn't an accident."

Amandine frowns. "Sorry?"

Eliot looks down into his lap. "I was sort of stalking you."

Amandine laughs. "What?"

"I saw you walking along Trumpington

Road and I followed you into the Fitzwilliam. I watched you there, for hours. I watched you while you gazed at all those paintings. I fell in love with you then. So of course I had to meet you."

Amandine smiles, thinking she's never loved her husband more than she does in this moment. "I don't believe . . . I can't believe you never told me that before."

Eliot shrugs. "I felt a bit silly. And I didn't want to give you airs."

Amandine laughs. "I've got something to tell you too," she says. "It's sort of . . . a slightly big secret."

"Oh dear," Eliot says. "Now I'm nervous."

"No, it's not a bad thing. Well . . ."

"Well, what?"

"You might not believe me at first," Amandine says, taking a deep breath. "But I promise —"

"Ah," Eliot says. "Is this about you floating about on rooftops?"

Amandine stares at her husband, speechless.

"Okay," he says, "so I'll admit . . . I didn't just stalk you at the museum. I followed you around a few other places too. I must admit, it was a bit of a shock at first. But stranger things have happened."

Amandine laughs. "Have they?"

Eliot gives a little shrug and smiles.

"Why didn't you ever say anything?"

"I thought I'd let you tell me in your own time," Eliot says. "I trusted you would, in the end."

"Oh," Amandine says, thinking of how she hadn't trusted him, how she'd thought he was having an affair, how she'd stalked him herself. Amandine squeezes her husband's hand, then turns and kisses his cheek. "Thank you."

Eliot smiles. "For what?"

"For everything. For this lovely, lovely life."

COSIMA'S FLOWERS
AND HERBS

Acacia — *Secret love*
Allium — *Prosperity*
Amaranth — *Immortality*
Baby's breath — *Everlasting love*
Basil — *Hate*
Bells of Ireland — *Good luck*
Bluebell — *Constancy*
Bougainvillea — *Passion*
Celandine — *Joys to come*
Chrysanthemum — *Truth*
Cinquefoil — *Beloved daughter*
Daisy — *Innocence*
Dittany — *Childbirth*
Fennel — *Strength*
Honeysuckle — *Domestic happiness and love*
Ivy — *Fidelity*
Jasmine — *Separation*
Laurel — *Glory and success*
Lily of the valley — *Return to happiness*
Lungwort — *You are my life*

Magnolia — *Dignity*
Michaelmas daisy — *Farewell*
Mistletoe — *I surmount all obstacles*
Orchid — *Refined beauty*
Purple rose — *Maternal/paternal love*
Scabiosa — *Unfortunate love*
Sorrel — *Parental affection*
Starwort — *Welcome*
Stephanotis — *Happiness in marriage*
Striped carnation — *I cannot be with you*
Trumpet vine — *Fame*
Tulip — *Declaration of love*
Witch hazel — *A spell*

A FEW OF COSIMA'S
FAVORITE BAKING SPELLS

Special Spicy Chocolate Cake — To Ensure Wishes Come True

200G CHOCOLATE (70%)
200G SALTED BUTTER
100ML ALMOND MILK
RIND OF 1 LEMON
100ML HOT WATER
200G CASTER SUGAR
4 MEDIUM EGGS
190G SELF-RISING FLOUR
3 TABLESPOONS GROUND ALMONDS
2 TABLESPOONS CINNAMON
1 TEASPOON NUTMEG
1 PINCH POWDERED PASSIONFLOWER (FAITH)
2 PINCHES DRIED BELLS OF IRELAND (GOOD LUCK)
5 DROPS WITCH HAZEL OIL (A SPELL)

Method:

Combine chocolate, butter, almond milk,

lemon rind, and hot water in a heatproof bowl over simmering water. Remove from heat when chocolate and butter are melted, and add sugar. Let cool. Beat eggs lightly, then add them to chocolate mixture and mix well. Add the rest of the ordinary ingredients and beat well. Sprinkle in the powdered flowers and, as you add the witch hazel oil, whisper your spell. Pour mixture into lined cake tin. Bake for 45 minutes at 170°C.

Breakup Brownies — To Cure a Broken Heart

200G CHOCOLATE (70%)
150G SALTED BUTTER
185G SELF-RISING FLOUR
285G GOLDEN CASTER SUGAR
3 TABLESPOONS GROUND ALMONDS
2 EGGS
1 TEASPOON BAKING POWDER
1 TEASPOON VANILLA EXTRACT
1 PINCH POWDERED MICHAELMAS DAISY (FAREWELL)
2 PINCHES DRIED MAGNOLIA (DIGNITY)
3 DROPS JASMINE OIL (SEPARATION)
CELANDINE (JOYS TO COME)

Method:

Melt chocolate and butter in a heatproof

bowl over simmering water. Remove when melted. Add flour, sugar, and ground almonds. Beat eggs, add to the cooled chocolate mixture, and mix well. Add the remaining ingredients and mix. Pour mixture into lined cake tin. Bake for 25 minutes at 160°C.

Chocolate Flapjacks — For Career Success

220G SALTED BUTTER

1 VANILLA POD

280G SOFT BROWN SUGAR

4 TABLESPOONS GOLDEN SYRUP

5 PINCHES SALT

60G COCOA POWDER

1 PINCH POWDERED LAUREL (GLORY AND SUCCESS)

3 TRUMPET VINE LEAVES (FAME)

1 PINCH ALLIUM (PROSPERITY)

300G LARGE ROLLED OATS

Method:

Melt butter in large saucepan. Take off heat and scrape vanilla seeds into pan. Drop the pod in too and leave to infuse for half an hour. Remove the vanilla pod and put the pan back onto low heat, then add the brown sugar, syrup, salt, and cocoa. Simmer and stir for five minutes. Add the powdered flowers and leaves. Add the oats and mix together. Pour the flapjack mixture into a baking tin and pat down to a thickness of 3/4 inch. Bake for 18 minutes at 150°C.

Blueberry Scones — To Elicit Marriage Proposals

8 OZ. SELF-RISING FLOUR

5 PINCHES SALT

1.5 OZ. GOLDEN CASTER SUGAR

3 OZ. SALTED (SOFT) BUTTER

1 LARGE EGG (BEATEN)

6 TABLESPOONS MILK

1 PINCH TULIP (ANY COLOR) PETALS (DEC-LARATION OF LOVE)

2 PINCHES DRIED LUNGWORT (YOU ARE MY LIFE)

1 PINCH DRIED STEPHANOTIS (HAPPINESS IN MARRIAGE)

30 FROZEN (NOT FRESH) BLUEBERRIES

Method:

Mix the flour, salt, and sugar together. Add the soft butter and crumb together by hand. Add the beaten egg, milk, and dried botanicals. Lightly knead dough and roll out onto floured board to 1/2 inch thick. Add blueberries and fold in. Cut out scones to 2 inches wide. Place on buttered baking sheet, then glaze with a little more milk. Bake for

12 minutes at 220°C.

Very Simple Sicilian Biscuits — For Domestic Bliss

100G GROUND ALMONDS
100G SELF-RISING FLOUR
25G GOLDEN CASTER SUGAR
25G SALTED BUTTER
1 EGG
1 PINCH POWDERED AMARANTH (IMMORTALITY)
2 PINCHES DRIED HONEYSUCKLE FLOWERS (DOMESTIC HAPPINESS)

Method:

Mix all ingredients together. Roll out dough to about 1/2 inch thick. Cut into squares. Bake for 12 minutes at 220°C.

Gustare (Italian) — to enjoy, taste, savor, relish

CONVERSION TABLE

Liquid Measures

1 cup = 8 fluid oz. = 1/2 pint = 237 ml

1 pint = 16 fluid oz. = 1/2 quart = .473 liters

4 quarts = 128 fluid oz. = 1 gallon = 3.79 liters

A dash equals less than 1/4 tsp.

Dry Measures

1 oz. = 28 grams

1 gram = .04 oz.

1 pound = .45 kg

1 kg = 2.2 pounds

3 tsp. = 1 Tbsp. = 1/2 oz. = 14 grams

2 Tbsp. = 1/8 cup = 1 oz. = 28.4 grams

4 Tbsp. = 1/4 cup = 2 oz. = 56.7 grams

Temperature

To convert Fahrenheit to Celsius, subtract 32 and multiply by 5/9 (.555). To convert

Celsius to Fahrenheit, multiply by 9/5 (1.8) and add 32.

THE GODS AND GODDESSES

Athena — the ancient Greek goddess of wisdom. Also the goddess of courage, inspiration, civilization, law and justice, strategic war, mathematics, and the arts.

Bes — Egyptian god of domestic protection, especially for pregnant women, childbirth, children, and families.

Hera — the ancient Greek goddess of love and marriage.

Isis — the Egyptian goddess of motherhood, protection, and magic.

Mama Quilla — the Incan goddess of the moon, marriage, and the menstrual cycle. She was considered the protector of women.

Minerva — the Roman goddess of wisdom, as well as of war and crafts.

Saraswati — the Hindu goddess of knowledge, music, arts, wisdom, and learning.

Satī — also known as Dakshayani. The

Hindu goddess of marital felicity and longevity.

Thoth — the Egyptian god of knowledge. Also associated with the arts of magic, the invention of writing, the development of science, and the judgment of the dead.

Tsao Wang — Chinese god of the hearth and family.

Vár — Norse goddess of marriage oaths.

■ ■ ■ ■

The Witches of Cambridge

MENNA VAN PRAAG

■ ■ ■ ■

A Reader's Guide

A CONVERSATION WITH
MENNA VAN PRAAG

Random House Reader's Circle: Where did the idea for *The Witches of Cambridge* come from?

Menna van Praag: It came from a conversation with my friend Amanda (to whom the book is dedicated), when we were chatting about setting up a book group. As we discussed the kinds of books we would choose to read, the conversation took a turn toward the colleges of Cambridge. Amanda told me she'd been taking walks about the city lately and had become enchanted by the exquisite college architecture of turrets and spires as she gazed up to the sky. We talked about how, although we found Cambridge so very beautiful, we rarely looked up to see the beauty above us and how much we often missed. Then — in one of those inspirational leaps that sometimes happens in conversations — we realized that, if a book club consisted of witches, they might hold meetings in those beautiful turrets. From there sprang the idea of these witches being professors, each with their own secret of one type or another. Amanda mentioned that she was scared of heights. So, naturally, when I wrote the main character — naming her Amandine in Amanda's honor — I added that she was also afraid of heights.

After that initial idea, I began thinking about the other characters — all professors, all witches — who might be in the book group. As I thought about characters, I thought about Cambridge. I've set all my novels in Cambridge so far. It's such a magical city and I love picking real places for the characters to inhabit. Sometimes I keep the original names — especially in the case of the colleges and streets — but sometimes I change them — in the case of the cafés. Gustare was actually based on my favorite Italian café in Cambridge, Aromi. It had just opened when I'd begun writing the book and I spent a lot of time in that café, sampling all their delights, purely for research purposes, of course!

RHRC: Do you have any advice for those

of your readers who'd like to become writers?

MVP: Oh, yes. In fact, since writing *Witches* I've started teaching creative writing courses, to individuals mainly, but also to groups. It's something I never thought I'd love — like most writers, I've always been incredibly shy — but I started a few years ago and I find it incredibly inspiring. Writing novels is such an insular occupation, so it's very gratifying to connect with other people, especially other writers, and to be able to explore my passion for the written word with those who share it. What's more, it's hugely rewarding to watch my students grow more confident as their work evolves, to see them take pride and pleasure in what they've created. It took me over a decade to get published and much of that delay was due to self-doubt and perfectionism. That's why I really love supporting other writers who might be suffering from similar afflictions. I recently coached a woman in her fifties who'd always wanted to write a book but had never managed to complete anything. We worked together for six weeks and, during that time, she wrote her first novel. And it's a marvelous piece of work. I'm looking forward to seeing it published. It was an honor and a delight to be part of the creative process.

It's shocking how many people I meet who tell me they've always dreamed of writing a novel but don't believe they can. And so they never do. Or they try but give up too quickly. When I ask these people what their proof of inability is — how many unpublished novels they've written — most of them haven't written any at all. It's sad that people give up on themselves so easily. But I understand it. I dedicated my twenties to trying to get published — while working as a waitress to pay the rent — and I had many a dark night of the soul filled with doubt and fear. So I always tell people not to give up, to keep writing, and keep on going through all those rejection letters. Although I also tell them that they should only keep going if they're writing because they love to write. If they're writing to get published, then I tell them that most writers never make much money from their novels alone. Aspiring authors tend to glamorize the lives of published authors, but the truth is that most of us will never earn enough to quit that day job. If you're not writing for the pure passion of it, then perhaps you shouldn't be writing at all. However, if you adore a beautiful sentence more than most things in life, then keep going because it's very likely that one day your work will resonate with someone who shares your passion and has the power to publish you.

RHRC: What are you working on now?

MVP: I'm currently writing a novel that's rather different from anything I've done before! It's not magical realism and it's a shade darker than my previous work. It's about a theater critic, called Aubrey H. Gagné, who has such high standards for literature and life than he's entirely miserable and can't connect to anyone. I'm absolutely loving the process of writing this story and am discovering that creating unlikable characters is a great deal of fun! In fact, I think this may turn out to be one of the funniest books I've ever written. This, in itself, is funny because I never believed I could create comedy — which just goes to show that we all have those erroneous thoughts about what we cannot do. So we really just shouldn't listen to them. Please don't listen to yours!

READING GROUP QUESTIONS AND TOPICS FOR DISCUSSION

Each of the witches of Cambridge has her own unique power: Amandine, the power to palpably feel emotions; Noa, the power to hear secrets; Kat, the ability to turn formulas into spells; Cosima, the ability to bake enchantment into her pastries. Which power would you find most attractive? Why?

George spends so much time trying to hide his true feelings from the world — and especially from Kat. How and why do you think that affects his ability to perform magic? Have you ever realized that by trying to protect yourself, you were isolating yourself?

Similarly, Noa has found safety in the number one. Blessed with the ability to hear — and cursed with the compulsion to tell — the most secret thoughts of those around her, she's driven away her loved ones by disclosing their infidelities, desires, and missteps. Do you think Noa has a right to blame herself for her parents' divorce?

Buried secrets can sometimes be more harmful than those brought to light. Do you agree that sometimes, as in George's case, and Noa's, the truth can set you free? Is honesty always the best policy?

Sisters Kat and Cosima are as different as night and day: Kat is mathematical to a fault, utterly practical, unwilling to use her powers to get what she wants. Cosima is creative, impetuous, and ready to let her heart lead wherever it wants, no matter the cost. Which sister do you identify with more? Is there a happy medium?

On the last page of *The Witches of Cambridge,* Eliot admits to Amandine that he knew all along that she could perform magic but that he trusted her to tell him in time. Consider the magnitude of the secret he kept from Amandine. Is marriage about assuming the best despite the worst? Does love conquer all?

After her husband's death, Héloïse forgot how to use her magic to see the future.

Although she eventually finds love again and unburdens herself of the misplaced guilt she has carried for Francois's death, her powers never actively return. How do you feel about that? Why do you think she never regains her power? Is the future less important than the present to two people in love?

As it's portrayed in this novel, is magic a blessing or a curse?

If you could be in a book club with the witches of Cambridge, what book would you choose to read? Why?

Cosima's recipe for an enchanted chocolate cake that makes wishes come true includes the requisite chocolate, butter, and flour, but the spell comes from the addition of "1 pinch powdered passionflower" for faith "and 2 pinches dried bells of Ireland" for good luck. Would you add anything else to this recipe, or are faith and luck all you need?

ABOUT THE AUTHOR

Menna van Praag is an author and creative writing consultant. She graduated from Oxford and lives in Cambridge with her husband and young son. She's also the author of *Men, Money and Chocolate; Happier Than She's Ever Been; The House at the End of Hope Street;* and *The Dress Shop of Dreams.* She's currently working on her newest novel, *The Lost Art of Letter Writing.*

mennavanpraag.com
Facebook.com/mennavanpraag.mvp
@MennavanPraag

The employees of Thorndike Press hope you have enjoyed this Large Print book. All our Thorndike, Wheeler, and Kennebec Large Print titles are designed for easy reading, and all our books are made to last. Other Thorndike Press Large Print books are available at your library, through selected bookstores, or directly from us.

For information about titles, please call:
   (800) 223-1244

or visit our Web site at:
   http://gale.cengage.com/thorndike

To share your comments, please write:
   Publisher
   Thorndike Press
   10 Water St., Suite 310
   Waterville, ME 04901